Praise for
The Rummy Club

Anoop Ahuja Judge shines at scene setting, in both India and the San Francisco Bay Area, with abundant, lush details.

In *The Rummy Club*, by Anoop Ahuja Judge, four high school friends from India reunite decades later in California, with old and new struggles, in a well-developed story about what binds us and how tenuous those ties can be.

Although the women have assimilated to American ways, their Indian ethnicity remains important. Indian food, religion, dress, and customs are integral to the story; the characters' broader social circle is primarily Indian. Ethnic references are smoothly, in fact beautifully, intertwined to be captivating and enlightening for Western readers. When ethnic terms are used, they are consistently italicized and their meanings are immediately woven into the text: "It was pat mangni, jhat shaadi—quick engagement, quick wedding."

The Rummy Club is a perfect book club choice that may just bring weekly card parties back into vogue.

THE CLARION REVIEW

★ ★ ★ ★ ☆

*In Judge's novel, four women share a bond that reaches from
their native India to Northern California.*

Judge's debut novel follows four Indian women who met in boarding school and reconnect as adults. The narrative shifts from one character to another, with Divya, Mini, Priya and Alka taking turns as narrator. When Divya moves from Queens to the Bay Area, where her perennially unsuccessful husband is hoping to start over in business, the four women begin meeting for a weekly rummy game, sharing their worries about their husbands and children, comforting each other through death and divorce, and keeping secrets that threaten to tear them apart. The four women are all distinctly drawn personalities, and Judge also has a way with the book's minor players; Divya's social-climbing mother, despite her brief appearance on the page, is one of the book's most vivid characters. Alka's high expectations for her only child, which drive the most dramatic episodes, seem at first glance to be part of the stereotype of the striving immigrant, but Judge develops the story fully, allowing Alka to become a rounded, plausible character.

Strong characters affectingly portray immigrant experiences.

KIRKUS REVIEWS

*Four high school girlfriends from India reunite in California
after decades and resume their weekly rummy night; a snapshot
of the Indian diaspora in the 21st century.*

PUBLISHER'S WEEKLY

The
Rummy
Club

Anoop Ahuja Judge

DAGGERHORN
PUBLISHING
Livermore, California

The Rummy Club
©2014 Anoop Ahuja Judge

DAGGERHORN
PUBLISHING

2150 Portola Avenue
Suite D224
Livermore, CA 94551

www.therummyclub-anovel.com

ISBN: 978-0-991081-01-1
E-book ISBN: 978-0-9910810-6-6
LCCN: 2013953996

Cover and Book Design: Peri Poloni-Gabriel,
Knockout Design, www.knockoutbooks.com

Printed in the USA

Dedication

To Tony, whose unflinching support
made my dream a reality.

To Amaraj and Ghena, who believed in me
and wouldn't let me give up.

And to my mom, who inspired me
with her own writing.

Table of Contents

Indian Terms Glossary

Acha Hoon—I'm good

Aloo parantha—whole wheat Indian flatbread stuffed with potato

Amah—nanny servant

Amchoor—spice made from dried green mangoes

Andhran fish curry—a type of fish curry originating from Andhra Pradesh, India

Arré—exclamation roughly meaning "Oh, my!"

Asparagus kofta—a vegetarian alternative to meatballs, stuffed with asparagus

Beti, beta—affectionate term for daughter; affectionate term for son

Bhagwan Jaane—God knows

Bhagwan ji—a term of respect for God

Bhujiya—crispy tea-time snack

Bidaii—traditional going-away ceremony for a bride

Bindi—mark (makeup or sticker) on Indian woman's forehead

Biryani—rice-based dish made with spices, rice, and chicken

Chaat-masala—a seasoning that has both a sweet and sour taste; mostly used as a garnish in salads, drinks, and snack foods

Chalo, chalo—move it, move it

Chee chee—an exclamation roughly meaning "Bad, bad!"

Choli—midriff-baring blouse

Chotu—a term of endearment for someone you care for meaning "little one"

Chutney—a sweet and sour condiment that is similar in consistency to jelly, salsa, and relish

Curry—a generic English term which is usually understood to mean vegetables and/or meat cooked with spices with or without gravy

*D*ada, Dadi—paternal grandmother, paternal grandfather
Dal or daal—thick lentils stew; a staple South Asian dish
Didi or Di—term of respect for older sister
Doli—a palanquin, one used for a bride
Dupatta—a long multipurpose scarf often wore over salwar kameez

*F*oreign-returned—A typical Indian English expression. Someone who is
 foreign-returned has returned to live in India, after living in a foreign
 country, usually because they have studied or worked there.

*G*aram-masala—a blend of ground spices used extensively in
 Indian cuisine
Gayatri Mantra—a highly revered mantra in Hinduism based on a
 Vedic Sanskrit verse
Ghanda Moola—according to the study of astrology, ghanda moola is
 when a child is born at an inauspicious time
Ghazal—a poetic form consisting of rhyming couplets and a refrain,
 with each line sharing the same meter
Ghee—butter
Goan fish curry—a type of fish curry originating from Goa, India
Gulab-jamun—cheese-based dessert similar to a dumpling

*H*ai Bhagwan—an exclamation meaning "Oh Lord"

*J*aan—my love, my wife
Jalebis—sugar-dipped wheat flour batter, deep-fried, in pretzel or
 circular shapes
Jeetay Raho—live forever
Ji—as a name suffix, respectful term of address
Jutis—type of footwear made of leather with extensive embroidery

*K*anjeeveram sari—one of the finest silk *saris* from South India
Kathak—one of the eight forms of Indian classical dance

Keema samosas—spiced ground lamb wrapped in a pastry shell and deep-fried

Kheer—flavorful Indian rice pudding made with coconut

Krishna Mantra—a highly revered mantra in Hinduism based on a Vedic Sanskrit verse

Kurta-pajama—one of the basic clothing of Indian men. The kurta is like a loose, long shirt almost reaching the knees, whereas the pajama is a lightweight drawstring trouser.

Kurti—tunic

*L*akshmi—Hindu deity Lakshmi, the goddess of wealth and beauty

*M*asi—mother's sister or maternal aunt

Matar-paneer—a simple North Indian food recipe prepared with green peas and cottage cheese that are cooked in a creamy, tomato-based curry

*N*amaste—common salutation originating in the Indian subcontinent. It is a customary greeting when individuals meet.

Nani—maternal grandmother

Nimbu-pani—lemonade

NRI—non resident Indian. In common usage, this often includes persons of Indian origin or ancestry who have taken the citizenship of other countries.

*P*allu—the loose end of a *sari*

Paneer pakoras—cottage cheese filling in chickpea flour batter, deep-fried

Pati Parmeshwar—a husband is Supreme Lord for his wife

Peshawari chicken curry—a type of curry originating from the city of Peshawar in Pakistan

Pipal—a fig tree native to India

Pooris—fried Indian flatbread

Puja—prayer ceremony

Pundit—a learned man, a scholar, and a teacher, particularly one skilled in the Sanskrit language

Punjabi chole—North Indian Punjabi-style chickpea curry with spices and ingredients

*R*aita—condiment made with yogurt and used as a sauce or dip

Rajma—Punjabi vegetarian curry consisting of red kidney beans in a thick gravy

Rotis—Indian bread made from stoneground wholemeal flour

Rupees—Indian currency

*S*aheli—girlfriend

Salwar kameez—a traditional dress of South and Central Asia. Salwar is loose pajama-like trousers worn under a kameez, which is a long shirt or tunic.

Sangat—a gathering of devotees

Sanskar—tradition

Sari or saree—traditional garment worn by Indian women. It is a strip of unstitched cloth ranging from four to ten yards in length that is draped over the body in various styles.

Sati—a social funeral practice among some Indian communities in which a recently widowed woman would immolate herself on her husband's funeral pyre

Sherwani—a long coat-like garment worn in South Asia, very similar to an Achkan or doublet

Sindur—vermilion, blood-red powder usually smeared at the forehead and at the parting of the hair of Hindu married women

Sitar—string instrument

*T*ulsi—Indian holy basil

*W*aheguru—reference to the Almighty God in the Sikh religion

CHAPTER 1

𝒟ivya

FREMONT, CALIFORNIA
JUNE 2005

I was always the outcast. At times, I felt like an untouchable.

No, no. I correct myself before the memories caterwaul away from me into a vortex of melodrama. *Not as bad as an untouchable. But an outcast, yes, most definitely.*

Did I always feel this way? Even before the accident of America happened to me? Or only now, since I haven't let them know I've moved across country. Near where they've been raising their families.

The monologue makes me so restless I step backward with a jolt. Right on the sidewalk in front of Bharat Bazaar. After driving around for half an hour trying to find it. Right here, about to shop for a special meal of *kadhi*—hot chickpea yogurt soup and rice— our first home cooked meal in the ten days since we left Queens. Even though our kitchen is tiny, and our belongings don't fit into the cramped town house Gopi rented for us. He has no idea how much space daughters colonize.

We've stored the oversized couch and a steamer trunk abandoned with the Raj in the guest bedroom of our only living relative in California. And my auntie Vimla was barely gracious about it. (I could see it in her disapproving face and pursed lips.)

"Thank you, Auntie. Thank you. Thank you. It's only until we get our own place." *Is appreciation enough to gratify Mother's cousin until our luck changes? Even with family I feel downtrodden.*

Sham's boyhood friend Gopi had promised him a managerial role in Gopi's trucking business, but now that we've arrived in California, he's demanding a stake twice what he'd initially stated. And gloom shadows the faces of our daughters as they trudge home from the bus stop.

Fatigue has settled on my skin like a rash. No more take-out from Von's. Food—there's a problem I can fix.

I've anticipated this visit with pleasure. I'm beginning to make the world right again. Bharat Bazaar, the premier Indian store in the East Bay, Gopi's wife advised me.

The string of brass bells over the door startles me. I'm used to the brightly lit mega-markets of Queens with endless tidy shelves, holding everything from stainless-steel cookware to plaster Hindu deities to jars of ghee and glass cases filled with trays of fudgy, syrupy sweets.

This jungle of a spice bazaar takes me back to the bustle of shopping in New Delhi. The heady aromas of cardamom, black pepper, perfumed incense, and rose-scented sweets fill the air. Wicker baskets overflow with slender gourds, plump eggplants, okra like ladies' fingers, and cauliflower heads white as the Himalayan snow I watched for hours out of my dorm window at Jesus and Mary. The strains of a *sitar* resonate from a far corner.

The rustle of a *sari* precedes the, "*Namaste.* Welcome." The storeowner's wife emerges from the aisle to greet me.

"*Namaste.* Thank you." I'm self-conscious at being caught gawking.

I have no list. I keep the ingredients in my head. Next to the orderly rows of spice blends for everything from *dal* to *chai,* I find what I am looking for. *Patak's achar,* the pickles Sham loves. I'm jubilant.

The tiny aisle is crowded with afternoon shoppers. As I reach up to pluck the mango pickle off the shelf, my arm accidentally brushes against another shopper.

"Oops, sorry." The woman turns toward me—a short, homely looking woman in jeans and a loose *kurti*.

Oh, shit. I wasn't ready to let them know yet. Just my luck—the one time I come to the Indian store.

"Divya? Divya Bhatia? Is it really you?"

"Priya Sharma?" I stumble backwards, exclaiming louder than is warranted.

"Yes!" Priya is already clutching my upper arm and enveloping me in her familiar, warm melting bear hug, as generously and lovingly as she always has. She squeezes my forearm so hard it will bruise.

"So many years." I wipe the sudden tears that gather at the corner of my eyes.

"Yes. Yes. How are you? The last I heard you were in New York."

"Um, yes. Fine, fine. We moved here ten days ago. And I'm Divya Kapoor now." There is a smile in my voice as I emphasize my married name.

"We have to catch up. We've all been here for years. You knew that, didn't you?" Priya studies my face, her tone shaming.

"Yes." I can feel my face getting hot, "but, but . . . I was planning to call once we're settled. But you don't live in Fremont, do you? Do you shop here all the time?"

"Actually, I haven't been here for ages. There's no Indian store in Danville where I live, and the one in Pleasanton doesn't carry this brand of coconut oil."

Priya holds up the *Amla* tin in her nubby fingers.

"But listen, we have to catch up. Look, I have to run to pick up my daughter, Anya. Alka's having a party on Saturday. You have to come. Call me, so I can send you the details."

Priya fishes out a dry cleaner's receipt from her massive shoulder bag and hastily scribbles her phone number and Alka's address. She thrusts it into the palm of my hand and hurries out toward her car.

I set my grocery basket gingerly on the floor and smooth the crumples out of the stained edges. *Alka, 824 Park Avenue, Piedmont.*

Ma's overbright voice reverberates in my head. "Divya, you must call Alka when you reach California. She lives in a huge house, I am told. Virry, virry rich. Your other friends are there too—Mini and Priya, all virry, virry happy, they are."

Oh God. I can't let them see that terrible town house! At least I was wearing my black patent Tory Burch flats. And my skinny jeans. Not that Priya would care. But I do look good, younger than thirty-eight. At least I have that going for me.

The dazzling colors and fragrances of India, of home, swirl about me—mounds of spices, piles of nuts, the wafting scents of ripe fruit. And especially curry. The last time all four of us were together was at Alka's wedding reception at the Taj Mahal Hotel, New Delhi's most prestigious address. Well, arguably. The extravagant, over-the-top affair had left me awed for weeks. Perhaps scarred?

I see us, best friends in high school, and after. Teenagers sprawled over the bed in Alka's dorm room, piles of coins jingling every time someone moved during our endless games of rummy.

Before dreams of foreign-returned, Jesus and Mary Girls' High School. Another time, another world.

CHAPTER 2

Divya

DEHRADUN, INDIA
1985

"It's like a dream come true," Ma says for the tenth time.

"Yes, Ma," I say, for the tenth time, even though it isn't my dream that's coming true.

My mother had always dreamed of being a boarder at a posh Anglo-Indian school in the northern foothill city of Dehradun. It was too late for her, of course, but with Papaji's recent affluence, she had turned to her youngest daughter—me—who had two more years of high school.

My dream has been different: to continue hanging out with my friends since kindergarten, growing up alongside dozens and dozens of cousins, practicing flirting maybe even a little kissing with Rishi, the boy next door whom my mother distrusts because his family was Gujarati.

That was Ma's rationale for the additional expense that, thank the gods, we could now afford after years of making do. I'd felt the gap keenly because all my friends were rich. My girlfriends got chauffeured around in cars of their own while I relied on erratic public transportation. They bought clothes in big city shops, unlike me and my middle-class cousins who wore simple cotton outfits made by the neighborhood tailor. They went for coffee at the upscale Bombay Café while I and my cousins hung out at the more affordable school canteen. *But not anymore.* I sing to myself.

I had argued with my mother at first, but it was not much use once she'd made up her mind. I reluctantly took the entrance exams for four different schools. The day the letter arrived announcing my acceptance at Jesus and Mary Girls' High School, Ma held me and kissed me as if she were seeing me for the first time. And perhaps she was—having a daughter, who would need a dowry, finally had some benefit.

We are cocooned in the luxurious feel and smell of the leather backseat of the family's brand-new car—a sleek, black-as-kohl Ambassador, driven smoothly by the brand-new family driver. My brand-new suitcases packed with brand-new clothes and other paraphernalia fill the trunk. Ma's wearing a deep maroon *sari* that sets off her tawny complexion, one of her many brand-new collections. She is luminous like a saint or guru with inner light glowing around.

She holds my hand the whole way out of Delhi, only relinquishing it when we stop for a wash and a thirst-quenching *nimbu-pani* halfway through the 150-mile journey. Being the fifth of six children, I am not used to her prolonged attention. The sixth child, the long-longed-for son, soaked up whatever was left of my parents' energy after all that trying. Ram, named for the prince of heaven. Moving away from that brat, who has become more arrogant and intolerable, was the appealing part of boarding school. But I worried about friends. Now I was going to be The New Girl in a place where friends have been living together for years.

I didn't dare talk about my concern. My mother had the obsession that I was destined to become best friends with the daughter of Somnath Aggarwal, publisher of *Savvy* magazine and brother of the publisher of the *Delhi Times* and one of the wealthiest men in India.

On the very day the acceptance letter came, Ma was on the phone all afternoon with friends and family to spread the good news and her discoveries. As soon as I walked in the door that evening, my mother burst out with it. "Do you know who also boards at Jesus and Mary?"

In the moment it took me to figure out what this question really meant, Ma answered. "Som Aggarwal's daughter, what is her name?" She beamed. "The Aggarwal girl. The one you had such a nice conversation with at her cousin's wedding. What is her good name, Divya?"

I suddenly understood. "I didn't have a conversation with her, Ma. She was complaining about how loud the music was, and we talked about loud music. For one single minute. Out of politeness."

"But what is her name?" Sometimes my mother's insistence made me want to scream.

"Alka," I said through clenched teeth.

"Yes, that's it. Well, it turns out that she is Class of '87 at Jesus and Mary, just like you, even though she is actually one year younger. But she is brilliant. A brilliant student. She will take over her father's publishing empire. And you already know her!"

I had never lacked for friends, boys or girls. They saw me as cute and funny. With four older sisters, I had learned a lot about clothes and love. I had worked hard in school for my A's and B's though my favorite activity was dancing—both structured traditional *Kathak* dance, which I'd been learning since I was six years old, and the loose, fabulous Bollywood style. I'd never hung out with a brilliant student—didn't know that I wanted to.

"Ma, please, I'm not going to be friends with Alka Aggarwal. We were standing in line at a buffet for her cousin's wedding and we talked about how loud the music is at weddings, and that was it."

"But think how nice for you to know someone already

established at your new school. It will be such an advantage to you." It was as if I hadn't even spoken.

It was a lost cause trying to talk my mother out of this obsession. Every time she brought up the brilliant Alka Aggarwal, I tuned her out, hoping Alka and my mother never came face to face.

We reach the quiet neighborhood mid-afternoon, passing large houses set back from wide, shaded streets. Several schools hover behind decorative iron gates. Ma reads the names of each, thrilled to feel the sound in her mouth. Finally, "Jesus and Mary Girls' High School," she intones, as if each word were a lick of ice cream. A high wall covered with magenta bougainvillea shields the school from the street view. We turn into the brick driveway. The car stops in front of a one-story white stucco building. *Jesus and Mary Girls' High School* reiterates the oval brass plaque above the green French doors. *Est. 1922.*

My chest tightens. I am scared and excited. It is so different from my Mater Dei school near Connaught Place in south Delhi with its small paned windows pressed against the flow of bikes, cows, cars, and trucks festooned with marigold garlands.

Between the car and the front door, Ma stops and grabs my arm. She straightens the new maroon school blazer I have just finished buttoning. She smooths sweaty curls back from my forehead and looks deep into my eyes. *Can she see my quaking soul?*

"I am so happy for you, *beti*. Your life is about to change. I'm so sorry your papaji cannot see you step through the doorway to your new life." Her eyes fill with tears.

I am touched—and embarrassed—my feelings jumbling together. I don't know what to say, but a young woman releases me from my quandary as she opens one of the green doors and steps down from the veranda to greet us. I think she is a student, but she introduces herself as Miss Prema D'Souza, the assistant registrar. "I've been keeping an eye out for you. The other five new junior class girls have already checked in."

Ma apologizes profusely as we follow Miss Prema, who assures us we were not late, only the last to arrive. She leads us into the Registrar's Office, past the oak counter. Seating us in front of her desk, she hands us a large manila envelope. Mine contains the School Handbook, a list of classes and available clubs, the calendar term, and a health form.

"You'll have time to look at all that later. You'll be eating today and tonight at Rosewood. Tomorrow is New Girl Orientation. All will be explained at that time." Her laugh makes me feel a bit less apprehensive. My mother has been thumbing through her copy of the School Handbook, nodding and smiling.

"We're just waiting for Mini Sidhu, who has been assigned as your Friendly Guide. It's a tradition here at Jesus and Mary that every new girl, whenever she starts here, has an older girl to give her a helping hand. Being a Friendly Guide is one of the service projects you can volunteer for as part of your curriculum."

Ma looks up at the word "curriculum." I have the strongest feeling that the next words out of my mother's mouth are going to be "Alka Aggarwal."

"My husband does business with Mr. Som Aggarwal, and Alka and Divya are already friends." My face burns.

"How fortunate! All the girls in the Class of '87 live in Rosewood Hall," Miss Prema responds. She steps behind her desk and opens up a loose-leaf notebook. "You will be in Rosewood 219, Miss Bhatia, and Miss Aggarwal is in—" She turns a couple of pages to find what she's looking for. "Miss Aggarwal is in 221, so you will actually be next door."

My mother beams. I pray my mother won't babble on about this. Luckily, the Friendly Guide shows up, and I'm spared that particular embarrassment.

"Hello. I'm Mini." She is slim and pretty, dressed in tight black jeans, penny loafers, and a boxy jacket with oversized shoulder pads. Her straight black hair is drawn back from her face in a French braid, and bangs poof out over her forehead like a tiny awning. A tiny diamond pin in her nose twinkles charmingly in the light, like a blush of sweat. She smiles broadly at me, and I immediately feel at ease.

Mini leads us out through a different door and into a lushly shaded green area. "The Quad. You'll see in term time, the benches and lawns are covered with girls."

I stick close to Mini, partly to hear her better, partly to prevent Ma from engaging in another conversation about Alka Aggarwal. Mini leads us through the mess hall, pointing out the tables assigned to our class. She rolls her eyes playfully when I ask about the food. "You'll survive it."

"We like to hang out at the Madras Café down the hill. They have pretty good veggie cutlets." Mini's voice is soft but melodious. I wonder who the *we* are.

We arrive at Rosewood 219, and my heart lurches as I turn the key. The room smells of disinfectant and furniture wax. Aside from the deep blue rug next to the bed, the room is unadorned, stark. One bed, one desk, one chair, one dresser, and one narrow book-case. The single window looks out on a high vine-covered wall. It's so empty, but my suitcases and boxes are lined up neatly in front of an open closet door.

"And I'm right across the hall." Mini opens the door as an invitation. I immediately appreciate her penchant for interior design. A simple desk and black office chair is backed against one wall separating it from a bed placed against the opposite wall. Red and white batik cushions and a twinkling red mirror work bedspread with matching curtains provide splashes of color. A brassy Ganesh, God of wisdom and intellect, crowns a magenta scarf across the left side of her tidy desk.

"Then you must know Alka Aggarwal." My mother's face is lit up with a 1000-watt smile.

"You know Alka?"

"Oh, yes. My husband and Mr. Aggarwal do business together."

I imagine myself pushing Ma out of my room and slamming the door shut. The last thing I want is for Alka herself to hear my mother's completely exaggerated version of reality. She had in fact little interest in that brief chat, which will be quickly made international news if Ma has a chance.

Luckily, only the half-dozen new girls and their Friendly Guides are present before classes started for real. Still, by the time we finish our tea in the Commons Room, I know all there is to know about Alka Aggarwal, for she is Mini the Friendly Guide's best friend—or rather, Alka and Mini and another girl named Priya. All three best friends live on the same small stretch of the second floor of Rosewood Hall. They have done everything together for the past two years.

I make myself as small as possible in my chair, curling up with embarrassment. My beautiful, charming mother could be a hostess on an interview talk show, the way she pumps Mini for information. I feel sick imagining Mini repeating all this to her best friends as they laugh their heads off about the gauche mother of the gauche new girl.

My ears perk up, though, when my mother asks, "And what happened to the girl who previously lived in Divya's room?"

"Oh that was Sonali. Her family moved to Boston, Massachusetts. In the US. Her father got a top job there."

"So sad for you, to lose your friend, even for such a nice reason."

Mini's face shows no signs of sadness. "I think the field hockey team will miss Sonali most of all. She was their star something—I don't know, is there a forward for hockey? I think that's what she was."

I breathe a silent sigh. At least I'm not replacing a beloved fourth musketeer in Mini's group.

Finally, finally, it is time for Ma to leave. Mini accompanies us back to the long brick driveway. The bougainvillea glows purple in the slanting sunlight. The driver springs out of the car and opens the back door. My mother hugs me and whispers a blessing in my ear. Tears actually fill my eyes.

But Ma manages to spoil the moment by enveloping tiny Mini and practically lifting her off the ground. "I'm so glad my daughter has found a friend like you, Mini *beti*. Please take care of her!"

I think I will die. The moment the car door slams, sealing my mother inside, I turn and stride away. I do not want to look at Mini. Calling Mini my friend! Asking her to take care of me, as if I'm some idiot child!

"Hey, slow down," Mini calls.

I can't look her in the eye. "My mother!"

Mini laughs. A pretty laugh. "Don't worry about it. I like your mom. And you're not going to see her again for a long time, so just relax."

I glance at Mini. I can't help but smile. She's relaxed, smiling, clearly not upset by Ma's brashness. She is one of the nicest people I've ever met.

As if she could read my mind, she says, "Why don't you come across to my room later? I mean, I know you'll want to clean up."

I wonder if Mini is trying to tell me something. That must show in my face because she laughs that pretty laugh again.

"You don't stink, don't worry. It's been a long day, a long ride from Delhi, no? Just knock on my door whenever, even just to tell me you're too tired to hang out."

I remind myself that Mini is my Friendly Guide, that she has two best friends already. I take the invitation for what it is.

When I'm freshly showered, hair gleaming, I knock timidly on Mini's door. She greets me warmly. She has brought some *bhujiya* and *Parle* glucose biscuits from home and spread them on a plate she must have snuck up from the mess.

"I hope I can keep my dancing going," I say. Mini's enthusiastic. She's a singer, and she has a lot to say about the dance and music program—and about Jesus and Mary. Most of it good, some of it gossip.

"We performed at the Grand Maratha Hotel in Bombay last year! Not everyone, just three singers and three dancers. Some rich alum paid for us to perform at some kind of political thing. It was amazing!"

She grabs a CD player of a kind I haven't seen before and pushes a button. George Michael blares out. Mini sings along, dancing around her room, shoving a half-empty suitcase out of her way with her foot. She pulls me up from her bed, and we dance and sing and clown for the entire length of the CD. We collapse, sweaty and laughing.

At tea I'm introduced to the other new girls. Maybe tomorrow I'll connect with them and start a new girls' clique. I fall asleep to Mini belting out "Wake Me Up Before You, Go Go" into her hairbrush microphone. She's helped me feel at home.

Mini knocks on my door at seven to walk me down to breakfast. The new ninth grade girls fill up three long tables on the far side of the mess hall. Mini and I join the new eleventh graders and their guides at the one other table set with dishes and cutlery. Reena who has long braids and cute red glasses calls out my name, so I sit down next to her, Mini on the other side and Reena's Friendly Guide beside her. Reena's from a small town between Dehradun and Delhi and is set on being a doctor like both her parents and her grandfather.

"Jesus and Mary has the best science program. And a brand-new chem lab. I could have gone to Welham, but their science doesn't compare." She's explaining, not bragging.

Later in the day, she gives us a tour of the lab. Air-conditioned, filled with filtered natural light and gleaming equipment. My stomach sinks. I barely made B's in science. I hadn't realized science was so important here.

That evening Mini knocks on my door again. "I'm just checking to see how you're doing." I can't believe how glad I am to see her in a T-shirt that says, "Save the Indian Tiger" and flowery pajama pants.

"I'm fine. You don't have to keep checking on me."

Mini looks at me strangely.

"I don't do anything I don't want to do if I can help it." She holds up a bag of chips. "Do you want some?"

I step back so she can come in. "I have to get everything in order before classes start. I can't stand chaos. I've always shared with my sister Aditi, who's kind of a slob. I'm really excited to fix my room the way I want it. I love what you've done with yours."

While she's helping me shelve my books, Mini describes her older sister Komal and their love/hate relationship. She talks about their trip to Singapore and how angry Komal had been to have her tagging along to the travel professionals' seminar.

"And then I met this boy," Mini's voice drops even lower, "while I was waiting to pay for some postcards at Archie's Gift Shop. We spent two afternoons together before Komal ran into us in the hotel coffee shop."

"A Malaysian Muslim!" her sister screeched when they were alone in the elevator. "You want to kill me? You want to kill your parents?" Mini is still crying about it.

I grab her hand in silence.

14

"Nobody knows. I couldn't write it to Priya and Alka. I didn't want to talk on the phone about it."

We were silent for a long time. I tell Mini about Rishi, about the afternoon my mother wasn't home—his was never around anyway. Nothing had happened that couldn't have happened with a million people around. "Someone told my mother and that's how I wound up at boarding school."

Mini squeezes my hand in understanding. "I'm sorry that's the reason, but I'm glad you wound up here."

By the end of the evening, my room is orderly and, if you asked me, I'd say I've a new best friend.

Priya likes me right away, no doubt because Mini's told her she would. It's obvious I'm comfortable with Mini, maybe even with a friend-crush.

Priya tells me Mini's the resident romantic. "Boys, boys, boys: what she will name her first son, where she will have her vacation house—because, of course, she will be a singing star of Bollywood and marry the handsomest hero actor. She does have a gorgeous singing voice, and her looks and vivaciousness are assets."

"Someone has to be the next big star." Mini's wicked smile erupts.

Priya has no such ambitions. She's content with average grades in most subjects. She took naturally to Math, but it doesn't interest her. She towers over us by five or six inches, and she looks five or six years older—with a superbly rounded figure, like a full-grown woman.

"You two are almost the same size," Priya remarks as she catches up with us at the mess hall for breakfast. "When Alka arrives, you'll be a set of triplets." Priya laughs pinching Mini's arm.

The mess hall is unbelievably noisy now that three hundred girls are shrieking greetings and clattering their forks and spoons, dishes and chairs. My face must look pained, because Priya squeezes my elbow lightly.

"Don't worry. This is the loudest day. Everybody has to tell everybody else how good they look, and where they went during vacation, and all the gossip they haven't shared for months."

She takes a bite of the *aloo parantha* and makes a face. "I've been cooking all summer with Sheela."

"Sheela is the *amah* who practically raised her," Mini explains to me.

"My chicken *biryani* is already better than hers." I can tell Priya's just stating facts. I don't think she knows how to brag. "In fact, when I went to stay with Alka's family in Simla, I made *biryani* one night and Aggarwal Uncle said it was the best he'd ever tasted."

Again Mini explains to me, "Priya loves to cook. And to eat."

Priya pokes Mini's ribs. "I'm not a bird, so I don't eat like one."

"When is Alka getting here?" Mini asks.

"Tonight or tomorrow." Priya explains to me. "Alka has been in California for the last week for her father's magazine."

"For *Savvy?*" I asked. "My mother subscribes to *Savvy.*"

"She's writing a big piece on the India-to-California brain drain. I mean," Priya corrects herself, "her mother is writing the article, and Alka went as her intern."

"Tough life," Mini smiles.

"You'll get used to it," Priya promises. "Alka lives in a different world from the rest of us."

"Divya knows Alka," Mini chimes in.

"No, no, I don't know her. I talked to her at her uncle's daughter's wedding. There were about a million people, and we happened to be standing next to each other. That's it." I speak fast and feel my cheeks going through a progression of colors.

"Her uncle's daughter's wedding? Her cousin Rita?"

"Yes, and I didn't even know the bride, but my parents brought

I and my sister to the wedding because . . . I don't honestly know why they brought us. My father does business with Alka's brother, I mean, father. But I don't know any of them."

On the third day of classes at breakfast, I'm sitting between Priya and Reena, with Mini and another girl across the table. Mini's filling in the new girls on the upcoming mixer with the boys from St. Joseph, their brother school. What kinds of clothes are allowed— and what kind of clothes the girls try to get away with. Which junior and senior boys to absolutely avoid. Which boys might offer something that looked like punch but might be spiked.

And then Alka staggers in, dizzy with jet lag. Priya jumps up and envelops Alka, who hastily backs away, almost prickly.

"I arrived from L.A. in the middle of the night and was whisked straight to Dehradun from Delhi airport. It's dinnertime inside my head."

"My head! My poor head!" she moans, dropping her black nylon Prada handbag on the table and collapsing into a chair.

Mini reaches across the table and pats her hand. "Hello, *saheli.* Do you want some tea?"

"Oh, yes, my *saheli,* I would love some tea."

"It was a nightmare," Alka announces, resting her forehead on her hand, her elbow braced against the table. "Our layover in Seoul lasted seven hours. There was nothing to eat except kimchee. I don't know how I'm going to survive classes today."

"She's not usually like this," Priya says, noticing that the new girls were watching Alka the way they'd watch a soap opera. I snap my mouth shut and stack my breakfast dishes. Reena tries so hard not to laugh that she sputters.

Immediately, Alka looks up. "Who is this?"

Priya starts to introduce us, but Reena speaks louder. "I'm Reena Chaudhury, one of the new juniors." She offers her hand,

Alka takes it but turns to me.

"But who is *this*?" Alka asks again. I look up.

"I'm Divya." I smile widely, feeling the dimples in my cheeks.

"I know you. You were at Rita's wedding."

My face flushes through the rainbow again. "Yes. Rita's wedding."

"Well, welcome to Jesus and Mary. What room are you in?" She is ignoring Reena completely.

By the time Reena stands up to stack her dishes, Alka has invited me and Priya to a little party in her room that evening.

"I have so many things to show you. I went to the authentic Levi's headquarters in San Francisco, and I had jeans made to order. And," she lowers her voice to indicate a secret, "I had a pair made for Mini. We're almost the same size. I just had to make the waist a little bigger."

"Divya," says Reena, "I'll see you in chem."

"Okay," I say, only halfway looking up at her. When Mini arrives with a cup of chamomile and a biscuit, I say, "I'd better go, too."

"Come at nine," Alka says. "I have food." I dimple at her and start to walk away, but Alka calls my name.

"You know," she says, "I bought four of those Levi's. Now that I see you full length, I'm sure one of them will fit you perfectly."

Ma would be thrilled that I have already received a gift from the daughter of Som Aggarwal. But if I asked Papaji for 50 US dollars to buy a return gift for Alka, I know he would say, "I will go broke trying the match the generosity of Aggarwalji's carefree daughter."

"Oh, that's so kind, Alka. But I can't accept them."

"Come, come. There's no need to be coy, Divya. See, we are already friends, and this is my Welcome-to-Jesus-and-Mary-God-Help-You gift." Priya and Mini crack up.

I suddenly feel let in on a private joke and break into a beaming smile.

"Oh, thank you, Alka." I fill with bliss.

I hear Mini ask, "What was that all about?"

"Isn't that the most amazing coincidence? That new girl, Divya, I knew her already. She was at my cousin Rita's wedding at the Taj Mansingh Hotel."

Alka's room looks like a bazaar when I arrive. Clothes on hangers swaying from the doorknob, the bookcase, and the top of the closet door. From a tall pile of books she'd brought back from the US, Alka pulls out one to give to Priya.

"Chez Panisse?"

Alka corrects her French. "Mother and I ate there. It's supposed to be the biggest thing in America. Maybe not for vegetarians. This guy from Delhi, his name is Raj Bajaj—he's making millions in Silicon Valley—he took us there with eight other people. My mother couldn't believe how much that meal cost."

"Was he good looking?" Mini asks.

"Oh, virry, virry handsome," Alka grimaces, mimicking someone's mother. "If your taste runs to frogs."

"Alka!" Mini giggles too, and I join right in. The Levi's fit me so well I wear them all evening. Alka adds sunglasses from Hollywood to my new image and an unused postcard of Beverly Hills.

She hands Priya a box. It contains two decks of cards, one with the Golden Gate Bridge, one with the Hollywood sign.

Priya starts shuffling them. "Let's play rummy. The cards tick and click in her nimble hands. "Do you play, Divya?"

I hesitate a second, then shoot them a mischievous look. Rummy was the one activity where I could trounce Ram. "Yes. I do."

We stay up way too late playing hand after hand. We devour all the snacks plus a chocolate bar Mini retrieves from her room.

Finally, Priya displays the winning hand, with four valid combinations. Alka falls asleep on top of the covers in her custom Levi's. Out in the hallway, Priya hugs us and we whisper, "Good night, good night. See you in the morning."

We didn't know it then, but the seeds of the Rummy Club had just been planted.

CHAPTER *3*

Mini

NEW DELHI, INDIA
MAY 1991

> *Mrs. Rani Aggarwal*
> *Requests the pleasure of your company*
> *At the wedding of her Granddaughter*
>
> *Alka Aggarwal*
> *(Daughter of Padmini and the late Som Aggarwal)*
> *To*
>
> *Raj Bajaj*
> *(Son of Kavita and Kamal Bajaj)*
> *On Saturday, 27th May*
> *At Hotel Taj Mahal*
> *Venue: Diwan-I-Am Banquet Hall*

The chauffeur-driven black Mercedes slithers to a halt in front.
Mini, waiting in her parents' rarely used front living room, jumps

up, her pink organza *sari* rustling, and runs to the window, peering out into the semi-darkness that covers the city.

"Inder," she shouts, "Priya and Vik are here."

Inder emerges from the guest bedroom sheathed in a navy pinstriped suit. He moves closer. Mini's nostrils flare.

Brut, she guesses. She smiles. He personifies the NRI, the non-resident Indian, in his appearance—even in the way he smells. If it weren't for the car outside, she'd allow herself to swoon into his arms.

He holds out his hand with the gold purse she'd left in the bedroom.

"Yours, I believe." American smooth at its best. Their eyes meet. Her smile widens.

Not bad for an arranged match. Mini puffs up with uxorial pride.

Take caution, young lady. Pride comes before a fall. From the base of her medulla oblongata where her subconscious is rooted, Mini's inner Sita, the Goddess who keeps good Indian girls out of trouble, admonishes in her commanding voice. Mini ignores her and tucks the purse in the crook of her elbow.

She's been living in California with Inder for three months now, and this is her first visit back—specifically to attend Alka's wedding, though she isn't above showing off her CPA husband to her friends.

Mini and Priya squeal in delight and hug tightly. It has, after all, been a full three months since Mini's wedding.

But the mood in the car speeding toward Number One Mansingh Road is somber. Priya fiddles with the pleats of her *Kanjeevaram sari*. Inder stares impassively in front of him. Mini seated between them in the rear of the car squiggles her nostril so she can see the light from the streetlamps glint off the facets of her diamond pin.

It feels as if they are going to visit a sick friend, rather than to share what ought to be the happiest day in Alka's life. Vivid

Bharati, India's most popular entertainment radio station, is playing a sorrowful love ballad. *Oddly appropriate.*

In the front seat, Vik Sharma swipes his face with a handkerchief. In spite of the air-conditioner, the heat comes in waves through the driver's half-open window—late May in Delhi is typically humid. Thunder is audible in the distance, and the stifling smell of a brewing storm fills the air. The heat will only be dispelled by a fierce, cleansing rain.

"Close the damn window," Vik snarls to the driver.

Vik turns sideways in his seat to look at his three companions. Mini lowers her eyes, embarrassed for Priya.

"Hell of a time to hold a wedding." The nasal twang is prominent in his whine.

"Hmmmph." Inder's grunt is possible agreement.

"I don't think that Alka knows what she's doing," Priya says quietly. She continues to play with her *sari.*

"So, is it really true then? Alka's sacrificing herself to save the family fortune?"

Mini's question conjures up the headlines they have all read, splashed across every daily, reported by every major TV news channel, fodder of almost all talk-show hosts. Everyone was talking about Som Aggarwal's sudden and fatal heart attack, followed by the disclosure that the publishing houses he and his brother owned were not only bankrupt, but mortgaged to the hilt.

Even in California, the news reached them. Priya had been the first to call and tell Mini. Then her sister Komal phoned, her disembodied voice confirming and expanding on what Priya had already said. The distressing news has even made it to "Namaste America," the Indian program on a local network that Mini watches avidly every Saturday for one hour.

"All I know is that Alka refuses to discuss it."

"Did you talk to her after . . . after?" Mini stops, not willing to bring up the media circus surrounding Som Aggarwal's death.

"Yes, yes, I did." Priya sounds defensive. "I called so many times to speak with her. I even went by her house. She wasn't home—or that's what the maidservant told me. I left a note, but I heard nothing back."

"And then, this. This wedding invitation." Mini can tell from the way Priya swallows that her friend is thinking back to the shock when the invitation arrived in the mail three weeks earlier. Along with the elaborate gilded invitation was a note in Alka's familiar handwriting: "Please come."

"I was shocked, too," Mini confirms. "It was difficult for us to drop everything and fly here on such short notice, but how could I ignore her message?" She leans back against the seat and lets her eyes close. Jet lag is getting to her, but even worse is her confusion, her inability to make sense of this turn of events in her friend's life.

The car lurches through traffic. Rush hour in Delhi. Cars, scooters, motorcycles, black taxis, all jostling for space on the road—the auto-rickshaws precariously putt-putting themselves among more substantial vehicles. The drone of large green buses, the constant honking—both familiar, yet already strange.

She sits upright and says to Priya in a confidential voice, "There's got to be more to this whole situation. What's the real story?"

Priya seems to hesitate. "I was going to tell you this later, not here in the car. My aunt, who's friends with Padmini Auntie—you know, Alka's mom?"

Priya shifts sideways in her seat to look at Mini directly. It is as if she thinks living in America might have addled Mini's memory.

"Anyway, my aunt told my mom," Priya's voice drops to a whisper, "that they had actually done all the paperwork to put their house and the businesses on the auction block when Alka received the proposal. This Silicon Valley millionaire. This Raj Bajaj . . . some kind of computer chip genius."

"His name sounds so familiar."

"He made the offer directly to Alka, then he met with Padmini Auntie and Alka's uncle. He agreed to pay off all their outstanding debts. Everything. And in exchange, all he wanted was to marry Alka."

"Ya, your precious Alka, sold to the highest bidder," sneers Vik from the front.

Priya shifts uncomfortably in her seat. The car falls silent. The notion of Alka being served up as the sacrificial lamb at the altar seems preposterous. In the old days, in high school, she had been the shining star. Her physical and intellectual accomplishments were so obvious that her friends did not even bother with jealousy. She had the most money, the best figure, the highest grades, the coolest clothes. There was no competition.

Back then Divya, Priya, and Mini speculated about Alka's future. To what heights would she ascend in Indian society? Which literary genius or entrepreneurial magnate would sweep her off her feet?

The crash of the Aggarwal family fortune ended all that. The year Alka turned twenty-two, her life collapsed in mid-leap like a cat frightened by a sudden loud noise.

Even so, Mini can't bring herself to believe that Alka, their brilliant Alka, would agree to marry a stranger just to save her family from ruin.

Bloody not likely, as Alka would have said. But Alka's silence is damning.

"*Chalo, chalo.*" The driver rolls down his window and shouts to a young man shuffling his ice-cream cart across the road. The poor man shuffles faster. The driver puts the indicator light on and begins the ascent of the two-hundred-meter ramp into the driveway of Delhi's premier social hotel.

A winding pathway beneath Mughal-inspired decorative domes of the sprawling marble lobby lead to the spacious hall where Alka's wedding is venued—the Diwan-i-Am. Hundreds of red roses adorn the facade and are prettily fashioned to say "Welcome." Live *ghazal* singers add to the mood of extravagant celebration. Liveried waiters glide by with flutes of Moët et Chandon, while others offer silver salvers of oysters nestled in beds of crushed ice. The aroma of the feast is tantalizing. Chefs at open air counters cook fresh tandoori *kebabs*, chicken and veggie *biryani,* as well as Italian staples like fettuccine Alfredo.

Mini and Priya stay close together through the maze of gastronomic delights. Then Mini hears her name being called. From across the wide crowded room a beaming Divya, hair flying, is charging toward them, followed closely by her parents, Bhatia Auntie and Uncle.

Divya practically screeches to a halt in front of them and flings her arms around Mini's neck. She then turns to Priya and pulls her into the embrace, all three of them savoring for a moment their affection. Mini feels tears pricking her eyelids. The familiar scent of Priya's talcum powder reminds her of what's been missing from her contented new life in California.

She is relieved to see that Divya has pulled herself together after her tragic romance. Her beloved Rishi, whom Divya picked up with for three years after high school, ended up jilting her. Poor Divya had believed with all her naïve heart that her marriage to him was a foregone conclusion, but his mother had other plans for her Rishi baby.

Mini gives her friend another squeeze, then steps back to take a good look at her. "You look adorable. Like your old self again." Her inner Sita is trying to conceal a small, goofy grin, with little success.

"Have either of you spoken to Alka?" Divya's anxious tone interrupts Mini's compliment.

Priya sighs heavily, nervously crossing and uncrossing her fingers. She is upset with herself for letting this go, for not badgering Alka enough.

"*Bhagwan jaane*, I tried." She lists all the phone calls, the visit, the note.

Divya shakes her head. "And now it's too late to do anything but join the celebration."

Mini is astonished. "What could we possibly have done?"

"At least we could be there for her, whatever is happening." Priya's tone is vehement. "At the very least we need to sit Alka down and get some answers before we let her out of our sight."

Mini responds emphatically, her nose pin shimmering as she bobs her head up and down. Her inner Sita looks tortured. For a moment, they could be back in the dorm at Jesus and Mary again.

"Divya *beti*, look." Bhatia Auntie has joined the three of them. She points to the podium erected at the end of the hall where a very dark man is standing, the mysterious Raj Bajaj, the obviously happy groom in a gold *sherwani*. In his hand is a garland of flowers in preparation for the traditional *Jaimala* ceremony, the exchange of wedding garlands.

The chattering crowd falls silent, then begins to part. Two waves of people somehow finding space to open up a path for the bride.

As Alka comes into view, Priya gasps. Mini puts a hand up to her mouth to stifle a sob. Divya bites her lip savagely. Alka's face is ashen, her skin as thin and colorless as skimmed milk, her movements slow and ponderous—one leaden foot in front of the other.

Stumbling, halting, Alka makes her way to the podium. The distance seems interminable. She is flanked on each side by her cousin-sisters, as is customary. But it appears to Mini that they are propping her up, each girl holding Alka's elbow carefully as they lead her forward.

Alka lifts her eyes slightly and faces Raj as she arrives at her place near the podium. Before she has even taken a breath, Raj places the garland around Alka's neck. His eyes shine, his hands are steady.

Her cousin hands Alka the ceremonial flower garland for the groom. Alka flinches, and Mini can see her hands tremble. In the background, the band plays some haunting film music.

Everyone waits for Alka to take a step forward and complete the ceremony by garlanding Raj. She stands motionless, a glass-eyed dummy in a wax museum. The moments tick. The guests' breathing is a vacant silence. Family members exchange nervous glances. The Aunties in the back of the grand room start to twitch and whisper.

Finally, Alka's mom, Padmini Aggarwal, steps forward. She places her hand on Alka's shoulder.

"Alka, *beti*. Raj is waiting." Her tone is clipped, authoritative, and loud enough to be heard through the crowd.

Alka blinks. She glances at her mother. There is grim determination in Mrs. Aggarwal's expression.

Alka's eyes flash momentarily. Then she turns slowly forward, her gaze appropriately downcast. She places the garland tentatively around Raj's neck, withdrawing her fingers quickly, as if burnt.

A relieved cheer ripples through the family members surrounding the couple. Raj's friends encircle him, clapping him on the back thunderously.

"Good job, man."

"Well done!"

Mini is lost in the nostalgia of her wedding to Inder. One week's holiday was as gracious as his accounting firm could stretch. It was *pat magni, jhat shaadi* – quick engagement, quick wedding. No grand Indian wedding like Alka's, but it was full of food, color, and fun. *Khana, peena, gaana-bajana*—food, wine, music, and dance. All her family had been there. Everyone had guffawed loudly when Inder quickly, too quickly, bowed his head to accept Mini's *jaimala*, so eager was he to make her his. She herself had laughed softly, her red *bindi* gleaming with delight, the tiny diamond that set off her perfect nose extra bright. The air was humid and heavy, filled with the mingled scents of sweat, incense, and wilting marigolds. Her *Dadi* clutched them to her heaving bosom when they bent down to touch her feet after the ceremony. Tears coursed down *Dadi's* cheeks, joining her murmured prayers for divine protection for Mini's well-being.

Is it only Indian grandmothers who get so emotional at a bride's bidaii?

Indian grandmothers have mystical powers, her inner Sita scolds her, making clear her loyalties. Mini hadn't realized then how lucky she was to have found such a good man like Inder. "Even if you go looking with a search party, you won't find a Punjabi boy as good as him," her *Dadi* grinned.

Priya yanks Mini's wrist, breaking her reverie. She uses her stature to plow a swath to lead Mini and Divya through the crowd. Alka stands surrounded by people, yet somehow alone. Priya steps forward and grasps Alka's wrist. Alka looks at her mutely, as if in a stupor.

"Alka, come with us to the ladies' room, please," whispers Priya urgently.

Alka takes a shaky breath and nods. She follows the three of them. They navigate their way back through the crowd.

Priya locks the door behind them and faces Alka.

"Why are you doing this?" cries Mini. She hadn't meant to be so blunt, but the sight of her beloved friend in this state of suspended animation is too much for her. She buries her face in the *pallu* of her *sari* and starts to sob.

Alka stares at the floor for a moment before replying.

"I had no choice."

Alka's defeated tone shocks her friends into silence. Priya is the first to revive. She draws Alka into an embrace. "Shh, Alka, it'll be okay." Mini pulls herself together enough to pat Alka's hand awkwardly. Divya looks on, wringing her hands.

There are no words for what they feel. It is as though this loss—Alka's future, her dreams, all their dreams for her—is so enormous as to be literally unspeakable.

Priya folds her arms across her chest and tries again. "It will pass," she says to Alka gently. "A child will come and love will fill your life." Alka says nothing, her eyes dull.

Across Alka's bent head the others exchange a look. Without saying a word, they understand the pretense Alka expects of them—don't feel sorry for her, don't ever talk about what she has given up, don't mention that she's marrying someone she looks down upon, don't ask about her dreams of being chief editor of *Savvy*, don't, don't, don't.

The vibrations of conspiracy are palpable among them. They watch Alka unlock the door, slowly disappear among the throngs.

Lying beside her sleeping husband that night, Mini feels it again, the sense that they have all made a vow of silence.

CHAPTER 4

Divya

PIEDMONT, OAKLAND, CALIFORNIA
2005

Coming up the tree-lined driveway of 824 Park Avenue in our 1999 Honda Accord, I'm overwhelmed at the majesty of the vista that opens up before us—the flats of Oakland, the bay defined by the Golden Gate Bridge, Mt. Tamalpais, the lakes of water—north and south of Bay Bridge, the city of high rises and wooded ridges. The personal residence of Silicon Valley entrepreneur Raj Bajaj and his wife, the gracious hostess Alka Bajaj, is landscaped around an array of massive native live oaks, scattered throughout the enormous estate.

The Greek revival home is adorned with six white columns dominating the breadth of its palatial scale. A balcony extends the full width of the second-floor facade. Before reaching for the brass door knocker, I pause to admire the commanding frame of the façade, appreciating how I would feel walking out this door each morning. Commanding is how I'd feel.

"Wow," Sham murmurs as we walk up to the imposing Honduran mahogany front doors. "These have got to be ten feet tall!"

My right hand is clutching Maya, and my left hand drags the squirming Serena behind me. I've been giddy with excitement since I ran into Priya at the market. But now, faced with the perfectly polished pair of brass lions' heads guarding the entrance to territory as I have never entered before, I suddenly feel a familiar lump in my throat.

The door swings open.

"Divya! Is that really you?" My memory banks struggle to match the familiar, boisterous voices with the two women beaming at me from the doorway.

"Mini!" I exclaim, filled with true joy at seeing my sweet friend. "You look beautiful!"

Mini's nose pin glitters over an emerald chiffon blouse with a low-cut V neckline and sheer tight sleeves. Her cream pleated skirt falls to mid-calf, placing those slender ankles and sexy black stilettos in full view.

I wrap her in a tight embrace. Stepping back, I look at her again.

"What a cool do!"

"Why, thank you." With a hand she props up a mop of curls cropped into a chin-length bob as buoyant as her personality. Her eyes still dance when she smiles.

I turn to the slim woman next to Mini. "Alka?" I indeed wonder.

While Mini has shortened her hairstyle, Alka has lengthened hers so that it falls an inch below her shoulders. Sleek and flat-ironed, it hangs like a black curtain around perfect features sobered by time. Her hair has thinned and is colored to cover the stray grays. Crow's feet fan out from eyes tinged with an inner sadness.

She is impeccable in tailored beige pants and a ruffled cream-colored blouse. Huge solitaire diamonds twinkle in her earlobes, and a heavy diamond and ruby bracelet adorns her left wrist. In my turquoise and white silk *kurti*, white pants, and a chunky gold pendant dangling from the black-and-gold beads on my traditional Hindu wedding necklace, I feel underdressed and out of place.

"Always the last one." Alka draws me inside and into a manicured hug.

I'm defensively annoyed at Alka's jab, but won't show it.

Mini appraises my shoulder-length, pixie-cut with designer-keen eyes.

"You look just the same." She is breathless and beaming.

We have not seen each other for fourteen years, not since Alka's wedding. But when I remind them, silence fills the two-story foyer and bounces off the marble walls.

Sham standing behind me, coughs discreetly.

"Oh, oh, this is my husband, Sham." I step aside, revealing the pleasant-looking man of athletic build. Serena leans against his leg in her striped fuchsia top, bright fuchsia leggings, and hair in pigtails. Her eyes are awed by the grand interior.

So much like me, I reflect.

Later, she will ask me, as only a seven-year-old can, "When will we have a house like Alka Auntie?" I will wince. It does no good to be reminded of dreams that have come to nothing.

Maya, dressed in a Rajasthani ankle-length skirt and blouse with tiny bells sewn on the sleeves, peeps out shyly from behind Sham.

"Come, girls." I beckon my daughters forward and make the introductions.

Priya comes charging into the foyer in a green *kurti* scattered with white dots. Her sweet, youthful face exudes good cheer.

"Well, hello, you. I see you found the house." I nod happily.

I make my way past crowds of guests. I accept a glass from a proffered tray. I let Maya and Serena be cajoled into visiting the Bajajs' theater, where other kids are enjoying Disney's latest animation. An hour later I'm sitting with Mini and Priya on Alka and Raj's deck, sipping Margaritas and facing the bay. Fog is beginning to flit across the Golden Gate Bridge, which only exalts its grandeur. *Alka's wound up with the life we all predicted.* My lip is curling.

"So, what brings you and Sham to California?" Mini breaks into my thoughts.

"Well, after Sham and I got married . . . I sent you all wedding invitations, but you'd all left Delhi by then." I say it off-handedly, but their absence had hurt at the time.

I'm sure mine was the most unglamorous of all our weddings—a simple Hindu ceremony in the mandir followed by a no-frills vegetarian meal at the local Sagar Ratna restaurant, but it would have been nice to have my girlfriends for emotional support. Ma wanted an extravagant wedding, of course, but Papaji insisted on a modest affair. More sanskar, less drama, he bellowed. Ma nodded dutifully, reminded of the Rishi disaster.

"Sham's work visa to the US came through in 1995, and we landed in Queens." My nose wrinkles in distaste. I'm not about to describe to them the modest apartment in the noisy immigrant neighborhood we'd lived in, or how Sham had tried hard to make a go of it in auto sales. A nasty worker's compensation claim by a former employee had left us bankrupt, so we'd closed shop at the urging of Sham's buddy, Gopi.

"Sham is starting a new venture here in sunny California." I gloss over the messy details.

Mini clucks her tongue in agreement. "Yes, it's the best place to live," she assures me, patting my hand warmly.

"What about you, Priya? We never really had a chance to talk at the Indian store."

"Oh, you know, Vik and I got married in 1991 . . . " Priya stares openly at him as he reaches into the pocket of his blue-and-white checked shirt and pulls out a cigarette and a red plastic lighter. With practiced ease, he lights the cigarette and pockets the lighter.

I can see the flutter inside Priya's breast as she watches him draw the smoke deep into his lungs, then exhale very slowly, like it is the most heady experience he's ever had.

Mr. Vikram Sharma, my pati parmeshwar. Priya's smile is joyous. Vik is engrossed in conversation with Raj and Inder and does not turn toward her.

I look at her questioningly.

"We have two kids, Sameer and Anya." Priya lights up—her children are the joy of her life. "They're here, probably playing those interminable computer games in Alka's basement."

A white-haired, elderly man approaches us with a tray full of *keema samosas* and *paneer pakoras.* His crisply starched white *kurta pajama* of fine eyelet embroidery complements the embroidery on his white cotton cap. His slip-on *jutis* of soft leather, pointed at the toe, are also white.

"I'm Kakaji." He places the tray on a side table and folds his hands in a *Namaste* to me. Then he lifts the tray toward me and indicates I should help herself.

"Thank you, Kakaji." I stumble over the words, not knowing how to address this graceful old man. *The Bajaj's actually have an Indian servant?*

"Where are you living now?" asks Mini, resuming the conversation as Kakaji moves away. Alka breaks away from her other guests and sits down with us.

"We're renting a house in Fremont," I say lightly, "while Sham sets up his business. I've applied at some of the local schools for a teaching position. Let's see what happens." I clasp my hands together over one knee, enjoying the cool breeze that lifts my glossy hair.

"And what's new with you, Mini Sidhu Singh?" I ask companionably.

"Not much, really." Mini's tone is carefree. "I work as a paralegal in downtown San Francisco. Two girls. Sophie's just finishing middle school and Rani's in elementary. Inder owns an accountancy practice with a partner. We live in Pleasanton. We must have you all over so the guys can get to know each other."

Her gaze drifts over to the men clustered around the bar—Inder, Raj, Sham, and Vik are huddled together as Inder recounts one of his famous *Santa Singh Banta Singh* jokes. The men break apart, guffawing loudly.

"Alcohol makes everything funnier," Mini observes, bonding with all her girlfriends. "Alka, you're such a good hostess. Your parties are so well-catered and the service . . . muuaah." Mini puckers up her lips and blows a kiss across the terrace to her. Alka sips tea serenely, beringed fingers clasping a fine china cup.

I nod. "Yes, yes, this is so lovely."

"No, no," Alka waves a hand dismissively "It's all Kakaji. I'm so glad you were able to make it today, Divya. When Priya told me she bumped into you literally," this with an amused glance at Priya, "I couldn't believe it. The four of us meet again in the US. What are the odds of that?" she asks brightly.

"I only wish Krishna was here, now," Alka continues. "I so wanted you to meet him, but he's busy with a school event. He's at Head-Royce Middle School. Such a good boy. Gets all straight A's. He's on the debate team, undefeated in his league. In the school choir as well. His dad's genes, I'm sure," she says flatly with a bark of laughter.

"Well, you were always the brilliant one in high school," I say kindly. I notice Mini and Priya exchange a look while Alka is bragging about Krishna.

"I don't know about that," Alka says testily—as if she doesn't want to talk about our high school days.

The giant clock in the foyer chimes 11:00 p.m. Only I, Mini,

Priya, and our respective families are left, sitting around the dining room table. The kids are gathered in the family room, watching a video on the Bajajs' sixty-foot screen. The evening temperature drop has brought everyone indoors.

Vik wanders in, a tumbler full of Scotch in his hand. He pulls out a chair next to me.

"So, how are you, Divya?" His words slur a little. "I haven't seen you since Alka's wedding." His eyes rake me in one slow, easy pass.

I bite my lower lip and try to ignore the warmth rushing to my face. Any fool can see he is drunk.

"Yes, Vik. We met at the wedding."

He sits so close I inhale his aftershave combined with cigarette smoke. I lean back for a breath of clean air. From the corner of my eye, I observe Priya, across from me, shake her head, almost amused. The last thing I want to do is alienate the amiable Priya.

I turn deliberately in my chair so that I'm facing Mini. "Remember how we used to play rummy?" Vik reluctantly gets up from the table and saunters away.

Alka plops down into the chair Vik has vacated and says, "Yes! You know what we should do—we should start a rummy group." Then everyone is discussing the details enthusiastically.

"Maybe we can meet once a week," says Mini.

"We can take turns hosting," says Priya. I crane my neck, looking to see how Sham is faring. He's deep in conversation with Inder at the other end of the table. Pieces of their conversation drift over to where I sit. Sham seems delighted—Inder has offered to introduce him to a couple of business possibilities. I smile contentedly—the evening has gone well.

Alka taps me on the shoulder. "Let me show you the house, Divya. Want to come, Sham?"

We follow Alka through the cavernous white marble hallway

that extends from the entry to the rear of the house, a foyer large enough for a ballroom. The hallway is alive with museum-quality lighting illuminating paintings by the renowned artist, M.F. Hussain. "*Detto* the Picasso of India," Alka remarks.

Twin stairwells arch upward and inward to form an elegant one-story balcony with waist-high white balusters, trimmed by a polished rosewood handrail extending across the breadth of the landing.

I want to find that splendidly bad taste, but I honestly can't.

"Just like the old Shangri-La Hotel in Connaught Place," I ooh and aah over every detail. Alka shows each bedroom, the guest suites. Sham keeps up a measured pace, but doesn't say much.

Everybody is waiting for us in the foyer, ready to leave.

"Bye, you guys," Inder waves to us and nudges Mini toward the exit. "It was great meeting you."

Priya's children are bundled up in their jackets, sleepily rubbing their eyes as the adults say their good-byes.

Maya is sound asleep on the sofa. She squirms and wails as I pick her up. "*Chup, chup*, honey," I say, shushing her. Her head lolls against my shoulder, and she falls asleep again, drooling a little from the corner of her mouth.

Sham gathers up Serena. We follow the Sharmas out into the fresh, clean air, thick with the scent of jasmine twining the railing on both sides of the broad stairs. Ours cars have been brought up to the front door.

I settle both girls in the back, then open the front passenger door.

Priya calls out, "Don't forget. Next Friday, 7:00 p.m. at my house. First meeting of the Rummy Club." She waves from the doorstep. I wave back until she disappears from sight.

CHAPTER 5

𝒟ivya

PLEASANTON, CALIFORNIA
APRIL 2010

My thoughts skitter like beads of water in a hot griddle, touching everywhere but settling nowhere. Sadness muffles my pulse. Almost every Friday night for five years, three weeks out of four, I have driven onto the lush and welcoming grounds of my friends' homes for our ritual of food, and cards, and gossip, and tears, and comfort, and laughter—always lots of laughing.

But each time I have to steel herself for the ferocious stab of jealousy I feel when I turn into Alka's monumental driveway in Piedmont or Mini's Victorian inspired home in Pleasanton or Priya's mansion in leafy Danville.

Our lives have grown so intertwined—a closeness the old Divya could only have dreamed about—that I wonder if some surprise is hidden behind the brambles. Yet every Friday night, and all the other days and evenings when I visit my friends, with and without my family, I practice a meditation of self-reassurance. *They are my best friends. They accept me for who I am. We support each other through thick and thin. The size of your house doesn't matter. Where you live doesn't matter.*

I don't really believe that last part. It matters to me. It matters a lot. Somehow, after five years, Sham and I and the girls are still squeezed into the temporary town house in Fremont. Though Sham's success was immediate, the bottom fell out of the economy, followed by a long, slow climb back. Taking on a mortgage was the last thing he wanted to do.

My friends have never said an unkind word about the town house or the fact we are still renting after so much time, but I can picture them shaking their heads and clucking about it when I'm not around. Since I feel the same way myself. That's why I developed my mantra—it allows me to walk into their houses calm and peaceful, smell fragrances like my mother's kitchen and see my beautiful friends gathered.

This time, though, this Tuesday, I don't need my mantra. Envy is the last thing I'm feeling. I gingerly open the back door to Mini and Inder's house. *No! just Mini's house now*, I remind myself, choking back a sob. The soaring melody of hymns greets me. I step inside softly and quickly slip out of my low heeled sandals. I cover my head with the shawl of my white silk *salwar kameez,* the color of the tunic and loose pants chosen to mark the somberness of the occasion. I have to encourage myself toward the front of the house where the *puja* for Inder's funeral is underway.

My eyes scan the spacious room for any of my friends among the congregation of mourners squatting on the polished floor. Sunlight pours in checkerboard beams through the French doors, landing in streaks on the wide walnut planks like lashings of honey. My wandering gaze catches the beckoning eye of Priya, who is sitting next to Alka. I circle the periphery of the room, comforted by the sight of my friends.

Although there is hardly an inch of space next to her, Priya attempts to cram her voluptuousness back against the wall. She clears a space barely bigger than a baby's pillow for me to settle on, but cozy enough for my size-two frame. With my knees brushing my chin, I lean into the comforting crook of Priya's hearty embrace. Seated beside her, Alka's head is bowed deep in prayer. We are joined in sorrow, gazing mournfully across at Mini, her lovely face devoid of makeup, and her still gorgeous black hair tied back severely into a ponytail. Her only jewelry is her nose pin. Her back is ramrod straight. She refuses to break down amongst the roomful of curious onlookers. Like a mare, her nostrils quiver nervously, causing her diamond stud to twinkle with a million facets.

All the times we've been together, we've never had to face something like this. Tears fill my eyes. I burrow my head in my lap to hide my tears. My lack of control is shameful.

"*Bhagwanji, help us get through this,*" I sob as the chanting rises to a crescendo, ending the prayers to aid Inder's soul in reaching its assignment in the afterlife.

Later, I join the queue toward the traditional buffet lunch—vegetarian and simple in its presentation. A gentle pat taps my shoulder.

Priya is looking concerned. "Are you okay?"

I wipe my wet eyes with my sleeve and sniffle. "Yes, as best as we can all be," I mumble.

"At least we're all together." A wave of nostalgia washes over me. It's comforting that the friends of my youth are still part of my life. By forty-one we've learned that life is unpredictable. A few people I'd grown up with have already died in accidents or from illness. Many more have married and divorced, or moved to such far corners of the world that their faces blur in my memory.

I turn gratefully to Priya and nod at my friend's caring rejoinder. The four of us are more like family than friends, right down to coded expressions—an arched eyebrow or a rolling of the eyes that no outsider can ever fully understand.

I'm about to say something, but I see Alka striding toward us.

"Divya. Priya."

Priya turns around at the urgent tone.

"Mini wants us. She's in her room."

The three of us walk briskly toward the interior of the house. The door to Mini's room is firmly shut. Priya taps on it—a tentative sound.

"Come in." Mini's voice sounds tremulous, almost wobbly.

She is sitting on the bed she shared with Inder. I look at her mutely. Mini looks at once pensive and defeated—like a beautiful Madonna, hair floating around her face. The white *salwar kameez* outlines her breasts, and her tiny waist curves into her hips.

Priya walks to her side and puts an arm around her. Alka sits down on the other side and clasps her hand. I stand next to Priya.

"I'm so sorry, Mini." I can hardly say the words.

Mini turns into Priya's embrace, openly crying. Alka continues rubbing her hand sympathetically.

My breath catches. In just seven days, everything has changed. The solid, dependable Inder is gone. His business partner found him slumped over his desk, the remains of a half-eaten Subway sandwich curdling under his lifeless fingers. A fatal heart attack.

"There's nothing you could have done," the paramedics assured him and Mini. "The poison must have been building up in his arteries for many years."

Mini looks up at us now, gaping like a gutted fish.

"What's going to happen?" she sobs, drawing the air in gulps into her lungs. Priya hushes her tenderly.

I understand what she means. Mini has lost Inder—and along with Inder, the sense that she understands anything in the world— or ever had.

CHAPTER 6

October 22, 2010

FRIDAY, 7:45 A.M.

Priya's right hand reaches toward the half-eaten banana nut muffin that her son so thoughtfully deposited on the counter before rushing out the front door for school. But her left hand pulls it away. Her hands jerk together in a dance of rejection and desire. Oh, how she wants to eat that muffin. She can almost taste the rich, buttery cake crumbling on her tongue, the crunch of the walnuts. The blended mealy mouthful.

She wrenches her gaze toward the window. Green and gold and white chrysanthemums are blooming in the backyard urns. Even her teeth hurt with longing. Her mind is whipped: she wants to be thin. She wants to eat. Anything and everything. She wants to look good for Vik. She doesn't want to lose her body. She wants to be her old, strong self. Sometimes she feels the river of her life is rushing into an abyss.

Only this morning she had been trying on a new outfit for Mona and Jimmy Vora's twentieth wedding anniversary party. She thought the black sequin-spangled *sari* with its dazzling array of metallic threads running through the flamboyant border was becoming—its own statement independent of the body it veiled. The mirrors that encased the bathroom on three sides reflected the ethereal chiffon fabric and the exquisite gold and silver embroidery encrusted with jewel-toned sequins, like so many tiny flower petals. She pirouetted this way and that, feeling glamorous for once.

"So how do I look?" she dared to ask Vik. He emerged from the shower, dripping water on the mat. He stopped and studied her. She felt her face getting hot, waiting for his verdict.

"Why a *sari*?"

"Fashion, honey." She didn't like her big hips, of course, but she admired in the mirror how the tight-fitting fabric accentuated her breasts and appeared to narrow her thick waist.

"Why would you want to emphasize the widest part of you?" His nose pointed at the spongy flesh protruding from beneath her short blouse, despite how carefully she had tied the *sari* high on her waist.

"The widest part of me?"

Vik gave a dismissive headshake and averted his eyes. She couldn't believe he would say such a thing.

"I'm just saying. You always look nice in a *salwar kameez*."

He changed the subject to blather about the busy day ahead, not noticing when she had removed the *sari*, replacing it in the closet along with her joy.

It was always the same. After every dinner party with their friends, he would remark with fervent admiration in his voice, "Divya is looking so thin," or so and so's wife was so HOT.

Once or twice she'd called him on it, but he earnestly exclaimed that he was only making polite conversation. "Don't all women enjoy a PPA?" He had once overheard her friends refer that way to a post-party analysis. "Well, that's all I was doing." If she didn't acquiesce with a quiet murmur, his face turned sullen. The drive home would hang under a churlish silence, the atmosphere heavy as the thick-cut orange marmalade she liked to slather on fresh bakery white bread. She had learned to let her mind drift away to the next delectable recipe she was conjuring up.

By now, Priya has convinced herself that she really doesn't mind. Nothing lifts Vik's mood as surely as a flirt with a slim and beautiful woman. The same way that Priya is turned on by a piece of flaky pastry crackling—one sweet slice like a long, screaming orgasm.

Enough of this daydreaming. Priya fiercely sweeps the half-eaten muffin into the dustpan. *Bhagwan Jaane, I really do need to lose twenty pounds.*

At that moment, Alka Bajaj is sitting in front of her computer, black arched eyebrows scrunched into a frown, reading the same essay for the fifteenth time, checking and rechecking for any lurking flaws. God knows, the essay has to be P-E-R-F-E-C-T. How many years has Alka waited for this moment—her beloved, her only son, her Krishna, heir to the Bajaj dynasty, groomed to take his bona fide place at Yale or Harvard.

Ever since he's been a toddler she's been dreaming dreams she thought abandoned when she was forced to marry. Now her son carries her dreams. She has scrutinized his grades since kindergarten, hired tutors in the fourth grade when his grades slipped to A minus. His leisure time was scheduled with chorus, piano, sports.

In just a few months, on January first, applications are due at all the Ivy League colleges.

In a suburb of Silicon Valley, Divya is bracing herself for the Friday morning rush of chattering kindergartners at Challenger Elementary School. She likes the morning hustle, the drive, getting to work, and the children. She thought teaching would be a soft job. But after eight years, she hates the routines. Like preparing twenty-eight five-year-olds for the trip home half an hour before the day's end bell. Coats zipped, shoes tied, backpacks strapped to the right child. "Oh, you need to use the bathroom now?"

Start the process over. Coming to work has become a struggle now, but the money matters if we're to escape the town house. I walk briskly into the teachers' lounge. I have always loved the quiet before the storm. A few moments to myself to sip *chai* and peruse the morning paper. As always, I turn to the "Homes for Sale" section. I study the now familiar ads for the charming three-bedroom, cottage-like property in expensive Danville with its leafy backyard, and the more affordable five-bedroom mansion with a bonus room and office in Livermore. But do I really want to uproot my family from the familiar, small-city rhythms of Fremont to cowboy country—Livermore with its vast spaces and brand-new, soulless tracts. Or to chi-chi Danville among snooty, upper-crust Indian families? Could my girls keep up with the Patels? And therein lies the catch—no place is just right for us.

The four-bedroom brick house in Pleasanton, which I loved was deemed too noisy by Sham because its back wall abutted a busy thoroughfare. The five-bedroom estate in the affluent Norris Canyon area of San Ramon was too far from the freeway—too long a commute for him. The three-bedroom fixer-upper in a quaint part of Palo Alto was too much work to renovate. Sham has no time to spare from his business activities, and not enough faith to entrust the entire job to me. And so on and so forth.

The list of homes we have viewed, debated, discussed, and mulled over throughout the last five years is endless. Twice in all those years we even agreed on a home and actually took the plunge of asking our agent to convey an offer to the sellers. But when the counteroffers came through, Sham froze, wondering if the house really was as perfect as we thought. Both times, he balked at making a final commitment.

Sometimes as I lay awake at night, I wonder why I'm still married to Sham after sixteen years. My yearning to have my own home seems to span a lifetime. The first years of our marriage,

Sham was investing in his business, so we really did not have the funds to invest in a property. But as friend after friend bought a house and settled down, my restlessness grew. Finally, Sham gave in to my pleas and agreed to start house hunting. After four or five Realtors and forty to fifty good prospects, taking the plunge remains scary to Sham.

In the last two years, with home prices at their lowest, nothing seems to please him. After chasing the American dream for so long, I don't want to settle for anything less than spectacular. But at least I'm willing to compromise on some things. Not so for Sham. So we keep rounding the corner, hoping the next house will have enough classy embellishments to wow not just us, but our friends as well. I hate to confess feeling that we have something to prove.

The sound of the school bell breaks into my thoughts. I circle the three-bedroom charmer in Danville with a red marker. I shove the newspaper into my crimson silk bag with mirror work that I bought in Jaipur when Sham and I were young and carefree and so in love. *I'll ask the others for their opinion when I meet them for rummy tonight.* The bell rings again as I stride into my classroom welcoming the noisy, rambunctious crowd.

That evening, guiding the Prius through commute traffic out to Danville, the blurb hums in my mind like a hamster exercising. "English country home nestled in picturesque Danville with views of Mt. Diablo, short walk to elegant downtown area." Sixteen hundred square feet is a little small for us. The girls will have to share a bedroom since the third bedroom needs to be available for the unexpected guest who might show up with a week's notice from India. But the large loft can be converted into a bonus room for the kids. *We have to start somewhere.* That's my line of argument with Sham.

Even he will agree that the stunning views of Mt. Diablo would silence any visitor rude enough to baldly ask us about the square footage. Moreover, Priya, who has been living in Danville for years, can be counted upon to extol yet again the virtues of the city's public school system. *Yes. I have to convince Sham that this is the right time and this is the right house.*

CHAPTER 7

Friday Evening

DANVILLE, 7:30 P.M.

It is drizzling, the tail of last night's downpour. Droplets shimmer on the leaves spilling out of terra cotta planters in front of Priya's home with its gray brick facade that provides a perfect foil for the wet, manicured lawn. I look at it hungrily, as I mount the steps with slow resistance. *These are my best friends. They support me through thick and thin. I don't have to be jealous. I don't have to compare myself.*

The doorbell is carefully camouflaged on the side of the substantial stained glass doors. A bartender leads me down the long hallway. My eyes adjust to the cavernous family room luminous with wall sconces, gallery spots, chandeliers, and floor lamps. With all that light, there's no place to be invisible here. Alka is sitting in one of the delicate, uncomfortable-looking Victorian-style chairs that fill Priya's sitting room. Her glasses are perched at the tip of her imperious nose, giving her once-beautiful face an owlish appearance as she furiously scrolls down her Blackberry.

I plunk my mirror work bag on the chair next to her. "Where's Priya?"

"No doubt fixing us a plate of goodies." She pats the chair on the other side.

"And Mini?" I can hear the hesitancy in my voice.

"I talked to Mini this morning, and she promised me she would make it this time." Both of us turn to look mutely at the fourth chair that has remained empty for the months since Inder's death.

The doorbell peals, and Priya comes bustling into the room with a platter of kebabs and tandoori chicken arranged around maroon and gold chrysanthemums.

Mini guardedly approaches the table. I jump up with a cry of delight and embrace her. Alka is right on my heels.

"It's been so long," says Alka, dabbing away tears. "And you're looking so good!" She hugs her again.

"Yes, yes! And we've missed you so much." I break off my babble as I realize that Mini is not alone. Behind her stands a petite woman, dressed elegantly, with her black hair tied austerely in a bun at the nape of her neck.

"This is my sister, Komal, visiting from home." Mini clutches her sister's forearm and pulls her forward. "She's always been fond of rummy, so I thought I would bring her with me."

Komal is beautifully put together in a smart pastel pantsuit, a fringed cashmere shawl thrown casually over one shoulder, and a profusion of gold and silver jewelry on her arms and around her neck. I study the newcomer from under my lashes. *Old money from New Delhi.*

Komal smiles pleasantly at us as Mini makes the introductions.

"Lead me to it, ladies. I can't wait to win money in dollars!"

Everyone laughs, including Mini and Alka, and almost by unspoken command we advance to the kitchen table, which is heaped with Priya's efforts since midday.

Komal surveys the over-laden table with wide eyes. Two appetizers. Three entrees. Four veggie dishes. A thick hearty stew of dal. Picture-perfect, separated grains of buttery, nutty basmati rice—queen of fragrance. A tower of round, light-brown chappatis. Komal is delighted to see her favorite chicken curry, garnished with fresh cilantro that smacks of lemon-pepper and ginger.

Her attention is diverted by a loud pop. The bartender opens the bottle skillfully. Champagne is de rigueur at our card parties, and before Inder's death, Mini had been the one among us always eager to imbibe. *I hope she has at least one glass tonight. She needs to loosen up.* I'm glad to see her accept the glass. Her eyes meet Alka's across the table twinkling a happy smile as sprightly as her nose pin.

"Cheers." Alka touches her glass with Mini's. I join in the toast, clinking Mini's glass lightly. "Here's to old friends . . . and new." I raise my glass toward Komal, who holds up her Diet Coke.

We settle into the breakfast nook with our glasses. Dinner conversation begins with compliments to the chef, then segues into family gossip, books and movies, and current events.

The end of dinner signals the beginning of rummy. We walk leisurely to the dining room table where we customarily play here for medium stakes—a dollar a point. Our husbands and our friends' husbands are known to play big money card games during Diwali season, when it is customary for everyone to play as much as a hundred dollars a point. But even the women who can afford it shy away from losing that much money.

Mini shuffles the cards. Alka busies herself setting up the bank—counting out one dollar bills that Priya has provided, and handing them out for change to those who need them.

Priya gingerly eases her large frame into the tiny Victorian seats wishing she could get rid of them. "God knows why Vik loves these uncomfortable chairs. No, I know why Vik likes them—he loves all things dainty and delicate."

"I've never seen a skinny chef," Komal responds. "I hope he appreciates your cooking as much as I do."

Priya concentrates on dealing the first hand, tossing cards to the five corners of the table. "One pure sequence, two impure, as usual."

As the great poet Kabir said, "The whole world is unhappy." Look at poor Mini. Mini's immersed in the hand that has been dealt to her, enjoying this reprieve, and misses the sympathetic glance Priya throws her way. Priya sighs. Imperfect as Vik is, she is happy to have a living husband.

DUBLIN, 8:30 P.M.

At that very moment, the object of Priya's thought is hunched over the smooth surface of the sweeping bar at On The Border, downing his fifth Scotch. The statuesque blonde in a clinging black dress at the corner of the bar has been throwing Vik covert glances all evening from under pale eyelashes. At first he ignored her, not believing that anybody so beautiful and so thin could be interested in his dark features and aging skin. The liquid fire translates the come-hither looks unmistakably. It is safe to make a move. He asks Harry the bartender to send her a cosmopolitan.

Harry is a good guy and never says a word to Vik about any of the women. He's been coming here every Friday night since Priya started her damn card group, even the weeks he isn't actually banished from his own abode. He looks down the bar again. She smiles when Harry places the drink in front of her. *Victory is mine*, he thinks jubilantly as he gets up from his perch with a swagger and begins to weave his way in her direction, careful not to stumble in his drunken advance down the length of the bar.

OAKLAND, 9:00 P.M.

Kakaji shuffles up the vast, curving staircase to Krishna's bedroom and knocks on the door. "Baba," he says softly trying to deduce the young master's mood from the silence. "Baba," he says plaintively as his previous call has gone unheard or at least unheeded. "Dinner is ready downstairs."

"Okay, Kakaji, I'm coming down." Kakaji drags himself down the staircase. *Poor Baba. He studies so hard, striving for good grades so his mummy and daddy will be proud of him. What's the bloody need?* Kakaji scans the 10,000 odd-square-foot mansion with a mixture of fascination and frustration. *Why does Bhagwan ji always sit with one leg bent? They have everything—money, servant (me), prestige. Why can't they let the poor boy be?*

Hearing the bedroom door close and Krishna's light footsteps on the wooden staircase, Kakaji retreats into the confines of the kitchen and busies himself making fresh *rotis* for the young scion of the house, glad that the boy is going to take a respite from his never-ending studies. As he places a plate of piping hot *rotis* in front of Krishna, the forlorn face dissolves Kakaji's characteristic reserve.

"Is everything okay, Baba?" He puts a diffident hand on the shoulder of the boy he has known since he was a baby.

"I don't know, Kakaji. I don't know what's going to happen." He shakes his head, casting his sorrow into the room like an aura. "I haven't dared to tell Mom that my SAT scores have not been the greatest and my GPA is only three-point-eight, and not four-point-three as she believes." He looks Kakaji full in the face, his secret safe with the manservant who practically raised him.

None of this is news to Kakaji, having found Krishna's report card balled up in the bottom of his backpack. He also knows that Alka had been asking for it. Krishna buries his head in his hands. Kakaji pats his shoulder comfortingly and squeezes it. He wishes he could do more, say more, but as a manservant, tradition limits him to a mournful shake of his head—though he's been more the mother than Alka Didi. And Krishna has given him the chance to be a father again.

If truth could be spoken, Kakaji would fill pages with the darkness sequestered under the wine red living room ceiling, in the grain of the oak paneling, and the elaborate crown moldings of the bedrooms. He could also tell how he came to raise this lonely, solemn boy whom he cares for more than his own son. He does send money to Shiv every month, though he doesn't really know him. He hasn't seen him since Shiv was small.

Just yesterday he tried to write a letter to Shiv. He would like to send a letter, but he barely can form Hindi letters, much less English to address the envelope. Instead, he imagines what he would say to Shiv if he could write.

Beta Shiv,

I haven't been able to talk to you in a long time. Ever since the corner paan shop was damaged in the last Hindu-Muslim riot and that number disconnected. Please let me know the new number as soon as the shop reopens.

Beta, I still see you like you were when I left. Barefoot and painfully thin, gripping your mother's hand. Your face was pinched and wan as you tearfully waved to me.

You were too young to realize that I was going to a distant land and would likely die there. Going there to provide you with a better life. What could I have hoped to give you if I stayed in our rat-infested slum. Do you know, beta, I have not seen a single rat in America, not in the eighteen years? A lot of years, but I still can taste the stench of our street.

Have no delusions of grandeur about your kaka. I am no big babu here. I cook and clean for the Bajaj family. My day is made if Alka Didi or Krishna Baba like my chicken curry. And take the time to tell me so.

Is it not enough that because of Raj Babu's generosity you will go to college? The first one in our family? Become an accountant in a good firm. Escape menial labor. That's how my father died. Precariously balancing two dozen bricks on his head for the high rise built next to Indira Gandhi International Airport. Under the sun blistering his back day after day. That would have been my life too but for Raj Babu and Alka Didi. Alka Didi's family driver knew me from the slum. Her mother taught me how to cook. They brought me here.

Beta, if I was not here, what of poor Krishna Baba? Have compassion for him. He is still the same as a baby—innocent, needy, and trusting. When I look at him and see the worry he tries to hide from his parents, I'm reminded of the stray dogs in your neighborhood. Their matted, mangled bodies. Their heartbreaking eagerness, the hunger for love in their eyes. Wagging their tails furiously each time I crossed the open ditch that separated Delhi's posh colonies from our slum.

Beta, I pray for Krishna Baba, for Alka Didi, and, of course, you my son.

Your loving father

Kakaji shuffles out of the room slowly, clamping down hard on the memories that have arisen from the dark landfill of his past.

DANVILLE, 11:30 P.M.

As Priya is clearing away the plates and utensils that night, she muses on how much better Mini is looking. After Inder died, she lost so much weight, but now the hollows in Mini's cheeks are beginning to fill out again. She feels so glad that her dear friend made the effort to come tonight. Dressed in a royal blue tunic covered with small white stars embroidered in silk, and paired with slim white trousers and diamond studs twinkling in her earlobes, Mini looked dazzling. *She's one of those women who gets more beautiful with the passage of time. I hope she remarries.*

It is clear that Mini is ready to rejoin the world of the living. "I'll host next week's rummy night," she'd said.

They all had demurred politely, worried that it might be too soon for her.

"No, no, I want to host while Komal's still visiting."

Priya finishes loading the dishwasher and snaps it shut with a clang. *Norma will be here in the morning to tidy the rest.* She climbs the staircase drowsily. The rhythmic beat of the grandfather clock in the living room reports that it's already one in the morning, and she wonders where her husband could be. She massages the small of her back and yawns widely as she pulls on her old "granny style," pajamas as Vik calls them affectionately, when he is feeling tender toward her. *Few and far, such occasions lately.* She snuggles deep into her down comforter with a happy sigh. *Mini is back among us—the evening went so well. Everyone raved about my brilliant addition to the raita—wild fennel pollen and a hint of lemon balm. I've finally found a use for those two pests that want to conquer the north side yard.*

CHAPTER 8

Mini

PLEASANTON, CALIFORNIA
NOVEMBER 5, 2010

"Mom, have you packed my lunch?" The shout comes from the kitchen. Mini is enjoying fastening the pearl-shaped buttons on the front of her ruffled cream-colored blouse. She frowns, grabbing her navy wool jacket from the front of the closet where it hangs, neatly ironed. She walks briskly to the back of the house.

"Rani, surely you're old enough to make yourself a peanut-butter-and-jelly sandwich." The words she's been composing in her mind start to slip out, but she bites them back hastily seeing her fourteen-year-old's pained face. The girls have gone through enough upheaval in their lives already with their dad dying too soon. She needs to be more tolerant with their mood swings, she reminds herself once again, and takes out the white bread and peanut butter from the refrigerator.

Rani hovers nearby, fidgeting with her paperback. "Mom, there's a dance this Friday night at school. Can I go?"

"Hmm, Komal *masi* and I are planning to go see the new movie *Love Happens* on Friday. But I'm sure we'll be done by the time you need to be picked up." She slices the crusty sides of the sandwich, just as Rani likes it. "What time does it end?"

"Probably around ten. And Mom, I need fifty dollars to buy a new dress for it." Rani's words are rushed. Her face is knotted as if she expects a denial.

"Of course, *beti*. Take it from my wallet. It's on my dresser." She hides a smile. Rani bounds up the staircase, humming happily.

So, that's what the moodiness has been about this morning. I'm not the only one in this house who worries.

Money has been a little tight since Inder's death, and only now is Mini beginning to set his affairs in order. She's attempted to shield the girls from the financial fallout of Inder's untimely demise and she thinks she's succeeded. Sophie is securely settled in her sophomore year at the Boston University, and Mini has managed to pay the mortgage, even if sometimes a few days late. Maybe she has not fully taken into account Rani's emotional sensitivity, so subject to her mom's day-to-day stresses of coming to grips with her new life.

But enough already with these gloomy thoughts. Of course, there were times I felt like I was drowning, but I've managed so far. Even her hyper-critical inner Sita isn't arguing.

Mini slips her own lunch into her briefcase, snaps it shut determinedly, and walks out the front door to deal head-on with the usual Monday morning press at the law firm in downtown San Francisco where she provides paralegal services. She'd fallen into the job by happy circumstances. Like many liberal arts graduates, Mini lacked real career goals when she entered the workforce in 1990 armed to take on the world with a degree in English literature from Delhi University. At Inder's suggestion, she did an online paralegal training. She was ecstatic when she got the job, and in the beginning, the work was intellectually challenging. In 1994, the BART train had come to Pleasanton, so commuting to San Francisco became a breeze.

What she doesn't like about the job is the isolation. As a specialist in insurance litigation, she spends most of her time condensing hundreds of pages of testimony into summaries for the lawyers to use in preparing cases for trial. The hours were compatible with the kids' schedules, and she likes the discipline of working in an office on specific assignments. After Inder's untimely death, she is too preoccupied to do any soul-searching about her career. It's a relief to have a job that fills her waking moments and leaves her little time to think.

Later that evening riding home on BART, she leans back on the headrest and remembers Rani's expression when she asked for a dress. The sudden attentiveness in her face, expecting Mini to say no. She needs to sit down with her younger daughter one of these solitary evenings and explain that Rani doesn't have anything to be uneasy about. Not anymore.

In the beginning, there had been a mess of paperwork to deal with, but Inder had left his affairs in pretty good order. And, of course, she had her own job. She had rearranged finances to pay down a substantial part of the loan on the house. Now, her paycheck covers both the mortgage payment and Sophie's tuition. Any extras, like school dances and the hot lunch program, are covered with the checks she receives steadily from the accountancy practice that Inder owned in partnership with his friend. His partner had come around one evening with his wife to assure Mini in no uncertain terms that as long as the practice continued the check for Inder's share would continue. She's grateful that Inder had the foresight to create such a partnership agreement when they started the business more than six years ago.

"Is this seat taken?" A deep masculine voice bathes her head and shoulders. Mini stares at the blue-eyed, salt-and-pepper-haired man smiling down at her. Mini smiles back tentatively. She shifts on the bench to make room for him. *Late 40s or early 50s*, she speculates, looking at him covertly from under her black eyelashes. *Good upper body. Must work out every day.* She blushes furiously. He's turned his bright-eyed gaze on her, grinning broadly as he catches her checking him out.

"Hi, I'm Tom." He extends a hand. Mini looks up gingerly, ready to politely excuse herself and bolt to the back of the train, but her eyes lock with his and a burst of heated desire courses through her, locking her breath. Her pupils dilate in unbridled longing. *To hell with it. Inder's been dead for six months now. I'm entitled to live a little.*

Her inner Sita glowers at Mini behind wire-rimmed spectacles. *Hai Bhagwan! This shameless hussy will disgrace us all!* she shrieks, looking heavenward for help.

Mini winces, but brings up her right hand and feels it disappear in his big palm. "Hi, I'm Mini."

CHAPTER 9

Alka

Dear Head-Royce counselor,

In your supplemental questionnaire, you want me, as Krishna's mother, to describe Kris's family environment to understand him better.

What would you like to know? Our scintillating dinner table conversations or lack thereof? Because the truth is that the rare occasions when Krishna's dad is not traveling on business and we manage to share a meal together under this gigantic roof are the worst. Our eyes skitter away from each other before they chance any contact. Each atom of air is tense, resists inhalation. The silences are thick as the dust on dead dreams. The only sounds in the room are that of the utensils clanging against each other. Real sterling on bone china.

Alka already knows that she will have to tear this up and start all over again, but the outpouring of pent-up emotions feels so good that she can't stop writing.

Had they always been so awkward with each other? Or has it gathered like tentacles of fog, an insidious animosity that squeezes them and stifles breath? Alka has tried without success to remember.

What she can remember is a time when she was nineteen and the world was hers for the taking. Pretty. Popular in college. Editor of the campus newspaper. Head of the graduating class. Dreams of the future beckoned. She had started the application process to Columbia University—a journalism degree from its prestigious program would be the unarguable credential to take her rightful place as editor-in-chief of *Savvy*.

At that moment if anybody had warned her about the games of Fate, she would have laughed benignly. Her dad, collapsing in a heap at his desk at forty-eight, brought down her house of cards. The business was mired in family squabbles and litigation that spawned a small industry in Delhi for over a decade. And then rescue—a balding, plump millionaire, ten years her senior, stepping in to save the magazine from grasping creditors. Herself the sacrificial lamb at the altar of marriage. Their consummation a series of halting fumbles. The images flitted through Alka's mind like vignettes from a movie whose name she could not remember.

Raj is no wife beater, nor morally bankrupt. Good husband material, if a tad short and too dark. But most women do not have to remember him as she does: a fat, little man in a dark, double-breasted suit, wobbling into the honeymoon suite. Smelling of cologne and too much Scotch. His small hands adorned with a pinkie ring of coral set in gold. His starched white shirt rumpled. His feet in black tasseled loafers too small for good equilibrium.

He slurred his words in attempting to break the ice with his new bride.

When she didn't respond to his overtures, he heaved his belly onto her slender frame. Her knees came up, her heels dug into the bed. He looked at her face. She was staring up at the ceiling, biting her lip. "I want you, Alka. So much. Ever since I first saw you so many years ago."

He wrenched her knees apart and shoved himself inside her. She stifled a scream and bit back waves of nausea that threatened to engulf her. His unrestrained explosion. The weight of his body, the frenzy of his excitement, the desperate push and pull inside her launched Alka even deeper into despair.

Instead of feeling closer to her new husband, the distance between them had widened. Raj rolled off her, walked into the bathroom, and shut the door. Alka, huddled under the cold, starched sheets, heard him turn on the shower. She was certain that no volume of dollars in his bank account would ever endear him to her.

The next night when he tried to climb into bed, Alka could not help herself despite the family assumptions. "Raj, please, I'm still in shock from last night. It's all so new to me. I need time to ease into this married life."

"And Raj Bajaj needs an heir, my wife!"

"Perhaps your son has already begun to grow, my husband. We will know in two weeks, and in that time, perhaps I will have adjusted."

Raj growled in disgust, but already was accepting the reality of his achievement.

She has tried to repress the memory of that first night many times since, but can never shake off the raw disgust she feels the rare times he enters her field of vision. She can't stand his loud guffaw at some crude joke. She averts her eyes from the small mouth working like a fish on Kakaji's meals he enjoys with such relish.

She felt blessed that the first night of their union had resulted in the Bajaj heir—the only goal of their union as far as she ever was concerned—so she could turn down his ungainly overtures with ease. Sleeping in separate bedrooms has become the norm of their daily routine. Soon his business trips became more frequent, and now their paths cross only once or twice a month. If he is getting his pleasure elsewhere, she doesn't want to know—nor does she care. Even living in the same house, they are like polite strangers, who draw back with a slight shudder to let the other pass.

Ever since Krishna was born she has poured her thwarted ambitions into him. He has morphed into a tall and graceful young man, handsome as his late grandfather Som, and golden-skinned like Alka herself. *It's true, he sometimes seems a touch too shy or sensitive. But being on a large, bustling Ivy League campus will draw him out of his shell. He just has to keep his SAT scores and his grades on track. I can make sure of that.* She crumples up the half-written letter to the high school counselor and begins another, one made up of rosy untruths. The various charities on which she served as a volunteer board member, the dollars she raised for the Hindu temple in Berkeley, the Breast Cancer Society, and the Museum of Modern Art. She mentions her giant sunflowers on dapper stalks in her well-tended yard, which took first place at Oakland's annual "Best Residential Home and Garden" competition for two years in a row. As a final beat, she talks of the trade shows she regularly attends in countries across the globe, from far-flung China to post-industrial Germany, in the company of her husband Raj, leading star of the computer chip industry, as he displays his latest Silicon Valley offering to the hi-tech world.

It is the very image of gentility and of a loving, happy home that she'd wanted to capture. Alka puts down her pen with a satisfied sigh, yet a bittersweet feeling lingers. It's not as if hers is the first marriage that failed. Many Indians whose matches were arranged are living a sham of a marriage—whether they have the modern opportunity to meet and talk to their future mate before their fates are sealed on the basis of common family backgrounds and the matching of astrological charts, or whether they catch their first glimpse of how tall, fat, or ugly their prospective spouse is only at the time of the *pheras*. *The only difference between us and those who serve up divorce papers like syrup-drenched gulab-jamun on a platter is that even when you know you have failed, you have to make it last.*

Her breath catches as the ground drops away for a moment.

She shakes her hands and arms until her torso joins in to dislodge the melancholy. She drinks thirstily from the tall glass of water that Kakaji has placed at her side, while his soft steps fade into the distance.

At that very moment, her son is in Berkeley. At the university campus for an informational open house. He isn't applying to Cal even as a backup, but it's something novel to do. Posters were all over school, and, on impulse, he headed for Berkeley instead of home when school let out. He didn't feel like hanging out with his friends who only talk about what school they're going to. Even when they're just goofing around, watching a DVD or playing games, the conversation always turned to THE subject. Two guys already had early acceptance.

There are dozens of schools that would be happy to have me, Krishna assures himself. But, as always, the next thought arises: *but I'm not allowed to apply to those schools.* He'd gone online and requested applications from Reed and Haverford and Oberlin, small schools that sound interesting to him in the many academic counseling sessions required of all Head-Royce students from ninth grade on. The queen of the mail and every other detail of his life met him at the door with the Oberlin packet.

"What are you thinking . . . Oberlin?" He turned red, as if she'd found a porn stash in his bedroom—which had happened to a couple of his friends.

"It's a good school," he'd protested. His mother wouldn't consider even Dartmouth and Cornell—Ivy League colleges, but not The Right Ones. Harvard, Yale, Princeton is where she's imagined him, and that's where he will be going. No one else had an Ivy League school like UPenn as backup.

He wanders away from the open house after a few minutes, through Sather Gate and toward the student union. He has no desire to be at home. It's one of those summery days that break through the drizzly gloom every winter to remind immigrants from Dubuque, New York, and Delhi that they really are in California. He'd grab a drink, sit in the courtyard, and look at girls. Or something. He kicks at a pebble on the path.

"Kris!" A girl's voice rises out of a cluster on Sproul Plaza. He knows nobody here, or so he'd thought, but Anya Sharma is striding toward him in a magenta camisole, skinny black jeans, and high black boots.

Krishna has always been a little bit in love with Anya, Priya Auntie's older daughter. Not the kind of I-want-to-have-sex-with-you love that teenage boys supposedly think about all the time, but more like the younger brother kind. Anya is really something in the looks department, tall and thin, all legs. Krishna is not immune to her. But more important, Krishna appreciates her kindness.

She is four years older, and if you judge her by her Facebook page, you'd think she's a party girl. Always smiling, black hair gelled and teased, toasting the world with a martini glass in one photo, wearing a low-cut red dress in another, dark curls tumbling over mesmerizing breasts.

In reality, Anya is a four-point-o in engineering, already destined for big things after two summer internships at Krishna's father's businesses. In reality, she has always looked out for Krishna. At those endless parties over the years at all the aunties' houses when he'd drifted off alone, she was the one who sought him out and brought him back to the crowd of kids—the almost-cousins and the real cousins and the kids he barely knew. She was the one who partnered with him for games so he wouldn't be left out, shimmied between him and the occasional bully, rescued him from the ritual grilling adults aim at kids to make sure they're doing right by their parents and their community.

"What are you doing here?" Anya engulfs him in a huge, sexy

hug, as if he isn't already flustered.

She takes his arm and steers him off campus, across the street to a coffee house on Oxford Street. It had only taken a couple sips of Americano for him to spill the whole sad mess to a sympathetic ear.

"She still thinks I have a four-point-o, but after this semester, calculus and physics—God, I shouldn't even be taking AP Physics." He catches his breath and barely manages to swallow a sob. "I'm more like a three-point-eight now." He hangs his head, unwilling to look at Anya.

Anya covers his hand with hers. "Just tell your mother," she says. Krishna's head shoots up. He looks at her like she's crazy. "Right," she laughs, "I can see it now, Auntie Alka clutching you to her heart and telling you everything will be all right." Krishna feels defensive, but he has to admit she knows his mother well. Priya Auntie would do just that—pull her kid against her pillowy chest and love him up. But his mother? He doesn't let himself begin to imagine what she would do . . . .

"Just a second," Anya says. "Let me think for a second." Krishna sits back in his chair and takes another sip of the cooling coffee. Anya sits forward and leans her arms on the table between them. "I owe you one, *Chotu*, and I'm going to pay my debt."

For the third time in just a few minutes, Krishna grows hot and embarrassed.

"You don't owe me," he mutters, but they are both thinking of the Diwali celebration at her home two years before. Krishna, doing his usual roaming away from the hordes of people and the noise of the DJ and the aggressive questions—"Will you be an engineer like your dad, *beta*? Ho, ho, those are big shoes you have to fill!"—had accidentally stumbled on Anya in some intense conversation with Rohan Chaudhury, a strutting jock Krishna couldn't stand.

The doorway framed them. Anya was up in Rohan's face. Krishna had never seen her angry, never seen her unkempt—hair disheveled, *dupatta* crumpled and dragging on the bright red rug of the guest bedroom. Frozen, Krishna watched Rohan jerk away from Anya, pull her hand from where it rested on his arm, and stalk from the room. He turned toward the kitchen and missed Krishna entirely.

Krishna ran to the guest room where Anya lay collapsed on the wide bed. His biting shyness dissolved, and he sat beside her, putting an arm around her shoulder.

"Anya *Di*, are you okay?"

That had been her turn to spill. The month before, she and Rohan had run into each other at an Indian party at an amazing beachfront house in Carmel—she coming out of a breakup with her forever boyfriend.

"I was feeling sorry for myself," she told Krishna mournfully. "I'm the one who seduced him."

Krishna had pretended to be cool, but his mind was in turmoil. Anya and that big idiot Rohan Chaudhury? It was too much to take in.

"And now my period is late and I don't know what to do." Her voice dropped to a sad whisper. The wildness in her eyes frightened him, but he was determined to stay steady with her.

"Have you done, you know, a, you know, a test?" He could hardly believe he was saying those words. Saying them out loud. Saying them to Anya.

"Not yet."

That was when Krishna surprised himself. He told Anya to go through the side door and meet him out front. He went into Priya Auntie's bedroom and dug through the pile of coats to find his mother's sequined butterfly purse. He removed her car keys and sauntered out through the crowd of people, through the front door, past a small clutch of smokers, out to his mother's silver BMW.

He was only fifteen, but Kakaji on the sly had taught him to drive years before—the way they do in India. Krishna was confident behind the wheel. He loved the sense of freedom to be able to move on his own. He made a U-turn and stopped in front of Anya, who stood shivering and hunched by a leafless princess tree.

He drove to the next town. He suddenly knew what he was supposed to do—a strange peaceful feeling. Less chance of being seen by someone you know. He pulled into the Walgreens strip mall in Alamo. He waited in the car.

She came out with a plastic bag and pointed to the Starbucks a few doors down. He followed her in and sat down at a table without ordering. A few minutes later, she emerged from the unisex restroom, her jaunty walk restored, a big smile on her face.

Even now Krishna couldn't explain where the sudden decisiveness had come from. They'd never talked about that night—Anya spending the last two summers out of California, so they hadn't seen each other often.

And yet here she is, eyes gleaming. "Yes, I do too owe you, and in a very short time, your fairy godmother Anya, is going to come to the rescue of the unfortunate prince."

She said no more, but entered his cell number into her phone. "Wait for a call from me, *Chotu.*" In spite of himself, Krishna felt better immediately.

CHAPTER 10

Divya

I grew up in the shadow of Pundit Jaiswal, a renowned Hindu priest from my ancestral town of Delhi, well-versed in the art and science of astrology. He came to our home often. Two months after our family moved into a new house and my grandfather died, Ram was diagnosed with epilepsy. Repeated visits to hospitals and doctors did not help. Pundit Jaiswal was called. "The family is suffering from the effects of the Ghanda Moola star." He shook his shaved head sadly.

All of us were summoned, all five sisters, Ram, Ma and Papaji, and my remaining grandparents. We crowded into the living room to listen to Pundit Jaiswal tell us gravely that the proper *puja* had to be done, as outlined in the Vedic scriptures. Otherwise, he foresaw trouble. Bad trouble. Hard times. Dark years dogged by poverty. And then the ominous, "There are indications." I was unconvinced, but who was I to voice my opinion?

Ma rushed to do the venerable pundit's bidding. It is true that the family's troubles subsided shortly after, but whether it is because Papaji netted a big client or because of Punditji's purported powers will forever remain a mystery. Ma had no such doubts. She regularly nags me during our Tuesday phone calls. "Punditji always says to me that the Hindu Vedas are so rich with information that they can easily help us all live in happiness. Why don't you ever listen to him?"

I don't even pay much attention to Ma's nattering. Then, a couple of months ago, Ma announced that she had made an offering to Pundit Jaiswal on my behalf. I could picture the thick envelope bestowed into his cross-legged lap.

"He told me," Ma says enthusiastically, "that he saw a home in your future, a beautiful home. It is your fate, he assured me. And there is almost nothing you have to do."

The nothing turned out to be something—to secure my future home and to ward off the evil spirits, I needed to carry out what was often referred to as remedies. Give up meat for a month. Wear at all times an amulet he supplied, which my mother will send to me. He also assigned a prayer for me to recite every morning after showering while facing the rising sun.

I barely listen when Ma tells me all this in a very long long-distance phone call from Delhi at nine in the evening, 7:30 a.m. in Fremont. I am frantically plowing through Maya's backpack, searching for a field trip permission slip. Tomorrow is the last day to turn it in, and Maya's homeroom teacher just e-mailed me with a subject line reading "URGENT!!!!!" I pull the backpack onto the kitchen counter, undo all the zippers, spread all the papers, wrappers, etc. I put my mother on speaker and say, "Mm-hmm" every now and then.

Maya comes down to the kitchen in pajamas. "My teacher said I can't go on the field trip if I don't bring it tomorrow!" Her shrill voice means she'll soon be crying.

My daughter often makes me feel like a criminal, even when I can't remember what sins I have committed. Just like when my precious brother broke the family's treasured Oriental vase and Ma blamed me.

"If you gave it to me, it must be somewhere in the house." I try to sound soothing. "We'll find it."

"You don't remember what you did with it, do you?" Maya shrieks.

"Shhhh," I hiss, "*Nani* is on the phone from India."

I manage to conclude the call just before Maya stomps her foot and wails, "You don't care about me. You don't care about anything! And now I won't get to go!"

I make a monumental effort to control my fury. Motherhood is a succession of Herculean tasks. "Not another sound out of you, Maya Kapoor, or I will e-mail your teacher that you can't go."

Maya stares back. She's silent, but her body vibrates and shimmers, blurred by the incessant needs that swarm about her. I have to remind myself, *This is my daughter. My baby.*

I manage to get Maya to return to bed. Back in the kitchen, I start rummaging through the junk drawer. I finally find what I'm looking for—in yesterday's trash, set aside for the recycling bin. I close my eyes with sheer relief, forgetting all about *pujas* and amulets.

But the next day on the way to work, Ma's words return to me. I don't know what to think. I grew up in a superstitious home, yes, but I was always skeptical of the supernatural stuff. I didn't really believe in it, but right now I have an uncanny feeling. What if the elusive dream of owning my own home is within my grasp but for some unknown obstacle that could be circumvented by Punditji's remedies.

Are there not always certain peculiarities, certain signs and portents connected with all persons destined to be really successful? Certainly poor Sham's business pursuits in the past had exhibited only symptoms of disaster. His educational qualifications were merely average, limiting his choice of careers. The car dealership he'd started in New Jersey had to be shut down at a considerable loss. Only now, after several years, are we beginning to feel comfortable with our finances.

Late afternoon, I'm driving home, crying with frustration. The traffic. My shortcomings as a mother. Another day of trying to do a good job with the kindergartners while my mind was off in a thousand universes. A motorcycle roars by so close that the vibrations from its engine shake the car and my brain. I glimpse the long hair of the driver blowing back from the bottom of his silver helmet. My heart pounds hard. I whisper a prayer. *I'm going to give it a try.*

For the fifteen days now my meals have been strictly vegetarian. And I'm wearing the amulet necklace—a small copper cylinder mounted with turquoise, suspended from a long black string. It fits right under my bra.

Sham, of course laughed his head off when he heard this. He was not raised with reverence for the sacred and the unknown. He has not tried to stop me, wary of the fury it would unleash. Nor has he agreed to join me—he works hard and he needs the protein.

It's 6:00 p.m. I'm running around the house wildly, juggling things about to go out of control. I consult my mental list of what must be done before the posse of ladies descends on our town house tonight. Kids' toys and sundry dolls (tossed back into bins hidden under the sofa). Check. Mushroom turnovers and cocktail samosas as appetizers. Check. Mixed greens salad with raspberry vinaigrette. Check. To be tossed on serving. Check. Hot lasagna bubbling in the oven. Check. Fresh sourdough from the Safeway deli. Check. Frozen tiramisu thawing on the kitchen counter. Check. Two bottles of Napa Brut Prestige champagne, just as our group likes it, cooling in the refrigerator. Check. Downstairs bathroom clean and guest towels in place. Check.

I take a quick glance in the gilded bathroom mirror and tuck the flyaway hairs into my ponytail.

Calm down. It's only us girls.

But the urge to compensate for the lack of my own home is so strong that it will not retreat with a few reassuring words. I always feel I have to offset its diminutive scale with unassailable housekeeping and culinary skills.

Why? Why? Aren't these my dear friends?

The answers remain a mystery.

I force myself to sit down. My stomach is growling. The vegetarian diet is probably to blame for that.

I pop a mushroom turnover in my mouth as I pass by the dinner table just as the doorbell peals. It is Alka, angular in slim jeans and cashmere sweater, a tasteful lavender scarf tied at her throat and two-carat solitaires twinkling on her earlobes.

I move to embrace her, but over the years, Alka has become ever more prickly, hard to draw out of her shell. Snappish and touchy for no apparent reason, though I suspect the reason lies within her loveless marriage. But even after so many years, that topic remains taboo. We exchange pleasantries, and just as we reach the kitchen, the doorbell chimes again. I scurry back. I hug both Mini and Priya and bring them inside.

The aroma of the hot food mingles with the lingering scent of jasmine incense that I light every morning with my prayers. A cluster of bronze statute of various deities are tucked neatly in a corner of the counter. A silver incense holder on a silver fluted tray lies in front of them. Prayers had felt to me like empty rituals, but with Punditji's recommendations, I'm filled with renewed purpose. Every morning after bathing, I perform *puja*. Not as elaborate as my mother's, but I'm finding comfort and serenity in many of the old rituals. Placing flowers on the shrine and the symbolic offerings of food. Chanting the Gayatri Mantra. Folding hands in front of a deity and making clear my needs and intentions.

The ladies exchange quick hugs and take glasses of champagne to the dinner table. Priya pulls out the cozy club chair covered in beige and Wedgewood blue tapestry and slouches down in it. As the cards are dealt and played, we chat, update, and ponder.

"Ladies, did you hear about the suicide of the young girl from Amador High?" Priya starts.

"Yes," says Mini, "Rani told me about it." She attends Amador. "It was such a tragedy. The girl jumped onto the BART tracks as the train pulled into the Pleasanton station."

"But why?" Priya's voice is shrill with anxiety. As mothers we are all stricken by a child's death, no matter what. Our deepest fear.

"Apparently, the parents didn't approve of the boy she was going around with." Mini has been regaled by Rani with the grisly details that afternoon.

"But there has to be more to it than just a romantic liaison." My practical teacher hat is on.

"Oh, yes. It seems the girl had been depressed for some time. The whole community is in shock. The school district sent all the parents an e-mail notification this morning, which listed the signs of depression we should be looking out for." Mini is glad that for once the focus is not on her. Since Inder's death, she feels everyone is watching her every move.

Alka is worried about Krishna spending so much time on his own. Mini thinks of her fatherless children. My fingers creep to my amulet as I remember telling Ma that my girls are growing up too fast. The table falls beneath a gloom as each of us sends a quick prayer to the various gods we invoke to keep watch over our families.

I notice Alka's subtle shudder before she asks in a voice barely above a whisper, "Can you please forward that e-mail to me, Mini?"

"Sure. I'll do that when I reach home."

While their mothers play cards and silently worry about them, Krishna and Anya rendezvous in the parking lot of a Safeway store near the junction of two freeways. "Like spies," Anya had whispered into the phone when she called to set up the meeting. She was enjoying herself.

"What's the secret password?" she asks him as he opens the door of her Audi A5.

"Don't joke," he says. "I could get killed for this." He hands her a manila envelope and folds himself into the passenger seat. She looks at the thin stack of papers inside and nods.

"Good job," she tells him. "I wasn't sure you'd pull it off."

Krishna shakes his head and shudders. Stealing several pieces of embossed letterhead with matching envelopes from the school office late yesterday afternoon has been the riskiest thing he's ever done. He had a whole story concocted to convince Mrs. Larter, the office manager, to give him a couple of sheets of the paper. He knew she'd believe him—he was a helpful kid who never got into trouble. He'd been even luckier though—she was with the principal when he ducked into the office, so he simply lifted them from the supply cupboard.

"This will do just fine," Anya says. She slides the big envelope onto the floor near his feet and, as soon as he clicks his seatbelt shut, she takes off with a squeal of tires.

"You still haven't told me where we're going," Krishna says. They are headed south, down the 880 toward San Jose.

"We're going to pay a visit to an old friend," Anya says. She looks over her right shoulder and angles across two lanes to exit at the San Mateo Bridge.

"This takes us to Stanford," Krishna says. His mother has been manufacturing visits to Stanford University since he was a little kid. The only acceptable alternative to the Ivy League would be the birthplace of Silicon Valley. Krishna, though, even if he had the grades for Stanford, would rather go farther from home.

Anya says, "That's right, *Chotu*, we're going to Stanford." A green freeway sign announces that the toll plaza is one mile ahead.

"Why do we have to go to Stanford? Are you going to hack the school computer to change my grades? Can't you just do it anywhere?" This is Anya's grand scheme: to hack the computer at

Head-Royce long enough to print out a fake report card.

"But I have to change the grades back," she told him on the phone two nights before. "The kids who hacked Diablo Junior College wound up in major trouble—jail, probation. One guy even had his degree canceled because he should never have gotten into wherever it was in the first place. Even though his college grades were good."

Krishna agreed. He doesn't want either one of them to get into trouble. He realizes that he's only postponing the moment of truth with his mother, but at this point he will take whatever he can get.

"I could break into that paltry system from my iPhone right here in this car," Anya says, "but just in case, on the infinitesimal chance our little stunt gets noticed, I don't want anyone to trace it back to my computer."

"So whose computer?"

"I told you, an old friend." Anya laughs. "Haven't you figured it out? We're going to use Rohan's desktop to cover our tracks." She takes her eyes off the road and peers at Krishna's face. "Don't you think that's a kind of justice, *Chotu?*"

Halfway across the bridge, Krishna looks north across the choppy water of the bay to San Francisco's lights glittering in the early winter dusk. He suddenly feels so tired.

When they get to Rohan's redwood-sided apartment building, Anya tries to convince Krishna to come inside with her.

"I just don't want to see him," Krishna says. He feels like a loser who needs Anya to rescue him from his own mother.

"He has no idea what I'm up to," Anya assures him, voice care-fully kind. "I just told him I need to do something without leaving my own footprints. He's cool with it."

Krishna turns away to cover his disgust. He doesn't understand how she can say Rohan is cool, how she could even talk to him.

Anya gives up and strides into the lobby, and Krishna gets out of the car to stretch his legs. His mother has left three voice mails and texted him twice. He doesn't reply. He plays a game, watches a stupid video. He has no idea how long it should take Anya, but this seems like way longer.

Then she appears, smiling mischievously. "Are you sure you don't want to come up and say hello? Use the bathroom? Eat some nachos? He actually has some pretty good nachos."

Krishna shakes his head and ducks back into the passenger seat. She hands him the manila envelope before walking around to the driver's side. The fake report card is printed on the creamy stationery he'd stolen instead of the regular form, so Anya has added a note at the top congratulating Krishna on making Honor Roll.

"Your mom will eat that up." Krishna doesn't know if she's right or not. He can't predict if his mother will be thrilled or suspicious. His brain feels shot full of Novocaine.

Anya is starving. Before they reach the bridge she pulls off into a Denny's. They both order eggs and toast and study their phones.

"You look miserable, Krishna. Are you sorry we did this? You don't have to give it to your mom. Maybe you should just suffer the consequences and tell her."

Krishna doesn't know what his face looks like, but it must be pretty bad. Anya slides over, puts her arm around him, and starts talking to him like he's six years old. He puts his fork down. It's all he can do to not start blubbering all over her suede jacket.

"I'll give it to her. It's okay. I'll just give it to her, and then I'll figure out what to do. I'll figure out something." He feels like he has to reassure Anya so she'll stop being so nice and just drive him back to his car.

In the Safeway parking lot, she says to him, "You'd probably love Cal, you know."

Krishna laughs. "Cal is good for you because you want to be near your mom."

Anya sighs and leans across the small space and kisses him sweetly on the cheek. "Good luck."

"Yeah, I'm good," Krishna answers.

"Call me if you need me," she says right before he slams the door of her car. He waves and sort of smiles.

It's Priya turn to shuffle. Across from her, Mini reapplies her lipstick in a thin sliver of mirror.

"Okay," says Priya to Alka. "Cut."

Alka divides the stack in two. Priya shuffles again, raising her arm high and bringing it down with a slap.

The talk moves to the recent spate of troubles Toyota is having, including the brake system on the Prius. They're recalling thousands of cars.

"Divya, you have a Prius, don't you?" Priya slips easily into motherhood. "Have you ever had the brake pedal fail?"

"I really can't say that I've had that happen to me," I reply through a mushroom turnover, "but I need to talk to Sham about it. We've just been so busy looking at houses that there's no time for anything else." I break off suddenly. The pundit has told Ma specifically that I should not talk about my house troubles with anyone, hinting that other people's negativity could taint the process.

Priya has not noticed my abrupt silence. We have moved on to their second hand of rummy and she's having difficulty trying to decide what to discard. "Yes, you should get that looked into right away. You don't want the brakes to go out on the freeway," she says absently. The others nod sagely without looking up from their hands.

I mumble that I'll bring more appetizers before anybody has a chance to question me on my house hunting saga. When I return with hot samosas, the conversation has drifted to sagging boobs and bras that help—a recurring theme at our rummy parties. Priya is extolling the virtues of the new Miracle bra from Victoria's Secret.

"Yes, I've tried that, too, but it didn't do a thing for me." Alka looks down at her spare bosom, and we all titter.

"Not an issue for you, Alka," Priya fakes indignation, "but my breasts spill out of their bra cups like Bundt cakes trying to fit into muffin tins."

Mini is laughing, too, but she makes a mental note to stop by Victoria's Secret after her haircut on Wednesday. Tom has asked her out for dinner on Friday evening.

The next night, Krishna hands the Anya-produced report to Kakaji. Biding his time until the main course of goat meat curry is served, Kakaji unobtrusively places the cream-colored envelope on the side of Alka's placemat. Two pairs of eyes look on anxiously. Alka picks it up a minute later, quickly scans the contents, and her eyes beam. Her Krishna can't be depressed.

CHAPTER 11

Priya

Thursday evening Priya's chattering to the passenger seat, though it's unoccupied as she drives home from the Hindu temple where she volunteers every week, preparing food for the *sangat* that throngs there on weekends to offer prayers.

"I wish Vik was home more often. It's been so long since we've even had dinner together. As for sex . . . " She blushes furiously.

"*Chee, chee.*" She can see Sister Grace, the Swedish nun at Jesus and Mary, referred to as "Durga" after the challenging Hindu goddess they'd learned to fear as children. *Such impure thoughts when you are just coming back from God's house, young lady!*

She furrows her brow to banish Sister Grace. But it is true that she and Vik have not even held each other in a very long time. He's been out of the house almost every evening lately. Last week when she mentioned it, he grumbled about pressures at work because of declining business. And it's also true that at his lucrative software company, with the economy continuing to falter, orders have slowed.

"Priya, you know I have to look for opportunities wherever I can grab them. There's no sign of things getting better. We've got the mortgage and college and you want to open a restaurant. That's a huge investment if you don't want partners wanting to use high-fructose corn syrup in *kheer* to save a few *rupees*." His tone was irritated. "You know that evenings are the best time to woo clients. It's like dating in

America. No family connections, no arranged marriages."

"Anya's at Cal, so she's not noticing. But your son gets moody and irritable when I say his dad is skipping the family dinner. Again." She is weary of an empty bed, but leaves her needs out of the discussion.

Thinking aloud as she drives, Priya concocts a plan. Whip up his favorite dishes, put candles on the table. Drape herself in something slinky that moves over her hips. Nature will take its course. Heat stings her cheeks with the image of Vik's bare, buffed chest heaving over her, his mouth emitting that loud, familiar sigh of satisfaction, as he finds release in her fleshy curves.

She smiles at memories of the messy passions of their youth. Of course, his interest has waned over the years, especially when she couldn't get rid of "the baby weight" since Sameer's birth. She has tried every diet known to womankind—from Weight Watchers to the cabbage soup diet, from carb free to a detox, liquids-only regime that left her weak in spirit and flailing of limb. No matter, her flesh has continued to stretch and spread. Vik often comments about her weight, but it never seems to stop him when his appetites need the release that only she can provide. At least once or twice a week, until lately.

Saturday morning, she's in the kitchen when she has absolutely no need to be, cooking up a storm. She hums softly, anticipating the evening.

By two, she's as limp as a rag. She's run out twice—for saffron from the Indian store for the chicken *biryani,* and for daffodils from the nursery. Vik is big on color.

Come to think of it, almost all Indians are fond of color.

She picks a kernel of rice from the pan on the stove and rubs it gently between nubby fingertips to see if it's done. A minute more to be cooked to perfection. Then she layers it with caramelized onions sliced thin and tomatoes cooked in their skin until the juices run dry, along with cardamom in its husk for that sensuous flavor, and a pinch of saffron for a warm yellow glow.

She massages the small of her back and looks around the kitchen. The rich flavors of the *biryani* mixed with the chicken tikka masala are bubbling on the stove. Stuffed eggplant with peanut sauce is warming in the oven, the cucumber yogurt *raita* is cooling in the fridge. Churned fresh mango ice cream is turning solid in the deep freezer. Norma stands at the sink washing the last of the dishes. Priya can count on her to lay the table with the good china from the cherry cabinet and her trousseau silver.

I'll take a quick nap. She pulls herself up the stairs, soft smile passing across the moon of her face. *After all, the night is going to be long.*

Priya is startled from the embrace of silk pillows. She's been having a nightmare of someone or something pursuing her through dark woods. She feels disoriented, her throat raspy. Looking beyond the massive frame of the window, she realizes she has slept for the better part of the afternoon. A soft light pools under the lamp on her nightstand. Her bedside clock reports 4:53.

"Oh my God! Vik will be home in an hour." She insisted he come home early today. She pushes herself off the bed and ambles to the master bath with anticipation brimming in her eyes. She puts on an old *Lata Mageshkar* CD and lights a couple of candles. Yes, it's romantic—but also because she loathes looking at her flesh in the unforgiving glare of the mirror.

Vik Sharma lifts himself up on one elbow and pushes the dark tousled hair off his brow. The blonde next to him stretches like a cat as wakefulness reasserts itself. "Darling." She is throaty. Her whisper brings them into conversation. Vik sees the clock on the cracked wall lit by a neon light trickling in through dusty blinds and heaves himself off the bed with a muffled curse. "Dammit. I was supposed to be home two hours ago."

Peggy places her long, red-lacquered nails on his muscled forearm. "Do you really have to go?" Her voice is still slurred with desire.

"Yes." His biting voice brooks neither argument nor question. But Peggy lacks subtlety. Her shrill protests grate on him as he laces his shoes. The door slams behind him with such force that the frame rocks its bedraggled hinges.

He strides through the dingy parking lot. His S550 Mercedes is parked under the only streetlight, whose flickering death throes render this adventure even more tawdry. Usually, he checks to make sure no hooligans have snuck into the motel parking lot and desecrated his precious vehicle, but today there's no time. Priya looked full into his eyes this morning until his gaze scampered away. Her expectation brooks no latitude.

He finds himself engulfed in a stream of traffic heading east to Danville. *Oh Lord, there'll be hell to pay.*

The tall old clock in the hallway chimes eight times. As the musical tones die away, Priya gets up unsteadily from the head of the massive oak table in the dining room and systematically empties the uneaten dishes into the Pyrex dishes Norma has left on the granite counter. Her face feels as cold and hard as the counter, though without the grainy pattern.

Several facts register in Priya's brain like the firing sequence of a handgun. She has been pushing away a niggling suspicion that Vik is cheating on her. His frequent absences in the evening. Calls when the caller hung up as soon as Priya answered. And a text on his phone. She had been in the master bathroom getting ready for a party when Vik's phone pinged loudly. He was taking a shower. She knew he was expecting an important phone call from his sister in Dubai, so she'd picked it up. The image of a blonde girl in black underwear flashed on the screen. She'd barely glanced at it before he grabbed the phone. The warning signs have been preying on her mind, but she's been refusing to pay attention.

I'll hire an investigator. Priya climbs up the stairs, lifting one leaden foot then the other. She restrains her mind from drifting beyond the simple acts of settling down for the night. She draws the red silk tunic, exquisitely worked with gold and silver embroidery on the neckline, gruffly over her head. She crumples it fiercely and tosses it across the room. She climbs onto the enormous four-poster bed and buries her face in 500 thread Egyptian cotton and down. She feels utterly alone.

CHAPTER 12

ℳini

Mini wraps her arms joyously around herself, feeling like the gorgeous woman Tom calls her. Inviting crisp morning air into her lungs, she walks briskly from the Powell Street BART station to her office. She and Tom are meeting for dinner tonight. *Our first date.* She's giddy with anticipation, and just a tad of trepidation. They have been talking to each other almost every day since meeting on the train, flirting up quite a storm when he calls her late at night, filling her lonely nights with laughter. After dancing around the question several times, she has consented to go to dinner.

Arré, what's wrong with you, young madam? her inner Sita asks, figurative eyebrow raised. *Don't you know pious Indian widows throw themselves on their husband's funeral pyre? And here you go, gallivanting with a strange man only six months after Inder's death?*

Mini swats her inner Sita down, scowling back ferociously. *The ancient Indian practice of Sati was outlawed years ago. In any case, six months is a long enough mourning period in America, even for a good Indian woman.*

Tom's made the reservations. She spent hours deciding what to wear and finally settled on a new emerald green satin top over her flounced black skirt and black heels. The black jacket is obligatory at the firm, but once the jacket comes off, the lacy corset will be peeking out from under the low-cut blouse. Intended to set any red-blooded man on fire. Now that her daughters are settled into their stable routines, she's determined to start attending to her own needs.

Harp arpeggios announce 6:00 p.m. Mini thrusts her chair under the desk and takes one last look at her cubicle to make sure all the papers have been stacked away neatly. She hurries out before some associate hails her with last-minute filing, or a demand letter to be drafted and sent this very second. She snaps her long, dangling earrings into place in the elevator down from the sixteenth floor and hails a cab.

"Chez Papa."

"Running late, but running." Tom texts back, "Slow down. Save your energy for me."

Mini enters the intimate dining room with an uncertain smile, but is set at ease by warm oak paneling and two picture windows over the bay. Both welcoming and homey. Tom beckons from a corner table. Even in Louboutins, there's a spring in Mini's step.

"Nice to see you. Very nice to see you." Tom's deep baritone is like lather as he helps her shed the jacket and pulls out a chair.

"I'm okay," she whispers, shy in the presence of this distinguished gentleman, so unfamiliar from what she has been used to all her life. She sits down awkwardly in the tiny French chair.

"I've ordered us a bottle of Domaine Chandon. Will that work?" he asks politely, bending his head toward her and looking deep into her eyes. Every flutter of her overwrought heart is magnified by black lace.

She shifts nervously in her seat and lifts the glass he pours her. She takes a big gulp. As the champagne courses through her veins, she relaxes into the story Tom is relating about a difficult client. Private wealth management is his forté—and from appearances, he makes a good living.

"Your clients sound like nervous fillies who need constant stroking and coddling." He laughs heartily, agreeing indeed that's true.

Old-fashioned courtesies of another culture—asking her solicitously about the entrée she's ordered, standing up attentively when she gets up to visit the restroom, pulling her chair out when she returns—wash over her like a soothing balm. How pleasant to be taken care of again. It's so nice to have a man to talk and laugh with—a gentleman like Inder, yet so different—beyond the (pleasant) surfaces of leaner, more muscular, straighter, taller. He even smells different, like windblown grass and Wood Spice, familiar and exotic at the same time, something preternatural. Two thumbs-up.

At the end of the leisurely dinner, Tom drives her to the BART station in Walnut Creek. He's offered to drive her all the way to Pleasanton, a half-hour out of his way, but she wouldn't hear of it. They share an easy silence. Lulled by the good wine and the commodious seats in Tom's luxury sedan, Mini dozes off. She wakes up as he cuts the motor. He has parked at a discreet spot, five hundred yards from the station. Tom's deep blue eyes are focused.

"Oh, boy." She starts to speak and is gently urged back into the headrest. Tom's warm lips melt fully into hers. His tongue is as passionate and urgent as hers. Heat suffuses her body, and all her senses dissolve into a single tide.

"Oh, boy," she says again when he lets her come up for a breath.

"No boy at all, if you've been paying attention.

That's exactly what concerns her inner Sita. She hasn't been kissed like this in ages. Tom carefully pushes himself off, back into his seat and starts the ignition.

"Much as I hate to," he says softly, "I'd better let you have your beauty sleep."

She has melted beyond words.

"I'm going to drive you home, and no arguments please."

She nods her head in silent acquiescence, not trusting her voice to speak. She tugs down her clothing and smooths her hair with agitated fingers. Being busy is good. Mini closes her eyes. She needs to make sense of things before it is too late.

This morning she'd read her stars in the *Tri Valley Times.* They were uncannily to the point. *You are going to make a decision that will change your life. It's now or never.*

Their attraction is unmistakable. She is bewitched by his chiseled cheeks, broad shoulders, and firm jaw. He's so different from Indian men she knows. Fresh air—but she has to think this through. She has two daughters of an impressionable age who haven't quite gotten over their father's early death. And her friends? What would they think? Traditional Indians want her garbed in plain white, not partaking in joyous celebrations. In the poorest sections in India, widows are still considered harbingers of bad luck. Granted, she's a modern woman of the twenty-first century, and neither poor nor in India. But choosing to date someone outside her religion, outside her country, outside her race? *Baap, re baap.* Loose translation: goodness gracious.

Do you really think the girls are ready to hear this? Clutching her hands and imploring, her inner Sita cautions, *Not yet. Not yet.* Mini decides she needs to keep Tom a secret for now, though it will be hard not to share this delightful tidbit. She will have to be discreet until she's sure her feelings for him—and his for her—are real.

CHAPTER 13

✐Alka

The day after college applications are in the mail, Alka cannot sit still. Some of it is excitement, but mostly she's nervous. She paces the expanse of the living room. She stops to gaze out the floor-to-ceiling glass window with its dazzling view of San Francisco Bay. Perched atop the ridge in the exclusive Piedmont district of Oakland, her home has grand vistas of the bustling downtown, with awe-inspiring sunsets from virtually every room. She turns back to glance at Kakaji chopping onions and garlic in the kitchen. His simple *kurta* hangs loosely from his stooping shoulders. The gaunt figure looks slightly incongruous, and yet perfectly at home, in the gleaming steel and granite kitchen. Her friends are coming over for their weekly fix of rummy, and Kakaji is preparing his most exotic delicacies. It's just the four of them—but as with everything in the Bajajs' home, it's got to be done right.

Alka's eyes flit from the kitchen to the formal dining room, and rest momentarily on the wrought-iron and glass wine cellar with its gold marble flooring. *I better get up and pick out the champagne for the evening.* That thought whizzes by in the cloud of swarming bees that fills her head.

What if Krishna is admitted to Harvard? Or Stanford? Such joyful news would even merit a call to Krishna's dad, out on a business trip as usual. For the thousandth time, Alka envisions opening the letter of acceptance. But try as she might, she cannot conjure up the feeling of delirium she has endlessly imagined, the years of her labor coming to fruition.

She closes her eyes, furrows her brow in deep concentration, and empties her mind of all random thoughts. Just as she had been taught to do in her weekly yoga class, she focuses on the image of opening the congratulations letter from Harvard University. But no feeling of ecstasy floods her soul. Nada. Only the sizzling sound of Kakaji's onions frying. And an odd feeling of disquiet. She shakes her head to clear the niggling worries. *We'll know soon enough, anyway.* She pads silently into the gold marble bathroom for the full body pleasure of a spa shower.

At nine that evening, the rummy ladies are gathered in Alka's living room. The floor is covered with a custom-designed Aubusson carpet. In the center rests a rich couch of pale gold damask, arm chairs in handsome chintz on either side. Along one wall a divan with round pillows of damask and silk velvet—the whole broad wall. The four friends have arranged themselves in a semi-circle and are discussing the comings and goings of their world while Kakaji serves up saffron lamb kababs and potato fritters.

Priya seems unusually quiet, nursing one drink and barely grazing the food that she normally devours. She is disheveled and unsophisticated in a baggy cotton top and a loose print skirt that hangs unevenly around her calves, as if she'd hastily thrown her clothes together, then brushed her hair into a semblance of neatness—not quite achieving the desired effect.

Alka rests her hand lightly on Priya's shoulder. "Kakaji especially made these lamb kababs because he knows how much you love them. Here, take some." Priya obediently takes one, but the bleakness in her expression doesn't change. Alka takes Priya gently by the elbow and turns her around so that they face each other. "Is everything okay?"

Alka notes wryly that the concern in her voice surprises as well as touches Priya.

Priya dissolves into tears. "Vik is having an affair." She gulps down sobs that cut off the last word.

Divya and Mini, wallowing in the disgust of Tiger Woods's latest exploits, whip around. They put down their champagne glasses and crowd around Priya. Mini strokes her back tenderly.

Priya tries to compose herself, embarrassed at the unplanned outpouring. Divya hands her a box of tissues. She dabs at the tears streaking her plump cheeks and blows her nose loudly. Three pairs of chocolate brown eyes look at Priya with concerned sympathy.

"I'm sorry to have ruined the evening," says Priya, her voice wobbly.

"Don't be silly," says Divya.

"We're here for you." Alka assures her with fiercely loving eyes. Mini takes Priya's hand and squeezes it gently.

Alka tries to transmit her concern and exasperation to Priya. *Really, Priya! We're are not going to sit in judgment of you and your failed marriage.* It must have worked, because Priya haltingly begins the story of what happened last Thursday.

"Maybe he really was at a business meeting," begins Divya carefully, but stops when Priya looks at her in anguish.

"Don't you think I've tried to tell myself that, Divya? *Bhagwan Jaane*, at least, a thousand times."

She nods her head, wisps of gray hair coming undone from the tight bun she had tied at the nape of her neck.

"But, I've smelled perfume on him every time he's come home late this month, and once there was purple lipstick on the collar of his white shirt."

They look at each other knowingly. Priya would never wear purple lipstick. Pink gloss is the most anyone has ever seen on her, and even that would be eaten away with her food before the evening was over.

"What are you going to do?" Alka is always the practical one.

"I have a meeting set up with a private eye on Tuesday, and then we'll see." She pulls herself up from the sofa and heads to the cards set up on the dining room table, signaling the end of the conversation.

After her friends have left, Alka helps Kakaji load the dishwasher. Being in silence with the old family servant always is grounding. Alka's thoughts turn from Priya's news to the admission applications that are surely being reviewed by colleges.

"Kakaji, do you know where Krishna is?" Earlier Krishna had stuck his head into the living room, dutifully said hello to Priya Auntie, Divya Auntie, and Mini Auntie, and then retreated into his bedroom. She had thought until a sweeping glance of his room at the end of the night revealed no Krishna.

"He told me he was going out," replies Kakaji quietly.

"Did he say where?"

"No, Didi, he didn't."

"That's odd." Alka wanders off to the *puja* room in the northeast corner of the house, the direction of Lord Shiva, expression of *shakti* or power, who shakes life up, the destroyer of things. She sits down wearily in front of the foot-high wooden *mandir*, which houses rose-petal-laden sterling idols: elephant-headed *Ganesh*, god of beginnings and remover of obstacles; blue-faced *Krishna*, god of love; sparkling-shawled *Lakshmi*, goddess of wealth and beauty; *Saraswati*, goddess of wisdom; dark *Durga*, mother of the universe; and regal *Lord Vishnu*, preserver of the universe. She closes her eyes and prays desperately for Krishna's acceptance at Harvard, at Stanford. Even at Yale.

"If not those three," she pauses, bobs her head, "even UPenn will do, Lord," invoking the name of *Ganesh* as she concludes her prayer.

Krishna, too, is praying zealously, leaning against an ornate pillar at their local Hindu temple some twenty minutes from the Bajaj residence. The temple is crowded, even at this hour. Visitors jostle in line to get a glimpse of the statue of Lord Vishnu to whom the temple is dedicated. Some of them openly gawk at Krishna. His slender body is pressed against the pillar, his head bowed in obeisance. Krishna is oblivious to all the stares.

"Dear Lord Vishnu," prays Krishna, his eyes squeezed tight, "I need your help. You know how my mom thinks I'm going to get into an Ivy League school, but I'm not so sure anymore. I feel awful for deceiving her. But I could never keep up with her expectations of me, her star student. In the last two years, I've realized that I'm just average. I know I should have told her then, but I didn't want to disappoint her. And now I'm afraid I'm going to break her heart. So, please, please, Vishnu, send me a miracle."

He raises his eyes, as if the skies will part and a bolt of lightning will strike, just like in the old tales Kakaji used to tell him. How Vishnu defeated wicked King Hirayanakashipu who had ordered his son Prahlad to hug a red-hot iron pillar. Prahlad prayed to Vishnu to protect him. Then he noticed a line of ants moving unharmed up the hot pillar, a sign that the pillar would not harm Prahlad either. As Prahlad hugged the pillar, thunder and lightning raged across the sky. The pillar burst open and there stood Vishnu himself—half-lion, half-human. In one stride, he reached the king as he stood in the palace doorway and tore him apart!

Send me a message, Lord Vishnu. Let me know you heard my prayers. Krishna waits. He turns despondently. Krishna descends the narrow, winding steps of the temple to begin the dreaded, silent drive home.

CHAPTER 14

Divya

Sometimes I feel like Sham and I are always playing catch-up with the others. Priya, Mini, and Alka had been in the same high school when I arrived. They are the same age as I, but each got married before me and started her family pretty quickly. I finished college and went home to fall in love with Rishi, the quiet Gujarati boy whose simple, unassuming family was quite unlike my boisterous Punjabi clan.

While my friends' parents were scouring the matrimonial ads for suitable matches, I was basking in Rishi's love and attention. Lying in his arms, I let myself dream of a life where love did not need to be kept secret, and children, when they came, would be welcomed warmly. I attended each one of my friends' weddings with not even a tinge of envy at their seeming good fortune. I was secure—Rishi and I would marry after he attained his engineering degree from the Indian Institute of Technology in Mumbai, India's premier engineering college.

Rishi's mother had long ago decided that a good Gujarati boy must marry a good Gujarati girl to live happily ever after. I could blame it on her. I could say that she used blackmail, tears, and tantrums to subdue Rishi to her strong will and possessive love. In the end, she won. But the truth is, in the end, Rishi didn't have the strength. The captivatingly gawky, soft-spoken mama's boy that I had foolishly been daydreaming over slinked off with his tail between his legs to marry the virgin bride of his mother's choosing.

I soaked my pillow every night with tears while my parents launched their own quest to find their daughter a match that would put to shame that "spineless Rishi" and "those brazen Patels." That would put an end to the town gossip, that would drown out the hushed whispers I heard, the sideways glances of the old ladies as I passed them grouped at the neighborhood market or the community temple.

Five agonizing, tortured months after Rishi broke up with me, I acknowledged I'd been stupid. "He chewed you up and spat you out to please his bleddy mother," Papaji flung at me vehemently. I bawled uncontrollably at the truth of his words. Having done such a miserable job at it myself, I decided to let Ma and Papaji find the right match for my flawed being. And so it was that Sham and I came to be married after knowing each other for barely a week.

Sham was a handsome Punjabi boy with oodles of ambition, but no family money or pedigree to boast of. His simple, middle-class family had lived their whole lives in a modest, rented apartment in an unpretentious part of New Delhi. Certainly not my equal in status. But my father recognized in him a raw hunger to succeed. And Sham, having secured for himself a sizable dowry from Papaji that included two coach tickets to the promised land of Queens, New York, USA, was willing to overlook my romantic indiscretions, euphemistically calling them "skeletons in the closet" that were best filed under the heading of "don't ask, don't tell."

I was resigned to my fate. At the arranged meeting Papaji set up for us in our living room, over *chai* and snacks, I changed my mind. Sham was a breath of fresh air in my moldy existence. He was only five feet nine, but broad shouldered. Short black curls framed large brown eyes, and he had a straight nose and a square jaw. He came in all-American dirty jeans and scuffed shoes that had seen better days.

But when he spoke about his dreams of settling down in America, his face lit up with anticipation and the fire in his belly was incendiary.

It will be a relief to get away from this town's small-minded bitches who watch my every move. I allowed myself a flicker of real, tangible hope, filled with the promise of new beginnings and a fresh start.

When we moved from New York to California six years ago, I had been thrilled to reconnect with my friends from high school. They welcomed me into their intimate circle of spouses and kids, and together we had come up with the idea of The Rummy Club. At last I felt truly one of them. All that remained was a home to call our own.

The circles in which we lived and moved, the relative worth of everyone shows itself in full only in the houses we live in. If you are determined to stay in the area, you could move to one of the outlying suburbs, as all the practical people do, and live there decently. Early on, I knew couples who had nosed deep into neighborhoods in Livermore or Antioch. The middle class extended its reach, reconfigured its zone of territories. Narrow Subway stores and Starbucks cafés grew on patches of street beside check cashing stores and rundown, walk-in pet clinics. Those neighborhoods were overrun with families now, and if the new residents were incidentally knocking out the low-income dwellers, we couldn't really think too much about it; that's how the big picture always worked. Gentrification.

The less adventurous couples I knew went to quaint and faraway towns with a single, narrow main street and one not-so-great restaurant that closed at eight. As if there were curfews against desperadoes roaming freely. But we would neither go to Livermore nor buy a house in an outlying town like Modesto. We would keep looking for the ideal deal, the promising house in foreclosure in Pleasanton or Danville or Oakland, the areas where our friends lived.

When will I get my own house? is the plaintive cry my heart beats out as I fall asleep every night and the first thought I wake up with every morning.

Now the whole family is touring an open house in Danville, as we are wont to do on practically every Sunday afternoon.

"And here's the huge loft I was telling you about. Look at the space it has! You can put in a pool table, video games for the kids, and you'd still have room for a couple of couches!" Our latest Realtor, Jackie, has a high-pitched voice that drones on as I close my eyes and try to picture myself in this expansive, sunlit home set in a newer part of the suburb.

The house is certainly big enough to comfortably accommodate our family, even with the addition of Sham's parents, who will be arriving next month for a twelve-week stay. Toll Brothers is responsible for the avalanche of cookie-cutter homes I can see from the kitchen window. They spread down the hill like fingers of an child's outstretched hand. I turn from the window, sweeping my gaze over the brand-spanking-new appliances, state-of-the-art cooktop in the gleaming granite island, and silver drawer pulls on the "one-of-a-kind" mahogany cabinets. I pick up one of the glossy brochures strategically placed on the counter.

Sham is nodding approvingly. He seems genuinely enthusiastic. Maybe, maybe this will be the one.

"What a shame they tore down those beautiful homes to build this new community," I say, more loudly than I realized. What I really long for is something less soulless, something more in keeping with my personal style—like the old houses these have replaced.

Jackie's accusing eyes swivel swiftly toward me. "Oh, not at all," she says rapidly. "There's still plenty of hills to look at, if that's what you're concerned about," she says with a slight emphasis on *you.*

In the great room, Sham lifts one eyebrow, no doubt surprised that I am uncharacteristically taking the role that usually belongs to him.

"I want to see something older, something with more character." I look at Jackie and Sham determinedly. Sham's shrug indicates *suit yourself*. He walks to the open back door and calls the girls in from the backyard where they are hanging and twirling on the recently installed swings.

A quintessential salesperson, Jackie is already rifling through her thick black binder of recently listed properties. "I can take you to this one." She enthusiastically points a long red nail to a charming bungalow in an older part of Danville. Sham comes back and takes a quick peek. The aging but pleasant looking home has 2400 square feet, four bedrooms, two-and-a-half baths. Asking price is 1.5 million dollars.

I look Sham full in the face. The complex expression says, *The square footage is a little less and the listing price a little too much, but if it has everything else we want, then we can make it work.*

"It's worth paying a visit," he says to Jackie. I beam rapturously at him, and the Realtor nods approvingly, her platinum hair bobbing up and down.

Thirty minutes later, we're standing at the open doorway of the house in the photos, looking out at the welcoming backyard with its massive sequoia tree in the far corner, the stone fountain with a lilting gurgle on the concrete patio, and masses of early azaleas in pink, purple, lavender, and a red only *Lakshmi* could create, in flower beds scattered throughout the yard. Behind the backyard, the double domes of Mt. Diablo loom. I have a sudden vision of myself lounging under the shady boughs of the ancient tree. My girls play hide and seek among the tall shrubs, squealing happily as they spray each other from the fountain though the January day is chilly. The picture shifts. Now, I'm serving iced tea and cakes to my card-loving friends on a hot summer afternoon while they gush admiringly over the riotous bunches of flowers spilling out of the stone urns that grace the entryway.

"I like it." Even I can hear the longing in my voice. I place an inquiring hand on Sham's arm. But he is examining the shag carpet fraying at the edges, the peeling wallpaper in the kitchen, and the green tile in the bathroom that screams circa 1980. He catalogs the items that will need to be replaced or repaired.

"They're only cosmetic changes," I interrupt excitedly. "The handyman at school would cut us a good deal."

"Okay." Sham's voice has a pause, imperceptible to anyone but me. "If we can get it for $1.28 million, we'd have money left over for the repairs." He turns his head to check the roof. It will need to be reshingled.

In a quick rush of words, I cut into his thoughts: "I know it's not half as spacious as the Toll Brothers property we looked at earlier. And your parents would have to share a bathroom with the girls. But there's the mature landscaping. And the girls can walk to downtown. The very quaint downtown." I lift my eyebrows for emphasis.

I picture Sham's mom chanting her daily prayers under her breath while Dad would have a peaceful place to scour the newspaper for stories of the drugs and violence of a Big Bad America to carry back to his neighbors in the small officer's colony where they still lived.

"Let's think about it a little more." Sham looks at my upturned face with a smile.

At least he didn't say no, I console myself, chewing my bottom lip. I follow my husband out to the car. "My Lord and Master and High Command of the Household," which is what I call him when I'm frustrated by his indecisiveness.

CHAPTER 15

Priya

Priya remembers her mother telling her this on her wedding night: "*Beti*, marriages are made by destiny, but what you make of them is up to you." *Did my mother know? A premonition born of experience and wisdom?* Priya is sitting on a dark leather couch in the small waiting room of the private investigator's office, wringing her ring-bedecked fingers nervously. Alka, seated next to her, reaches, puts her hand over Priya's, firmly stopping the nervous motion. Priya looks down at the two clasped hands and swivels her head to look at her friend. Her eyes are swimming with tears.

"Thanks so much for coming with me, Alka," she whispers. Alka nods reassuringly and gives her hand another squeeze before withdrawing it as the receptionist beckons them inside.

"Bad news, I'm afraid," says Derek Bensimon, private investigator, without preamble. He pushes a manila folder toward Priya with one pudgy finger. Priya picks it up with trembling fingers and a pounding heart. She quickly skims the contents. The report is brief but conclusive. Vik is having an affair with one forty-something blonde named Peggy. There is a picture of her, and Priya can see at one glance that she is indeed Vik's type. Blonde, buxom, and pretty in a brassy way. For a terrible moment, she thinks she's going to be sick.

Snap.

Priya shuts the folder. Her face is ashen as she gets up, ready to leave. *In our Punjabi culture, we believe that whether or not a daughter's doli leaves from her parents' home, her corpse must be lifted from her husband's home.* She shivers. *It is what it is.*

"Thank you, Mr. Bensimon, for your time and for this. I'll put your final check in the mail."

Derek Bensimon nods as Priya turns to the door purposefully, Alka hot on her heels. Priya feels icy-cold but oddly relieved as well. This charade of a marriage has been going on for too long. She knows now what she has to do.

Alka drops her at home twenty minutes later—the Hollywood hacienda of stucco, red tile, and wrought iron. It usually gives Priya a thrill to see it. Today she wearily climbs the stone steps to the front door. Her insides are still shaking, but her mind is oddly at peace. Alka suggested she have a cup of tea and lie down for a nap, but she feels oddly energized, even full of vigor. She needs to cook her adored childhood dish, *sambhar.* She needs to. The South Indian lentil soup is her best comfort food, no matter the season. Vik doesn't like South Indian food, so she hasn't made it in years. Now she's free of the burden of always pleasing his highness.

At twenty to six, Priya is patiently wading through her cookbook journal, a dog-eared collection of recipes passed down by her mother and grandmother, smeared with food stains and barely held together by a frayed ribbon, once pink, now more the color of curry. With the recipe clutched in her fist, she triumphantly launches herself into the rhythmic motions of chopping up onions and tomatoes, humming an old Indian song from the movie *Muqaddar Ka Sikandar* that she thought she had long forgotten.

Everyone arrives crying, but the one who exits laughing
Will be called the king of destiny, my dear

Life is unfaithful, one day it will leave you
Death is a lover, it will take you with it

At precisely 7:15 p.m., Vik walks in the door, car keys jauntily dangling from one finger. He stops short at the scene in the kitchen. Priya is bustling around as frenzied as the two pots simmering on the range. *Sambhar.* The heady smell of curry leaf wafts to the hallway, all with peppy tunes reminiscent of Indian film songs from the 70s—Priya's favorite type of music—playing on his son's CD player. And Priya herself, when she turns to look at him, is wide-eyed, flushed, and full of a spirit he has not seen since the early years of their marriage.

"*Sambhar* smells good," he says tentatively, advancing toward her. The joie de vivre that emanates from her draws him in. He toys with the shocking idea of kissing her, an urge he hasn't felt in years.

"It'll be ready in ten minutes," Priya returns coolly. "Why don't you go up and freshen yourself? I'll call you when it's ready. Let's eat early—I need to talk to you after dinner."

"What about?" Vik is not liking the fact that he will have to wait until after the meal to find out what's on his complacent wife's mind.

But Priya puts up a hand imperiously. "After dinner."

Vik skulks off grudgingly toward the staircase.

Dinner passes in total silence. Vik attempts some desultory conversation once or twice, but when he sees that Priya is preoccupied, he relinquishes the effort and indulges in chewing his food noisily. When he gets up to leave his place at the head of the table, Priya places a hand on his arm, restraining him.

"Wait, Vik. I have something to show you."

He looks at her blankly as she pulls out the private investigator's report from the buffet. Priya opens the folder slowly and out spill a stack of photographs of Vik and Peggy. Lots of pictures. Kissing in the parking lot of Motel 7. Going into a room there hand in hand. In his Mercedes exiting the parking lot together.

Vik winces, then looks up to meet Priya's steady gaze.

"I want a divorce," she says flatly.

Though the truth is evident, right there on the dining table in living color in a way no one but a blind man can mistake, Vik tries to deny it.

"It was just a one-night stand," he sputters. "She doesn't mean anything."

Then, "It was nothing but a stupid mid-life crisis." And, "I was going to break it off anyway."

When her resolve doesn't waver, he breaks down. Crying unashamedly, he keeps repeating, "So sorry, so sorry." He even moves as if he's going to lay his head on her ample lap—as he used to a decade ago—but she pushes him away. The marriage has run its course and nothing he says can change that.

The only time Priya feels her decisiveness weaken is the next morning when she tells the children. Vik had stormed off early in his Mercedes, dark circles under his eyes announcing a sleepless night. In the warm kitchen Priya sits down with Sameer and Anya, who's home from Cal for the weekend, and breaks the awful news. They are shocked to the core. Sameer's lower lip quivers. Anya tries desperately to hide her tears. At the sight of her wounded children, Priya crumbles, weeping loud uncontrollable sobs that she tries to rein in because she doesn't want to scare her children. Anya flings her chair back and joins her mom in the armchair, cradling her as if she is the mom. It takes a few minutes for Sameer to join them. He strokes his mom's back tenderly. Priya cries and cries, spilling out the sorrow of a decade.

When the storm of tears abates, the three of them shove the heavy Victorian furniture out of the way and sit down in a semi-circle on the Tibetan rug that covers the floor of the family room. Priya asks her children to link arms with her. She chants a mantra, asking the good Lord Krishna for strength in this desperate time.

Om Tat Purushaya Vidhmahe
Mahadevaya Dheemahe
Thanno Rudra Prachodayath
Om Panchavaktraya Vidmahe

On and on they recite, just like they used to every week when the kids were little and Vik was just starting out his business—when he had more time and inclination to be with his family.

The comfort and familiarity of their prayer calms Sameer and Anya. Priya's glad. They have been frightened by her outburst, she knows, but after the initial shock they both comforted her saying, "It's for the best, Mom."

"We know how Dad treated you, Mom. We've hated seeing you so unhappy. It's okay to leave him," says Anya. Sameer nods.

Priya turns around in stunned disbelief and gathers her daughter's tiny frame to her bosom.

Since when have my kids got so intuitive? She sniffles loudly into her crumpled tissue, looking at them gratefully for their understanding.

$\mathcal{M}$ini

It's Saturday, and Priya's already called Mini five times. She's called Divya and Alka as well—twice each—reminding them all they'd promised to accompany her to Jimmy and Mona Vora's twentieth wedding anniversary. When Priya was married to Vik, they lived down the street from the Voras and moved in the same social circle, so, of course, the invitation was expected. But Priya is in a tizzy after Mona told her there was no way to not invite Vik.

Priya tells Mini for the umpteenth time, "I can't bear to be around him at a social affair with all our common acquaintances. It's embarrassing, and he'll probably bring some tart."

"So what if he does? You have to get used to seeing him around, unless you plan on moving. Come on, it'll be fun. The last time Mona had one of her fabulous parties I met Sonu Sood—you know, the cute actor from *Dabangg*." Mini prompts helpfully— Priya is often behind on the latest Bollywood trivia and has to be brought up to date by her personal celebrity hound.

"He was so hot. He ogled me all night. Unfortunately, I was married then," Mini finishes dramatically, as if yearning for lost opportunities. "Let's just go."

They agree to meet at 8:30. For a formal party in celebration of a milestone, the dress code is Indian—women in *saris* or *salwar kameez*, but the men could get away with a suit and tie. Mini had gotten rid of her ostentatious *saris* after Inder's death, and her jewelry was stashed away in the bank vault—which is closed on the weekends.

After prowling through her closet, she settles on a pink *sari* with a broad gold border. The fabric has a subtle paisley print. She is a widow in the eyes of the celebrants, after all. But it is a celebration. She adds gold hoop earrings and puts up her long hair in a chignon. In the pink georgette, her body shimmers like spun glass. Even her inner Sita looks at her approvingly. *You look like an Indian princess, a lotus flower. Virry, virry nice. Maybe a good Indian man will sweep you off your feet.* Mini rolls her eyes.

Priya looks stunning in a white chiffon *sari* with a design of hand-embroidered roses. Her short red *choli* is shot with gold, and she's donned a gold filigree necklace and earrings to match. The jasmine wound around her hair draws attention away from the sagging middle to her cherubic face, still youthful when she flashes her brilliant smiles.

Mini looks at Priya surreptitiously as they enter and is happy to find a small smile playing around her lips. She can tell it's for show in case they run into Vik. But still, it makes her face glow.

Alka is always invited to these events. Her wealth and status make her a sought-after guest, but she almost always declines since Raj is never in town. On this evening, she's putting in a rare appearance to lend Priya moral support. She bypasses the traditional *sari* for a more casual *salwar kameez*. *The color suits her*, Mini muses—a bright blue silk with the silver border of the kameez complementing the *dupatta* she wears, draped across her shoulders. Since she hates excess of any kind, Alka's only jewelry are three-carat solitaires twinkling in her earlobes. *Very classy.* Mini gives Alka the thumbs-up.

Divya has been invited—not because she is in the same social strata as the Voras, but probably because of her friendship with the other three women. She and Sham are expected later, after she's settled her girls in for the night.

The three friends enter the Voras' home through a white foyer. In the middle stands a round, rosewood table, with a huge and exquisite arrangement of intoxicating red roses. Oil paintings in a variety of styles grace the walls. A hired man, dressed in a white frilled shirt and a tuxedo, leads them through the set of double doors that open upon the white-themed wide corridor. At the far end is the entrance to the living area. Its double-high ceilings are lit up like a football field at a night game. The far wall is glass opening to a balcony that overlooks Danville and the foothills of Mt. Diablo.

As the three women walk into the Voras' living room, heads swivel. Almost everyone, men and women alike, look at them—*with cash register eyes swiftly totaling up our assets*, thinks Mini. *It's like let's give the face an eight, the ass a seven, the grand total being . . .* Penetrating the social jungle as newly single is unnerving. *Be nice, beti. Enjoy the celebration.* Her inner Sita is cool. Perhaps cold.

By unspoken agreement, they head toward the bar. Its 9:30—time for some fortification.

"I'll be right back," Mini hisses to Priya and Alka. "My bladder's bursting."

On the way back from the ladies' room, she stops to admire the Hussain painting of Goddess *Saraswati*.

"Ah, I see you've found Mona's naked *Saraswati*," says a voice in her ear. It's a tall, dapper-looking man in a well-cut suit. "This one was very controversial in India, but Mona liked it anyway—or because of that." The man laughs heartily.

He has a nice laugh. Not bad-looking for an Indian. Mini gives him a quick look-over.

"We haven't met before, have we? I'm Mona's brother from Chicago. Dr. Tarun Rathore at your service." He gives a small bow.

Mini bats her eyelashes, enjoying herself. He doesn't wear a wedding band, she's noticed. "Mini Singh."

She proffers her hand, and he bends over it with a flourish.

"A beautiful name for a beautiful woman."

Mini can feel her cheeks tingling, but before she can think of a witty comeback, a plump, diminutive woman with very pink lips and frosted blue eye shadow emerges from a room. Her arms are heaped with gold bangles that match her glittery *sari*.

"Ah, there you are Tarun." She tucks a possessive arm in the crook of his elbow, then looks suddenly suspicious. A swift appraisal of Mini's simple pink *sari* and ringless fingers find her wanting. "Has my husband been behaving himself?" she asks Mini with a low growl.

"Yes, quite so," Mini returns calmly. She nods slightly toward Tarun, a gesture which discourages further conversation, and turning on her heel, walks out, her back erect.

A few minutes later, comfortably ensconced in a corner with a gin and tonic in her hand, Mini looks around. She recognizes the satellite TV talk show hosts, the Danville pack, the hi-tech crowd who've made it big in Silicon Valley, some socialites—the usual suspects who drift from one high society Indian party to the next, often flying private to southern California and back for the evening if the host is important enough.

Mini notices the feigned aplomb as Sham and Divya make their entrance. Mini can tell Divya's nervous the way she flicks away imaginary locks of hair as she takes in the posh surroundings which enhance the chiffon draped around her slim figure—a gorgeous turquoise and cream *sari* flecked with gold.

"You look beautiful, darling." Mini gives Divya a welcoming hug.

"Thanks, Mini." Divya gains back her equilibrium as Mini leads her to the others.

"So, is *he* here?" Priya jumps in.

"I don't think he's coming." Sham has already been to the bar and came back with drinks for all of them. "I just heard Jimmy tell Mona he had a text from Vik."

"Not unexpected," Mini comments to support Priya who has visibly relaxed. She leads Priya by the elbow to a large, white tent set up in the backyard. Three enormous shallow chandeliers throw rainbow sparkles over the ivory silk lining of the ceiling and walls. Beneath the domed ceiling shines a black-and-white checkered dance floor, the right side occupied by a stage where a saxophonist plays a haunting solo from an 80s Bollywood movie. The rest of the stage is commandeered by a console, but there's no sign of the DJ yet.

Free-flowing cocktails and catered *kebabs* slip the four friends into party mode. Munching hors d'oeuvres, checking out the couture, and catching up on gossip are the only agenda of the evening against a backdrop of laughter, Bollywood, and bhangra music.

Mini watches Alka rub a hand across her forehead as though it hurts. *It can't be easy for her. Daughter of the Aggarwal family, wife of Raj Bajaj—having to put up a pretense all the time. But Alka had to be here today—for Priya's sake.* Mini knows that. She's not surprised when, a minute later, she sees Alka square her shoulders, and, attempt to focus on the chatter around her.

Priya's in the middle of a story about an unfortunate encounter.

"Ya, that one—the Indian manager from Citibank," she points to a short, dark balding man ensconced at the bar eyeing every pretty girl who walks by.

Mini takes in his toothy grin and the nuts he keeps stuffing into his crane-like mouth and cringes. He'd followed her earlier as she emerged from the bathroom. "The one who insists on stripping every woman with his eyes?"

"Ya, the every same. He came up to me when I was getting appetizers and said, 'I'm Rajat from Citibank. We've spoken on the phone.' And before I could respond he asked me, 'Care to dance, sweet melon?' squeezing my elbow in that touchy-feely way . . . Ufff." She finishes in a spate of giggles.

"You don't need another Vik in this lifetime," Mini warns, too familiar with the jerks of the invasive male species that has taken root in pools and mud holes all over the world.

"And what did you do in your last life to deserve Vik in this one?" Divya's tongue is not used to a second glass of champagne.

Mona comes over, always the solicitous hostess, asks if we need anything. "*Chai*, coffee, or a bit of wine—for you and me?" She laughs at her own joke.

She lingers, admiring the enamel peacock comb in Alka's hair and the embroidery on Mini's *sari*. Finding nothing to admire about Priya or Divya, she leans over Mini, elbow to shoulder, as if discharging a secret. "By the way, if you ever need a fourth for your rummy night, ping me. I love, love, love to play Rummy. Not that I need the money my analytical mind will garner." She tosses her head. "My *Dadi*—who's from Mumbai and I used to play together when she visited us in the States."

Mini nods. "I would have called you if I'd known."

"Next time." Mona smiles indulgently. "Divya, anything I can do to make you feel at home, just let me know. You'll find me by my laugh."

Divya tries not to hunch her shoulders apologetically, feeling hopelessly inadequate as Mona saunters off. Being at this party has reminded her of all the wonderful things Mona has and all the wonderful things *she* wants to have.

Mini, glancing her way, can read Divya's tension from the way her collarbone sticks out. She draws Divya into a clasp—not the airy clasp they've been getting all evening from Mona and her guests but a real one. Divya instantly feels better.

After midnight, the four of them stagger into the cold clear night with Sham bringing up the rear.

"Thanks for coming to the party with me," Priya slurs sleepily. "I'm glad Vik didn't show up so I could hang with you, my girlfriends."

Mini grins at her. Divya leans sleepily into the crook of Sham's arm stumbling, and the normally taciturn Alka is smiling good-naturedly at Priya.

"Now if we were back in Rosewood dorm," says Mini, her diamond nose pin exaggerating the starry sky, "I'd invite you all to my room for snacks and a hand of rummy."

Even Sham cracks up! A sweet evening.

CHAPTER 17

Mini

FEBRUARY 19TH, 2011

Mini is putting the finishing touches to the picnic basket. The weather has been perfect for ten days—warm and dry, but not summer scorch. She and Tom are going off to Tilden Park in Berkeley. Since he's master of the wine and the dessert, she offered to bring sandwiches and a salad.

She slathers mayonnaise on two slices of white bread, topping it with ham, cheese, lettuce, tomatoes, cucumbers, and pickles—just the way Tom likes it.

Slap, slap. She stops. *I'll make an Indian chutney sandwich, too, and see if I can convince Tom to try it.*

Harumphh, her inner Sita snorts, but mercifully remains silent.

She takes out the jar of mint chutney hidden behind the white take-out boxes of lasagna and pasta Alfredo, leftovers from Bruno's Pizza and Pasta where they ate last night in downtown Pleasanton. Mini has never been averse to the occasional Italian meal when Inder was alive, but all Tom ever wants to eat is good ol' American. Sometimes he'll stretch to Italian fare when they're out. She's beginning to miss her curries and spices.

She spreads mint chutney on one slice of bread, mayo on the other, heaps spindly thin slices of cucumber, sprinkles some *chaat masala* on the top, cuts off the crusts, like her mom used to, which her mom must have learned from the days of the Raj, humming under her breath as she works.

Tom arrives looking distinguished in crisp white trousers, white leather loafers, and a sky blue Polo T-shirt, the collar lying flat against his neck to reveal curly, silver tendrils.

My, my, he's early, and not for the first time. Mini runs to the powder room to check that the pink lipstick is on her lips and not her teeth. Tom turns on his heel and walks back to his car. Grabbing a turquoise chiffon scarf from the closet, she scrambles out the front door before Tom becomes impatient and starts tooting his horn, which he's done once. Patty Powers, the octogenarian neighbor who lives two doors away, had smiled at her broadly the next day when they saw each other near their mailboxes.

"He's an impatient one, isn't he?" She shook her white hair a tad disapprovingly. *Good, I can use some reinforcements*, her inner Sita had beamed approvingly at Patty.

Tom has put down the top of his dashing red convertible.

Mini pretends not to notice the keen look of admiration as he holds the car door open for her. She's wearing khaki drawstring capris and a floral chiffon blouse in multi-hued shades of orange, with penny loafers. Her long hair is drawn back in a French braid, accentuating her features and her pretty rosebud mouth, glisteningly pink. Her nose pin flashes at the sky.

"You look great, sweetheart." He kisses her forehead tenderly. Her inner Sita frowns. Too much PDA (public display of affection), even if he is white! Mini blushes and scampers into the front seat, suddenly self-conscious that the geriatric Ms. Powers might have witnessed this sweet exchange.

They talk and talk. He tells her about his divorce. How he and his wife grew apart from each other after the kids moved out. How his wife cheated on him with a former classmate whom she'd run into shopping in San Francisco while he was away on a business trip. She talks to him about her job. The gripping cases she's working on. There's the elevator case—woman accuses co-passenger of assault/molestation while they're riding together in the elevator. Jury's still out. She speaks of her arranged marriage, the Rummy Club—how for decades they've remained close, sharing secrets and customs. So engrossed have they been in conversation that Mini barely notices the half-hour drive. Tom deftly parks the car a few rows away from others and opens her door with a flourish.

I could so get used to this, Mini muses. Inder, yes, a loving husband and a wonderful provider, had lacked the small courtesies that seem to come naturally to Tom. Walking around the car to open the passenger door and seat her first. Holding open doors to let her pass. Putting down the toilet seat in the bathroom after using it. Bringing in the groceries from her car.

"Mini." Deep in her musings, Mini's been lagging. She runs to him, beaming, and he catches her in a wide embrace, bending down to kiss her lips.

"Slowpoke," he rebukes gently. "What were you thinking about?"

"Nothing really," she returns guiltily, for a moment feeling disloyal to Inder's memory. She shrugs the thought aside. Tucked among the ridges of the Berkeley hills, the magnificently wild park is scattered with inviting lawns and stunning views over the flatlands and the bay. The sounds of children at play drift though eucalyptus trees groaning in the sea breeze. Mini drinks in the sweeping views of the woodlands and the city beyond. Tom sets off in search of a more secluded spot on the grassy meadow for their picnic.

Mini busies herself spreading their repast. Appetite quenched, they sit with their backs against a broad oak, holding stemmed crystal brimming with Clos du Bois Chardonnay. The breeze ruffles the tendrils of Mini's hair that have escaped from her braid. Tom tenderly settles her head on his shoulder.

"Did you like the *chutney* sandwich?"

"Hmmm. It was okay." Then seeing her crestfallen face, he turns her shoulders around to give her a tight hug and whispers huskily, "Give me time, Mini. I'll get to like what you like."

That's all Mini needs to hear. She turns her face up to him with a radiant smile, and when he takes her offered mouth into his own, she deepens the kiss by winding her arms around his neck and clinging fiercely to his hard physicality. Tom pulls her tighter into his lap so she can feel his arousal. When Tom's right hand begins caressing her hip, the breath leaves her throat in a strangled gasp.

Try to remember who you are, her tortured inner Sita begs on bended knee.

"Tom, stop. It's too public," Mini says breathlessly as kids approach.

Tom lifts his head and sees a group of raucous teenagers, feet noisily trampling the undergrowth.

"You're right," he growls in frustration. He pulls her upwards in one smooth motion. "Let's go to my apartment."

Mini hastily sweeps up the trash and leftovers into a brown grocery bag. Tom holds out his hand. She clutches it tightly and follows him out to the parking lot. She makes a quick call to her carpool mom to bring Rani home with her. The drive to his apartment is tense with excitement. The ten minutes seem like a lifetime, both still caught up in the passion.

Mini's mind drifts back to Singapore and her first crush. She'd noticed him when she entered Archie's gift shop. Tall and slim, with a headful of tight curls. She'd suspected he was Indian. He stood in line behind her and asked her for the time. The oldest pick-up line in the world, but she gladly fell for it.

"Its 3:55 p.m." She could see a Motorola cell phone peeking out from the back pocket of his gray twill pants.

"Are you here on holiday?"

Soon they were walking into the brilliant sunshine, laughing like old friends over being undercharged by the teenage boy behind the counter who couldn't count in his head and wasn't yet savvy enough to master the calculator.

Her sister's scowl stopped her in her tracks. Mini introduced Ahmad.

Komal's scathing words still echoed in her brain. "How could a beautiful Sikh girl, daughter of a devout Sikh mother and father, fall for a dirty Muslim?" she asked, her cynicism born of the mental divide wrought by partition and the constant reiteration of difference. Subdued by the thought of family chaos, Mini tearfully rejected Ahmad's calls to her hotel and boarded their glinting Pan-Am plane back to Delhi, leaving her heart behind in Singapore.

Mini knows that Komal would still disapprove of what she's about to do. Tom looks over at her, his eyes rabid with lust. He takes her palm from her lap and presses it to his lips, misunderstanding the source of her anxiety. "We'll be there soon."

Her inner Sita throws up her hands in despair. *Is that all he thinks about?*

She has a brief view of big windows in the comfortable living space of Tom's apartment before he catches her in his arms and begins kissing her intimately.

"Mini," he groans, tangling his hands through her hair. Kisses trail down her throat to the hollow where her pulse throbs. She curves her head down and kisses his neck. She lets her teeth and tongue graze the sensitive skin just beneath his ear. He moans.

Tom gathers her to him, and she wraps her arms around his neck as he half carries her to the master bedroom. They fall on the voluptuous bed in the middle, desire pulsating like the static charge before lightning. Mini presses against Tom. She can't catch her breath. His warm body presses into hers, the familiar smell of Wood Spice on his neck envelops her. Her breasts flatten against his chest, and his heart thunders in counterpoint to her own. She tugs Tom's shirt from his belt as his fingers open the buttons of her shirt.

Almost unconsciously she drapes one leg over his and curves against the muscles of his thigh. He groans, catches Mini's hand in his, and presses it down between his legs. There is no doubt of his desire. For her. One of his hands slips behind her, unhooks her bra, and frees her breasts. Still high and taut. Mini tips her head back to give him the best view of them.

I wonder what Komal would think of blue-eyed Tom? is the last thought as Tom takes one chocolate nipple into his mouth.

A beam of sunlight reflected from the mirror plays on their tangled limbs. Tom intertwines her smooth, brown hand and marvels huskily, "Just like coffee and milk," before bending his head to kiss her again. Mini thinks she might be a little offended, but she lets it pass. God, she loves his smile. The way it softens the hard contours of his features. The light in his eyes, the slightly wicked curve of his lips. She loves it all. *Too fast. Inder had taken things slow, too slow.* Mini cups Tom's face between her hands and kisses him back with wild abandon.

They wake up late the next morning. In the dispassionate light of morning, Mini turns shy. Tom laughs at her awkward bolt to the bathroom, but it's a gentle laugh. She brushes her teeth and fixes her hair. *Now I'm ready to be seen by my lover.* She studies her face in the mirror. "Lover." She says it out loud, a delicious, embarrassing word that conjures up confused images and feelings. She was a girl, a virgin, when she married Inder, an arranged marriage that, while satisfying, never aroused the steamy feelings that Tom's touch brings forth.

"There's no milk in the house," yells Tom from the kitchen.

"Let's walk downtown for breakfast."

Mini joins him in the open, airy kitchen. Floor-to-ceiling windows look out on mossy, wooded hills. Tom has the makings of an espresso laid out on the green granite counter. She's going to have to help him remember her likes and dislikes: mornings she prefers scalding hot, cardamom-infused Indian tea. For now, though, she nods.

"Let me get my purse."

In the bedroom, Mini finds herself face to face with an array of family portraits on the maple console. Here most certainly is Tom's twenty-something daughter—blonde and athletic in a way that resembles him. And one with her tall husband good-naturedly grinning, their beaming son on his shoulders.

"Mini." She starts guiltily, as though he's caught her doing something forbidden. Tom wordlessly hands her a white and navy windbreaker. It covers up her hopelessly crumpled coral blouse.

They walk downtown at a brisk pace while Tom recounts the history of the earthquakes in the area. Mini's glad she has the jacket against the morning chill.

"Don't you think the international community could be doing more for the victims of the recent earthquake in Japan?"

"Mini! Mini!" Divya is calling from the other side of the street. Grinning from ear to ear, waving madly. Mini squeezes her eyes shut.

Ah ha. That's what comes out of all this dating nonsense. Didn't I tell you it was too much too soon? Her inner Sita is glowing triumphantly.

Divya doesn't wait to reach a crosswalk. She strides across the road, practically pulling her daughter with her.

"Helloooooooooo, Mini." Divya barely conceals her examination of the blue-eyed silver-haired man standing next to her friend.

"How amazing running into you here. Serena just had a tryout for a dance competition right up the block here."

"What a coincidence. Tom, this is Divya. Divya, Tom."

Ignorant of her discomfort at introducing him to her closest friends, Tom is his usual courtly self. Even Mini's stiff posture, her downcast eyes don't clue him in that she's upset.

"We're headed for breakfast at the English Farmer. Why don't you two lovely ladies join us?"

There is little for Mini to do except smile through gritted teeth.

"Lovely, we'll stay just for a cup of tea."

Tom and Divya are already chatting about the latest vagaries of the stock market. Divya hangs on his every word. Mini has little appetite, despite rigorously exercising right through dinner last night. Of course, her two worlds would come together at some point. But not like this. Her inner Sita nods with a satisfied grin.

Finally, Divya remembers that she and Sham planned to go house hunting this morning. Regretfully, she and Serena say good-bye. Hurrying to scoop up the crumbs of Serena's half-eaten muffin into her handy hold-all, she refuses Tom's sincere request to stay longer.

"I'll call you later, Mini." She kisses her friend lightly on the cheek. The glint in her eye promises Mini that an inquisition is sure to follow.

CHAPTER *18*

Alka

Alka's eyes crinkle at the corners, squinting against the afternoon glare as she peers into the empty mailbox. She inserts one thin arm and pats down the frame of the steel box. The sun pulls a rain cloud over itself like a blanket. Her eyes relax. She searches inside the mailbox again, her eyes wide open. There are no errant letters that Kakaji mistakenly left behind when he brought the mail in this morning.

Other than an acceptance letter from the University of Pittsburgh, which Krishna is going to refuse anyway, there have been no letters from Harvard, Stanford, Yale. Not even from UPenn.

Her mind races as she walks back to the invulnerable massive oak door. *Maybe they don't have the correct address,* but she had checked each application herself, word by word. *I'll call them to see what's going on.*

Still in her gingham pajamas, Alka tiptoes stealthily into the house, not wanting to be caught unawares like yesterday when she walked into the kitchen, yawning widely. The unfamiliar sight of Raj prowling around looking for tea bags was a shock—she didn't remember that he'd e-mailed her to say he'd be home that day. She doesn't pay much attention to his wide-ranging travel plans anyway.

There was a short, awkward pause as they looked at each other tensely, not knowing how to make polite talk like the strangers they were, yet weren't. Alka broke the silence with a stiff smile and reached past Raj to ring the bell to summon Kakaji to make the tea. She hastily retreated upstairs to her own room, the corner bedroom with the view she loved. Reminding herself of what the *Bhagavad Gita* says. *The soul floats like the lotus on the lake unmoved, unruffled by the tide. Unfortunately, her soul slipped away from consciousness as inevitably as sand from a fist.*

Raj's bedroom is across the landing, Krishna's in the middle. The master bedroom stands unoccupied, as it has for eighteen years. Raj had moved out of it after Alka repeatedly rejected his sexual overtures. Not once since their wedding night has Alka let Raj make love to her. In retrospect, Raj has been amazingly patient with her, but she's glimpsed the frustration on his face at times, watched it increasing in the first month of their marriage. He'd started working longer and longer hours, probably to avoid the daily rejection. Raj was not devoid of feelings, she had to admit.

The very idea of being naked with him makes her feel ill. Even his passionate fingers made her jerk away. She said she was sorry, but she just couldn't. When he followed her into the shower one morning, she slammed the glass door so hard his leg spurted blood. Soon they were no longer speaking. Raj moved out of the master. Soon after, Alka took over the unobtrusive guest room to escape the ornate, cavernous master bedroom that echoed with disappointment.

They stopped pretending to each other long ago. Krishna accepts the arrangement as normal. At least Alka assumes he does. Sometimes it strikes her that she knows nothing about what's going on in her son's head. She shakes off a momentary sense of dread. When she checks with Kakaji, he assures her Raj left hours ago for his office. Relieved, she sits down at her desk. She has phone calls to make.

If she had binoculars, she might notice Krishna sitting on a bench at the Berkeley Marina throwing pebbles in the water. The bright sun glints like broken glass on rippling blue waves. A picture perfect day. Pebble after pebble breaks the gentle lapping to disappear into the dark undertow. Resting next to him are a pile of thin, cream-colored envelopes, embossed with gleaming crests: Harvard, Stanford, Yale, and UPenn. The letters within are similar: "We regret to inform you . . . "

A toy sailboat is blown between breakwater rocks below him. A child tugs at the line to draw it out. The father stands behind him, encouraging him in his valiant struggle. The line snaps, but a swell lifts it free and breezes send it determinedly out toward the Golden Gate. Before they lose sight of it in the wake of a speed boat, it capsizes and disappears.

Krishna watches, too. He watches the father squeeze the son's shoulders and guide him away from the scene of disaster. Krishna imagines it going down, down, down; imagines the undertow pulling and pulling it into dark bottomlessness. A strange peace settles over him. Anything can disappear like that—a boat, a person, even lies and deceit.

What is that Indian adage Kakaji is fond of reciting? Wherever you roam, your deeds will follow you as the shadow follows the substance.

He stands up slowly, dusting the dirt off the backside of his designer jeans. For the first time in ages, he feels calm.

CHAPTER 19

Divya

"Third time's the charm!" Jackie sings as she unlocks the door of the charming fixer-upper she'd first shown us a month ago. I answer Jackie's fixed white smile with my own tight teeth. Luckily, the Realtor remembers an errand she has to take care of in the neighborhood and leaves us to walk through the house by ourselves. Though I'm in love with the property, I hold my feelings strictly in check, refusing to ooh and aah over the tunnel arbor of roses and vines in the garden, the chamomile lawn, or the hanging baskets of lobelia and geraniums.

Sham comes outside to stand next to me. The late afternoon light bathes the lush garden in a rosy hue. He puts his arms around me, and together we gaze over the oak-studded foothills to Mt. Diablo.

"What a fantastic view." His mouth is soft against my ear.

My phone rings.

Jackie's voice blares into my other ear. "So Divya should we write up an offer for one-point-two-eight?" I hate when Jackie calls me Devvy-yah, and I hate even more the over-bright smile. I can't stop myself from imagining Jackie standing in front of the bathroom mirror every morning practicing how to speak with her lips pulled wide in a scarlet slash.

"I'll call you this evening." I click the phone off and turn to follow Sham back to the house. When I catch up with him, the expression on his face comes as a shock. He knows what the phone call was, he knows what I'm about to ask him, and he's looking guilty. I haven't even opened my mouth, and he's looking guilty.

Sham peels a strip of yellow paint from the kitchen wall with one long brown finger. "The exterior needs paint, too."

I have a ready response. "I know that." I lay a soothing hand on his arm. The muscles beneath are taut.

"And that's why I'm going to have an estimate drawn up tomorrow by Villenada Painting. They just painted Priya's house, and she's already talked to them for me."

"She's decided to sell the house?" He's taking an unhealthy interest in every detail of Priya and Vik's impending divorce.

"I don't want to discuss that now!" I need Sham's undivided attention focused on this charming house of two stories with a semi-circular railing that I have fallen in love with.

He throws me an amused look. "Well, you know we'll have to rip out this wall to let more light into the kitchen." His knuckle knocks against the low-ceilinged wall partition that's a throwback to the 70s. Very dated.

"Jackie already faxed me an estimate for this one, since we talked about it at our last visit." I dig around in my big accordion file for the quote from the subcontractor. I bought it almost five years ago and it's now coming apart at the corners, overweighed by the brochures of countless houses we've seen. Five years! I had been so hopeful when we began.

Concentrate, concentrate. No use crying over spilt milk. Focus on the present. Good clichés work like a mantra. Half-calming technique whenever Sham exasperates me, half-prayer.

Sham studies the quote, lips pursed, eyes traveling down over the figures.

"Hmmph." He finally breaks the silence. "I guess this doesn't look too bad." I give him a demure smile, but my insides are doing cartwheels on both hands.

"What color tiles do you want in the bathroom?"

"Jackie said we're looking at an expense of five thousand dollars max to change the tiles in both."

"Both?" There's another heavy silence as Sham digests this piece of information, crossing his arms on his chest. "No problem. Okay, okay." He's run out of steam for the moment.

"So should I ask Jackie to write up an initial offer?" I literally hold my breath.

Sham raps the kitchen wall again with his knuckle. He doesn't look at me.

"Nah. I need to think about it a little more." He strides out of the house, closing the door behind him with a conclusive bang.

I angrily wipe away my tears. Neither of us speaks a word during the drive back to our cramped rented town house.

Sham's parents have already arrived for their annual three-month visit. I feel like a complete failure. Instead of my fantasy of welcoming them to my spacious new home, we are once more crammed into the town house with *Dadaji* and *Dadiji's* suitcases and numerous bags overflowing the tiny den.

To my Caucasian colleagues, having in-laws that live in India seems wonderful—until they move into our town house for the hot season in Delhi. "What's the point of traveling halfway around the world for only a week or two?" *Dadaji's* smile is exaggerated by Skype. Forty weeks a year, Sham and I are an independent family living on an island of uninterrupted bliss. But, from the moment the 747 jumbo jet touches down, until the flight attendant announces the in-flight movie options on the return trip, it's a whirlwind of dinners, tours, and extended celebrations with the family.

It's as if a comet crashes into your life, burns through your refrigerator, and obliterates everything you saved on TiVo. You wake up at the crack of dawn to prepare a vegetarian meal for your in-laws because they can't, or won't, eat meat. You point out Ferry Building Marketplace on the map for the fiftieth time. You repress the urge to sigh loudly and say, "Please! Can't you read a guidebook?" It is only day four, but one glance in the mirror and you see puffy eyes, dirty jeans, and bedhead. What happened to you? You try to wipe the sleep from your eyes, but there's no time. You're already late for the year-end appreciation breakfast in the teachers' lounge.

Three months a year, I put my life on hold. Three months in the year, I crack and snap at Sham, my daughters, and anyone I can project a judgment on. *It isn't pretty.*

The half-bath downstairs is theirs by default creating what my girls refer to as "*Dadaji's* Gasbomb Invasion." *Dadaji* spends hours in the little bathroom, leaving it redolent of the sandalwood cologne he favors, a scent which takes hours to scrub away. And yet I'm grateful that he's at least using deodorant this year. Last year he had not, leaving behind a sulfurous cloud when he emerged from the downstairs powder room.

The first time the Rummy Club met after their touchdown at SFO, Alka (of course, it had to be Alka) headed straight to the bathroom before I could redirect her. I saw her back hastily away, the delicate tip of her elegant finger pressed to her nose. I cringe every time I remember that scene.

At my next turn to host the Rummy Club, I get creative. I arrange to have the game at Edna's Tea Tyme, a quaint shop in downtown Sunol. For fifty dollars over the snacks and drinks, the owner set us up in our own quiet corner where we can play all evening undisturbed. It's a small price for my peace of mind.

Everyone enjoys the change of venue and agrees that it might be fun to go to a restaurant for our games every once in a while.

The cucumber sandwiches and petit fours are to die for. "And no cleaning up afterwards!" chirps Mini as she pushes her chocolate-smeared dessert plate to one side.

"But no leftovers, either," Priya counters. "I feed my kids for days on our leftovers." We all laugh, acknowledging Priya's famous feasts.

"I'm so glad you don't mind," I say. "You know I'm always happy to host, but with my in-laws here, well . . . . "

"No need to explain to us." Priya pats my arm. "Did you take them to see the house in Danville?"

"Oh, my God, my mother-in-law hated it. 'Why do you want to force my son to spend so much money on an old house? What's wrong with the place you live in now?' On and on and on. She won't be happy until we move back to India!" All three of my friends sympathize. None of them have this kind of pressure from family. Most Indians who move to the States make it their first priority to save enough money to buy a house. America allows them to create a life they couldn't have dreamed of in their home country. A house means much more than shelter—it's a stake in their new country. Thus my constant needling sense of failure.

"You don't think Sham would actually want to move back, do you?" asks Mini.

"Sham doesn't want to move back. He loves it here. But my mother-in-law! She calls three times a week, at least. 'When are you coming to visit, *beta?*' 'Oh, my back, my stomach, my who-knows-what! Who will take care of me?' And Sham gets off the phone with that look on his face, you know, guilt! Last night he said to me he thought he should at least check out the business climate back home before we make a final decision on the house!"

"He said that?" Alka is astonished.

"Oh, he didn't mean it, I'm sure. Having a house is priority, is ensuring that the atmosphere is soft, warm, and peaceful. " Priya says.

"He's just trying to show he's a good son," Mini says.

My head droops. "I know he doesn't want to go back, but . . . . "
I swallow hard. "We have the money. It's sitting there in the bank."
I shake my head, unable to lift my eyes to look at my friends.

Alka shuffles the cards and passes them out quickly, efficiently.
She picks up her hand and glances at it, then places it back on
the table.

"So, what's stopping you?" she asks.

"What . . . What do you mean?" I stutter. My eyes sting. My throat
feels thick. "Come on, Alka, why don't you say what's on your mind?"
Rage is seething inside me, bitter in my mouth.

"I wasn't going to say anything, Divya . . . but I wouldn't be a
friend if I didn't say this. I think you should make the decision for
Sham. I mean he's forty-something years old. He's lived most of
his adult life in this country. He has two girls, a complete family.
When will he agree to buy a house? When he's sixty? You let Sham
push you around like a male chauvinist pig."

I push back my chair and wring my hands in anger. "Is that
what you think of me? A loser and a wimp?" My voice has grown
low and rasping.

"Of course not." Alka knows instantly she has overstepped her
bounds. "I'm sorry." She reaches for my hand. "I didn't mean for it
to come out like that."

The whole table sits in silence. I keep my fists tightly clenched
under the table to control my kaleidoscoping emotions, to stop
myself from lashing back at Alka. Words swirl around in my head,
their colors bleeding into each other.

Priya puts her arm around my hunched shoulders and says
loudly, reassuringly, "I'm sure it'll happen soon."

"I . . . I guess so," I finally say, trying to keep my tone light
even as my eyes mist over with pain. I smile uncertainly at Priya,
grateful for her kindness.

But that night I toss and turn, Alka's taunt echoing in my head. Ma always used to say, *Those whom God blesses with beauty, He also gives them pride.* Sham is awakened by my restlessness. He rolls over onto my side of the bed to ask what's wrong. The whole story tumbles out then, my voice breaking as I repeat Alka's put-down.

Sham's face is a mask of cold fury as I finish the sorry saga. He hugs me close to him, his lips drawn tight. "That bitch." I pull slightly away from his embrace, looking into his face worriedly.

"No, no, Sham."

But Sham's words are as hard as his stony face. "I don't want you to associate with her anymore." I recoil from his anger, laying a placating hand on his arm.

"She's a very old friend, Sham. Sometimes she doesn't know what she says because she's so unhappy herself."

"She's no friend of yours." He turns his back to me, and in a few minutes he's fallen asleep again, guttural snores keeping a steady beat with the turmoil of my racing thoughts.

CHAPTER 20

Alka

"Alka, don't you think you were just a little too harsh on Divya?"

"I don't think so."

Of course, it was Priya who would call on Divya's behalf. Alka didn't know why that should irritate her, but she can feel her body stiffen.

"It's obvious what Sham's reluctance—let me be specific, his refusal—to buy a home is doing to Divya."

"You're right. But knowing that's her weakness, your naming it only hurts her feelings, don't you think?" Priya is deliberately keeping her tone light.

Alka rolls her eyes. What was up with these women wanting to sweep everything under the rug?

"I'm just saying . . ."

"I know you, Alka. You're only trying to help by suggesting she take a different course of action. But as my mom used to say, sometimes being a good friend means saying nothing."

Alka is ready to pounce back at Priya. But there's something in Priya's voice, a barely there quaver. And the truth of Priya's words suddenly strike her. *Who is she to say anything? Her own marriage is a sham. Her family life nonexistent. None of the others have pointed a finger at her own loveless household. Even though she's often moody or melancholy because of the dynamics with her absentee husband, she hasn't felt judged or censured by them at our weekly rummy sessions.*

Over the phone line she can hear Priya exhale. It must have taken a lot of nerve for Priya to call. Unlike Divya, Alka knows she's reliably unpredictable. She's been known to snap a waiter's head off and send him scampering if her coffee is not as scalding hot as she likes it.

"Hmmph. Okay. Let me give it a thought." Alka is breezy as she snaps off the connection.

Maybe she was at fault, but no use magnifying a molehill. Hell, she's apologized already, hasn't she? She'll give Divya a hug the next time she sees her, which is (mercifully) in a week's time, and things will be back to normal. God knows, Divya needs to develop a thicker skin anyway. She's always kow-towing to that spineless husband of hers. If they have the money to buy a house as she claims, Divya should just decide for him. Forge his signature if need be.

Alka bites her lip. *It was okay for me to say those words to Divya, right? Right?*

No, it wasn't, she's surprised to hear her inner voice admonishing her. She's good at willing it out of existence—like Raj who's always intruding on her love for Krishna. *Could it be that you got pissed off because you were wanting to confess your worries about Krishna. But just when you were ready to share it all, Divya took over the conversation?*

As usual, but it wasn't like that, Alka protests. *Don't be ridiculous! I'm not so petty. I was trying to be a good friend.*

She hadn't wanted to hurt Divya's feelings or upset her, but what kind of friend lies? The truth is that she enjoys Sham's company, but whatever his insecurities, he always resists when it's time to sign on the dotted line. Alka had seen this pattern with the Kapoors—Divya falls in love with a property, but the house is either too big, too small, too ugly, too beautiful, too expensive, too cheap. Even preoccupied Alka can see the physical toll it's exacting on Divya. She's become an empty shell of the confident, bubbly girl she was at seventeen.

Alka remembers the words of an old poem her *amah* used to recite, "Where Reason makes kites of her laws and flies them The Truth sets Fact free from its fetters."

I was right to tell her that. She should learn to stand up for herself. Alka crushes her inner advisor ruthlessly and tosses her black braid over her shoulder with a decisive movement.

CHAPTER 21

Priya

"Happy birthday, Mom."

"Thank you, sweetheart."

"So Mom, have you got any big plans for tonight?"

"I wouldn't exactly call them big, but it's our rummy night at Auntie Mini's house and I know all the girls will make a fuss."

Silence on the other end. From the sound of the wind in the background, Anya is rolling along a freeway somewhere at high speed.

"Well, Mom, you know I could always skip my dance class and come over to take you out for dinner. Or if you're willing to miss the cards session, you could drive over to Berkeley, and I'll take you to that fab tapas place on Grant Ave. All my friends have been raving about it for weeks!"

Priya smiles at the thought of celebrating her birthday at some joint suggested by Anya's friends at Cal. She's not overly fond of the crowded hole-in-the-wall restaurants they frequent. But it's sweet of the child to think of her.

"No, my dear. It's totally fine. I know how important the dance class is to you. Besides, you and Sameer are coming over on the weekend anyway."

"Oh, yes! I'll see you then." Priya hears her daughter's relief. The road noise vanishes in the background and she guesses that Anya is closing the window.

"Hey, Mom, remember I told you about my roommate Anjali? I was telling her about your potato paranthas with homemade *ghee,* and she got all teary-eyed. She misses her family so much. So is it okay if she comes home with me for your birthday?"

"Of course, you can bring her, Anya baby. Where do Anjali's parents live?"

"Somewhere on the East Coast. Mom, I've got to run. I'm late for class! But, I LOVE YOU! Hope you have a wonderful time tonight with your friends."

Priya is still smiling when the phone goes dead. The last three months have not been easy on any of them, but for the moment, it seems that her kids are getting settled back into their old routines and the upheaval in their lives has subsided somewhat.

It's been harder for her. Priya can't bear to be near Vik, though he's tried—many, many times. Wooing her with her favorite white lilies and with Godiva chocolates. Reservations for romantic dinners at old haunts where they had cozy meals in happier times. Priya remained unswayed.

He descended into angry tirades—obscenities over the phone, calling her "a fat garbage of a woman." Priya restricted all communication to e-mail or text. *Enough, Vik. I've had enough. We have broken our hearts, we have broken our home, and we have broken our marriage. We have nothing left. It's time to go.* Punditji's words from the Vedas finally register: "Look at the clouds, how they roll on. Look at us, how soon we're gone."

It wasn't until she hired a divorce attorney who sent Vik the dissolution of marriage papers that he realized she meant business.

Of course, Vik hired his own attorney, a blonde playboy with flamboyantly starched shirt cuffs and a cocky swagger in the courtroom. Priya observed the lawyer's sly glances to see if his threats and accusations were having their intended effect.

After one month of letters, motions, and conferences, Vik received the playboy's first bill. Always the practical businessman, he let Priya and her attorney know that he was ready to settle. In less than an hour's conference, they had agreed on what to do with the assets and how best to provide for the kids.

Their huge house in Danville was sold, and a trust fund for tuition was set up. The rest of the money was split evenly between husband and wife per California community property law. Priya consulted with her financial adviser, an old family friend, one evening over wine and her special samosas. He had sound suggestions for parking her money until she discovered what more life had in store for her.

Left to her own devices, without Vik's peacock primping and posturing in her life, she's found that she's a woman of few needs. No prime postal address in the East Bay to feel relevant—she's more at home in the two-bedroom condo across town than she had been in the eight-thousand-square foot house. Her rummy friends and her temple community have sustained her through the turbulence and grief. Just as important for her, though, is her passion for cooking: samosas, potato paranthas, kababs, fish fry, lentils, zucchini pomegranate casserole, and whatever else catches her fancy at the farmers' markets she visits faithfully every week.

Thursday evenings, she throws her organic mesh produce bags into her Honda Civic—she has downsized from the gleaming Mercedes that Vik always preferred—and drives the ten-odd miles to Livermore to forage for fresh vegetables to work her alchemy on. And on Sunday mornings, she saunters three blocks to the farmers' market in Danville. Her floppy hat bobs past the shops and little houses whose front yards are bursting with flowers. Humming happily, she wanders among the stalls of fruits and vegetables, cartons of fresh eggs and local cheeses.

Nothing seems to bring her more happiness than finding the perfect squash, carrots, spinach, lettuce, peas, or long-stemmed okra, and turning them into a casserole with a hint of Indian— that touch that brings whoever tastes it to their knees.

In the last three months, Priya has gradually shaped a new life for herself and her kids, pulling herself back into the world. She's joined the India Community Center in Milpitas and begun volunteering at the seniors' club. Every week she cooks potfuls of her sublime dishes to stock the freezers of the elderly uncles and aunties. They pat her on the back with a blessing of "*Jeetay Raho, beti.*"

"No, thanks! I don't want a long life," she mutters under her breath, but she knows when you're too old and feeble for anything, you can at least offer a blessing, for the sacred force of grace to flow through. *Bhagwan Jaane*, she needs all the blessings she can get to turn her life around.

So she cooks up a storm, and then cooks a whole lot more. When her rummy friends wistfully turn down huge servings, she carts her dishes to the farmers' market to share with the vendors whom she knows by their first names now and has an easy camaraderie with. Vik always made her feel gross and unattractive, but with these men, it's the taste of pastry imbued with cinnamon and *garam-masala* crumbling upon the tongue and not her utter lack of concern for cosmetics, or disheveled hair liberally sprinkled with gray. When she brings piping hot vegetable stew or steaming samosas, it's about the aroma of fresh-cooked food, not her girth hidden beneath colorful tunics. She beams amidst her appreciative new circle of friends.

On Thursday evening, her mind bustling with happy thoughts, Priya rounds the corner as a farmer from Fresno comes striding up. "Let me help you with that." Miguel carefully pulls the heavy bag from her right shoulder and hoists it easily on his own. The sunlight hits the sweat-stained brim of his cowboy hat and glints off the sterling silver buckle of his belt. Tanned muscles glow beneath the white sleeves of his shirt. He walks lithely through the crowd of shuffling buyers.

Priya follows him slowly along the aisle between the rows of booths, admiring the spring vegetables—shiny oranges, crisp romaine, rotund English peas, and juicy strawberries. Miguel arrives at his own stand and waves his arm. She hurries in his direction, a satisfied smile on her face. She knows just what she's going to make for the girls at their next rummy session.

CHAPTER 22

Divya

I'm sitting on the floor of the classroom surrounded by twenty children, reading aloud to them a second book. The room is boisterous, as it always is the half-hour before dismissal. On a low table off to a side, goldfish crackers and juice have been set out. In the far corner a few less social children are playing with some of the toys I've filled the shelves with. Still others are finger painting on a makeshift table that a parent volunteer has built. The room is all about color—the shelves varied as crayons with no theme other than brightness.

My eyebrows scrunch in a horrendous frown, trying to keep my mind on the book rather than the row I nearly had with Sham. Again. A week ago, when I mentioned the next rummy session at Mini's, Sham forbade me to go. Not in so many words, but he made his displeasure very clear.

"Don't tell me you're planning to go after you were violently insulted by that Alka woman."

I fell silent, not knowing how to counter this charge. True, I'm still smarting from Alka's thoughtless comment, but the ties that bind the four of us are irrevocable. We have known each other so intimately for so many years that there's a subvocal language of understanding among us. When Alka is edgier or more sarcastic than usual, it's invariably because Raj is back, disturbing the uneasy alliance of their marriage. Or when Priya constantly moans and unloads the burden of her mounting weight on us, it's because Vik has thoughtlessly crushed her by flirting with some skinny woman at a party. And of course, we wouldn't even play until Mini had healed enough to rejoin the living world after Inder's death. But in the months since she met Bart Tom (as I teasingly refer to him), Mini's laughter again fills our conversations with mirth, her hands swift as she deals the cards with careless joy, her face animated as she discusses the latest designer jeans to mold her hourglass waist or this month's eyeshadow color ("African sunrise").

Yes, I know all my girlfriends' moods and secrets, and even though Alka's bitchy comments have hounded me, I'm not ready to give up the bonds of old friendship.

Before rushing out of the house this morning, I reminded Sham that I'm going over to Mini's for cards this evening. "You'll have to heat up the dinner."

I had prepared it that morning for the whole family, gearing to my in-laws' preferences. I had momentarily toyed with the idea of leaving a note on the kitchen counter along with the freshly made *rajma* and rice, slinking out the door before the torrent of questions pelted down upon me. But I straightened my spine. *I'm not going to be scared to speak up in my own home.*

Over the years, I've learned to ignore the snort of disapproval that invariably erupts from Mommy Dearest whenever I announce I'm going to play cards. My mother-in-law always mutters something about gambling being a vice, according to the Vedas. In truth, she has very little to say to me on any given day except to criticize. I'm not about to let Sham's blade of disapproval cut into the bonds of friendship. *What gives him the right to control my life? To wall me up in the name of wife-duty?*

"You're going after all?" he asks sharply.

I turn and look at him, unflinching. "Yes, I am." My tone allows no room for argument.

"Suit yourself, but don't come crying to me if you get hurt again."

Not choosing to dignify that with a response that can only lead to one of us saying something we'll regret later, I park my sunglasses firmly on my nose and wave him a jaunty good-bye.

CHAPTER 23

Mini

Mini curls her hair on big, electric rollers and sprays it to keep it in place. It takes only a little mascara, blush, and lip gloss to accentuate her refined features. She slips the flowing fuchsia silk paisley dress over her arms and lets it slide down her body. She encircles her waist with a crystal-encrusted belt and steps into black embellished sandals. Finally, she mists Chanel No. 5 behind her earlobes and on her wrists. She's singing in her off-key voice to a popular song from her childhood. She's feeling happy again. The gray, leaden skies have finally parted, and the sun is peeping through the clouds. The ladies are coming over to her house tonight to play rummy, but beyond the excitement of catching up with her girlfriends, she has a secret that lights up her face every time she remembers it.

She and Tom have decided to go public with their romance. For her, that means introducing Tom to her daughters and her girlfriends. The family dinner with Sophie and Rani will take place on Sunday when Sophie is home from Pepperdine University. As for her girlfriends, Mini and Tom decided tonight would be a great time for him to make his entrance. Mini figures the ladies will be all settled into the throes of gossiping, or lamenting the latest hassles in their indulgent lives when Tom will casually drop by. She will formally introduce him as her boyfriend—how delicious that word sounds, how unlike her mundane life as Inder's dutiful wife.

Of course, her girlfriends already know of Tom's existence—the gossip grapevine must have been busy at work after Divya ran into her and Tom in downtown Oakland several weeks ago. To their credit, neither Priya nor Alka have bombarded her with queries, and, aside from a knowing glance anytime Mini utters the word "Oakland," Divya has shown unusual restraint herself.

Tom has fallen happily in step with her plan. There had been only one slight hitch: Tom is unaccustomed to eating dinner at such a late hour, and Mini had to work a bit to convince him that it would be rude not to take part.

"Yes. It will all be Indian food and spicy, but you just have to take a little of everything and admire the flavors." She thought it was a good sign that he grumbled only a little.

Divya arrives last. Through the living room window, Mini spots her stopping on the steps of the wraparound porch and gazing out at the view of the mountains. Divya always says how much she loves Mini's house—its Georgian style, the quiet street, the great location. *Poor Divya!* Mini forgets her own exciting drama for a moment, remembering Divya's discomfort at their last game. *At least she's here! Priya and I had our doubts.*

She throws open the door before Divya even rings the bell and envelops her friend in a hug as big as her five-foot-something frame will allow. Divya holds back from entering the family room, cautiously poking her head through the doorway to get the lay of the land. Alka is sipping a glass of wine on the other side of the great room, staring into the fireplace. Priya is positioned solidly behind the granite countertop, putting the finishing touches on the kababs and samosas she has brought to celebrate her birthday.

Divya grits her teeth but proceeds forward. She's enveloped by the aroma of the chicken vindaloo Priya has left simmering on Mini's Wolf range. She moves gingerly across the room and gives

Priya a quick, sideways hug.

"Hi, Alka." Divya stands awkwardly, shifting her weight from one foot to the other, poised to take flight depending on Alka's reaction.

"Oh, hi, Divya." Alka finally notices her.

Mini, uncorking a bottle of Veuve Clicquot, can't hear them from the kitchen, but she can't miss Alka's expressionless response to Divya's graceless greeting. And Divya's flushed face telegraphs her discomfort. She heads in their direction holding out a full glass of wine to Divya and tops off Alka's glass.

"Come on, ladies, rummy time."

The familiar rituals bring a return to harmony. Every time they make the same jokes about playing styles, sore losers, sore winners, and the beneficiaries of Lady Luck, they laugh at themselves and at each other. Tensions fall to the side for the duration of the game.

"Rummy." Mini's triumphant voice discarding her last card. She lays out her hand, fanning the cards in a semi-circle—one pure sequence and the three impure sequences that she needs to win. Priya, Divya, and Alka calculate their penalty points while Mini beams broadly. Alka is the biggest loser. At a dollar a point, she owes Mini fourteen dollars just for this hand. Her usual cutthroat strategies haven't been in evidence so far this evening.

It's Mini's turn to deal. She gathers the cards and shuffles them. As she begins to distribute them, Priya says, "I want to tell you something I've been thinking about."

"Is it about food?" asks Divya. Mini laughs, and Priya, too.

"Actually, it is. I'm thinking of maybe opening a restaurant."

"Seriously?" asks Divya.

"A restaurant?" asks Mini.

"I've been thinking about it for a long time, but Mr. Bigshot Vikram . . . " Priya's voice trails off.

"But now," says Mini, just as the doorbell peals. The ladies look puzzled. Mini's inner Sita looks as if someone has made her bite a lemon. She's been hoping Tom would text Mini to say he suddenly fell ill/suddenly fell asleep/suddenly got hit by a truck and can't make it after all.

Mini walks quickly to the front door and throws it wide open. Tom stands on the doorstep, a bunch of yellow peonies outstretched. He takes her shoulders and pulls her close. He hugs her tightly and kisses her on the lips. Blushing furiously, Mini disengages herself and leads him inside to her friends.

Tom moves into the group easily, charming them as he chats. He's tall and lean with precisely combed silver hair that must have been a beautiful gold blonde at one time, a good-looking fifty-something—in a starched, buttoned-down way, or maybe that's the impression Priya got from his blue Polo shirt and pleated khaki Dockers. He chats familiarly with Divya about the latest trends in the real estate market, and patiently explains to Priya the merits of funds, equities, and some of the edgier new stocks. Mini watches with anxious pride as he connects with her friends. Even Alka pays some attention when Tom just happens to mention that he's a Dartmouth alum. Mini's inner Sita huffs away, muttering something about men who are too smooth to be trusted.

Tom catches Mini watching him and throws her a look she can only describe as lustful. It pulses into her like a physical force.

"Time for dinner!" she calls out, surprised at the breathiness of her own voice. Priya charges into the kitchen to do the honors.

Cooking was never Mini's forté. When Inder was alive, she had relied largely on Chinese take-out and Indian food made by old Punjabi ladies who cook for their livelihood for two-income working families. Now as a widow with only one daughter at home, Mini has given up all pretense of culinary abilities—and Priya is happy to step in with succulent dishes from her own kitchen.

Tonight there's cinnamon squash stew, hot potato paranthas

with mango-ginger chutney, and the chicken vindaloo—an aromatic blend of spices with potatoes cooked with meat on a slow-burning fire until the flavors all mesh together in a delicious whole. To the side rests the birthday cake that Mini picked up at the supermarket bakery. Above it is a small banner that yells: HAPPY BIRTHDAY. The smell of spices and the sound of easy chatter fill the kitchen. Mini stands to one side, smoothing down her flaming silky dress with dancing fingers. She soaks it all in, a beatific smile on her lovely face. Her nose stud seems enlivened by the heat of her emotions, like an opal.

CHAPTER *24*

$\mathcal{A}lka$

"He seems like a good man," Alka whispers into Mini's ear as they hug good-bye. Mini draws back.

"And so handsome, too," she says, trying for a lighter tone.

"Alka, are you okay?" Mini is looking right into Alka's eyes.

"Of course," Alka lies. She extricates herself from the happy Mini and her handsome boyfriend, and strides across the stone driveway to her car. She might as well have skipped the rummy game this week. The whole evening she couldn't get her mind off Krishna and the fight they'd had right before she left for Mini's house.

All dressed up and ready to go, she had sat herself down at the kitchen table where her son was eating his dinner and reading one of those ridiculous Japanese comics.

"Krishna," she said, laying her hand on her son's arm. She could feel his bones through the sleeve of his Cal sweatshirt.

He had looked up at her, his eyes blank and distant.

"Hi, Mom. Are you going somewhere?"

"It's rummy night, like every Friday night."

He started to make a joke about his lousy memory, but Alka interrupted.

"Kris," she said again, "I'm really worried about those acceptance letters. Priya's niece heard from Penn and Yale, and you

159

haven't heard from any of them. Maybe you should e-mail them again, maybe they . . . . "

Krishna explodes from his chair. "Stop asking me about the f***ing letters. Just leave me alone. Leave me alone." He stomps from the kitchen and out of the house, banging the big front door behind him.

Alka can't move. Every cell in her forty-two-year-old body is rigid with shock. Voices are not raised in the Bajaj household. She can't remember a day in his life that she got angry with Krishna. She has showered all her attention and adoration on her only child. With Raj gone most of the time, Alka and Krishna have spent most of their time together. They read books and snuggled and studied bugs in the backyard and played endless board games like Ludo and Snakes and Ladders, Kakaji making a third when needed. On cold winter days, they wrote long letters to his Nani, Alka's mom, who lived in the ancestral home in New Delhi with Alka's uncle and his family. Even now, wracked by worry about her son and the mystery of the silent Ivies, she thinks back with maternal pride to Krishna's endearing letters, the well-formed characters lined up across the page, bringing joy to both his grandmother and his mother. And now this cursing, door-slamming boy.

Throughout the entire evening, through Mini's chirping excitement and Priya's culinary parade and Divya's pathetic attempt at conversation, through the losing hands of rummy and the so-called surprise entrance of Tom, Alka kept seeing Krishna's furious face, hearing his furious voice. All the while she kept smiling, kept pretending that everything was just fine. These were her supposed best friends, but they were so preoccupied with their own drama that she didn't feel free to tell them her fears about Krishna. Nor would she even know how to begin.

When she reaches home, she stays outside in the car, unwilling to enter the house. Something's wrong. Raj had remarked on it

Wednesday morning before he left for his twice-monthly trip to Nexnet Ventures' headquarters in Boston. At the front door, beyond his usual parting list of instructions, he added, "That boy is being whittled away before our very eyes. It's time to bring him to a doctor, Alka." In the driveway, a town car waited to whisk him away to San Francisco International Airport.

Alka bristled at the imperious note of command in his tone. *You're hardly ever here to notice what's going on.* Her hackles always rose at any criticism, implied or otherwise, of her chief occupation: the nurturance and cultivation of the Bajaj heir. She nodded, schooling her face into an impassive expression. Wednesday, she still was not convinced there was a problem.

By Friday night, though, she has to face it.

"I'm sorry about yesterday," her pale, sad son mumbles to her the next morning. Alka and Kakaji are in the kitchen chopping onions for *Peshawari chicken curry* when Krishna enters hesitantly, a drooping smile pasted on his face.

Alka's heart hurts to see his state. She instinctively reaches her hand up to check his forehead for fever, almost hoping for some simple illness to explain his appearance, his strange behavior.

"I'm okay." He pulls away from her touch.

"I am worried about you, Kris."

"We all are, *beta.*" Kakaji abandons his characteristic silence.

"I'm fine," Krishna insists. *What can I say to you, Mummy? What words can I speak with my throat, which has turned blue like Lord Shiva's from the poison of deceit I've swallowed?*

Alka now sees what she hadn't let herself see before: the circles under his eyes, the slumping shoulders, the jeans sagging off his body.

Rubbing his temples, Krishna pads as silently out of the kitchen as he had entered. Alka, immersed in her thoughts, continues chopping tomatoes for the dishes Kakaji is preparing. Raj's aunt is visiting from India, staying with her sister in Fremont, and Alka has invited her for dinner at their home tonight.

Alka hastily dries her hands on a towel. She walks into the backyard to collect her thoughts and meditate on how best to deal with Krishna's growing moodiness. She stops short seeing her son at the end of the curved flagstone walkway that opens up to a terrace overlooking the Oakland hills. Krishna is standing with his hands on the railing, looking bleakly into the distance.

Approaching him noiselessly, she places a tentative hand on his arm.

"Kris, *beta*. Maybe you should go out with your friends—not study so hard."

"As a matter of fact, Mummy, I'm going out." He turns quickly on his heel without meeting her eyes.

Remembering the cloud that covered his face, Alka admits something is wrong.

CHAPTER 25

Alka

11:21 P.M.

Alka can't escape the ghastly yellow gleam of the clock by her bedside. She's been tossing and turning for hours. Usually, when she can't sleep she distracts herself with her favorite fantasy: Krishna showing her around Harvard Yard or introducing her to his roommate at one of those beautiful new dorms at Yale. But the niggling feeling she's had since morning gets in the way. Her chest is tight with fear.

Throwing off the goose down comforter, she pulls her gray cashmere robe from the settee at the base of her bed and belts it firmly around her waist. Jamming her feet into the slippers that Kakaji always leaves outside her room, she pads silently across the landing and stops in front of Krishna's bedroom.

I'll check in on him, and then I'll make myself a hot cup of tea.

She closes her eyes and takes a breath, trying to picture herself sitting in her dimly lit kitchen, smelling the *Tulsi* ginger cinnamon tea Mini brought back from her latest trip to India.

She feels calmer. She reaches for the knob on Krishna's door, turns it slowly, and opens the door. She can't breathe. Krishna's bed is immaculate, the covers smoothed down perfectly and the decorative pillows plumped up by Kakaji that morning.

Krishna drives across the Bay Bridge at breakneck speed. When he woke up at 7:00 a.m. that morning, it was clear: *This is the day.* He has carefully done the research. The Golden Gate Bridge is closed off to bikers and pedestrians at 9:00 p.m. on weeknights, and there is no security barrier at mid-span. He's relieved, almost euphoric.

In less than an hour, he's there. It has been a beautiful day, not a cloud in the sky. But at the Vista Point, it's cold and windy. Hazy moonlight illuminates the parking lot. He sits in the driver's seat, his thin arms draped over the steering wheel, and peers through the windshield at the fog.

He takes the bottle of Absolut Vodka from a brown bag—liquid courage he and his friends call it—and some food he's brought from home. He raises the bottle to his lips and chugs down several gulps, almost gagging up the last mouthful. He coughs as the alcohol burns its way through his gullet and into his stomach. His eyes tear up from the fumes in his mouth. He takes a large bite of the Tandoori chicken wrap Kakaji packed for him and leans his head back so that his dark hair rubs against the headrest, letting the horrible feeling subside.

After a moment, he raises his head and fortifies himself once again. Feathery fingers of the evening fog wrap around the car, obscuring the view across the bay. He shivers. It is time. He opens the door of the Mercedes, tosses the remains of his feast onto the passenger seat, and hoists himself out the door.

He walks through fog without incident. He loves, he needs the dark feeling. It contains more safety than the small circles of orange light beneath each streetlamp. He pulls the collar of his black leather jacket closer to his neck and stalks through the blustery cold into the roadway to bypass the barrier. He reaches the span on the side facing the bay. There are no people, almost no cars. Krishna is the last person left on earth.

The words of an old song run through his mind.

I want to swim away but don't know how
Sometimes it feels just like I'm falling in the ocean
Let the waves up, take me down
Let the hurricane set in motion (yeah)
Let the rain of what I feel right now . . . come down
Let the rain come down
Let the rain come down
Into the ocean (good-bye), Into the ocean (good-bye)
Into the ocean (good-bye), Into the ocean (good-bye)
Into the ocean (good-bye), Into the ocean (good-bye)

At the point where the cable dips lowest to the railing, he stops. More than two hundred feet to the water. He stares over the railing and counts to ten. He's surprised at tears streaking down his face. He counts to ten again. He hesitates. Minutes fall around him like clumps of hair at the barber's. *Focus. Focus!*

He can faintly hear a voice from the city side yelling. He has no choice. Afraid that his commitment might falter if he lets himself perch for a moment on the steel beam, he takes a few steps back, runs, and vaults over the railing.

His body clears the railing as he hears the hard breathing that accompany the rapid footfalls. The last thing he sees are his hands releasing the railing. The words swirl around in his head. He tries to make them sound right.

Into the ocean (goodbye), Into the ocean (good-bye)
Into the ocean (goodbye), Into the ocean (good-bye)

He tucks his body instinctively as the water rushes towards him. The frigid ocean shocks him into aliveness for a moment, then envelops him mercifully in nothingness.

CHAPTER 26

Alka

Maybe he's out with friends. Alka tries to calm her frantic brain. Her heart knows with a sinking feeling it isn't true. Krishna has hardly any friends—that's part of the problem. Certainly not someone he would be taking a romp with in the middle of the night.

When the phone rings, Alka is jolted, like sticking her finger in a light socket. *Who could be calling at this hour?*

Raj is three thousand miles away. "Tring. Tring." The ring of the house telephone is maddeningly loud.

She seizes the extension in Krishna's room with quivering fingers and presses the TALK button.

"Yes." Her breathing sounds like she is in full scuba gear.

"Is this 1250 Skyline Boulevard?" asks a clipped voice at the other end.

"Yes."

"Are you related to Krishna Bajaj?"

"Yes." Alka is annoyed that the person mangles their last name. She doesn't notice how tightly she's clutching the phone to her ear, can't figure out later where the red welt on her cheek has come from.

"I'm calling to inform you, ma'am, that Krishna Bajaj has been in an accident."

"What? What? Is he okay?" The room is spinning. "Tell me he is okay. Tell me." She's shrieking now.

"He's been brought to Highland General Hospital . . . "

Alka feels the phone drop from her nerveless fingers. Her brain explodes in a thousand fragments. Knives stab her belly. A cramp wrenches her whole body downward.

Kakaji appears. He plucks the phone from where she has dropped it.

"Hullo?"

His wizened fingers cradle the phone to his crumpled old ear. Alka notices that a few white hairs are poking out of the shriveled skin of his earlobe.

As if from a thousand miles away, she hears Kakaji speak in halting English. He writes something down. The words she hears are random shards. White noise fills her head so loud she can't identify beyond her pulse.

Didi. Didi. Kakaji is shaking her shoulders. "Krishna is in hospital. He's in a coma. We need to go to him." Kakaji gulps down convulsive sobs.

He continues talking, but she is able to block out his voice. Closing her eyes helps. The hiss in her brain condenses occasionally into a clumpy fog that turns into letters and then words which link themselves to form an unceasing beat in the depths of her ear canal: *Krishna, Krishna, Krishna.*

Kakaji shakes her more vigorously, and the fog suddenly clears from Alka's brain.

"We must go. Kakaji lock up the house and bring the car out front."

Kakaji flees down the stairs. Alka runs to her room, willing her brain not to think beyond the immediate moment. She peels off her robe with trembling fingers and casts it aside in one quick movement. She jams her legs into black sweats, and pulls a white T-shirt from the rows of blue and white T-shirts lined up on one orderly shelf after another. She grabs a heavy jacket from the back closet and thrusts her feet into ballet flats. Snatches her purse from the entry table in the foyer and runs out the side door.

Kakaji opens the driver's door of the BMW and comes around to take his place in the passenger seat next to her. Wordlessly, Alka slides in, releases the brake, and jams her foot down on the gas. Rubber grinds heavy into the flagstone, a terrible screech that severs the quiet night air. In silence, she and Kakaji arrive at the Emergency Department of Highland General Hospital.

CHAPTER 27

Mini

Mini is resting back into a plush corner of Tom's sofa with one foot tucked beneath her, while he's getting dressed for dinner, admiring the panoramic view of the Oakland Hills beyond the floor-to-ceiling windows. Feeling smug is a new emotion for her. She's enjoying it. *All American*, she thinks.

When Tom heard that Rani was sleeping over at a girlfriend's house, claiming they needed to study together for their big science test, he immediately invited Mini to spend the night with him.

"I'll take you out for a nice dinner. Italian? I know you like that. Hmmm? How about it?" He coaxed her, and she had acquiesced. She admitted she was glad to not be eating alone in her gray stone Georgian, which has grown even larger since Inder's death.

She feels at home in her boyfriend's condo. *The unexpected things life brings you.* She absently fingers the hole where her diamond pin had lived for almost forty years. Tom had said, almost carelessly, that it made her look "very Indian."

A cool, damp breeze has found its way through an open window somewhere in the hall. Mini wraps a shawl over her gray and black satin sleeveless dress. She reaches for the TV remote.

"No update on the Piedmont boy who jumped from the Golden Gate last night. He remains in a coma. His parents have refused to comment, but the Wisconsin couple who saw him catapult over the railing had this to say . . . "

The air is a dense black sphere around her. It's impossible to breathe. Even though no names are mentioned, Mini can't shake off the eerie feeling that it's Krishna Bajaj. A few words bleed into her awareness. The lights of San Francisco . . . help from passing motorists . . . frigid water . . . a Coast Guard ship trawling for illegal crab nets.

This is crazy. Calm down and don't jump to conclusions. Her inner Sita is supportive for once.

Only the Piedmont address points to Krishna. But the clench in the pit of her stomach won't go away. The words play through her head like a camera shutter clicking at a fashion shoot.

Tom pokes his head out of the bedroom to say he has to make a short call and then they can go. Mini can't imagine confiding her fear to Tom, but she doesn't want to be sitting with it either. Priya's in India. Divya and Alka are hardly speaking, so there's no way Divya would know something before Mini did.

She remembers that she has Kakaji's cell in her contacts. She waits with a pounding heart for him to pick up.

"You have reached 510-583-3555. No one is available right now."

Mini cuts off the robotic monotone and keys in his number again, jabbing in the digits ferociously.

"Hullo." Kakaji's tinny voice is no more than a strangled whisper.

"Kakaji, this is Mini. Is Krishna okay?" No need for preamble with Kakaji.

"No, Didi." There is a catch in his voice. Then he's crying muffled, racking sobs that terrify Mini. What she had feared is true.

Mini pushes through the double doors of the hospital and races along the hallway to the reception desk. The inside of the hospital smells like old leather preserved in formaldehyde. Tom is two steps behind her.

"Where's intensive care?" Mini addresses the ample-bodied

woman sitting behind the admitting desk. The woman's dyed-black bouffant and milky white face around vermilion lips make her look like a ghost from some Far Eastern tragedy.

"Third floor East. Take the second set of elevators." The woman points a stubby finger toward the front of the building, barely looking up to acknowledge her presence. Mini speeds toward intensive care, hair streaming behind.

The elevator takes forever. When the door opens on the third floor she sees the unmistakable figure of Kakaji standing by the hallway window, head bowed into calloused fingers. Oblivious to the deepening twilight. Oblivious to the hum of machinery, the dinging of buzzers and alarms. Oblivious to the soft tread of aides and nurses, the crisp click of doctors. Oblivious to the crackling static of fear.

Who does Kakaji beseech? Vishnu to arouse our Krishna? Gentle Ganesh to dissolve his pain and overcome all obstacles? Shiva to destroy his inner demons and the anger that drove him to choose obliteration? Hanuman to build his strength?

Mini cannot wait for his prayers to end. She taps him on the shoulder. His face crumples with pain, but the ancient barriers between servant and master forbid him to share his sorrow. He turns his face, rigid and embarrassed, until his features are under control again. Mini's heart goes out to this wizened man who left his own son to look after Krishna from his very birth. But she's not the one who can bridge the space between them.

"Where's Alka?"

He nods silently toward the double doors. ICU. ENTRY BY PERMISSION ONLY.

"You must say you are Didi's sister," Kakaji tells her.

Mini looks at him, the always proper, always dependable rock of a family not his own. "Did you go in there?"

Kakaji turns a color Mini can only describe as purple. "I said I was her uncle." The nurse at the desk on the other side of the double doors doesn't blink when Mini introduces herself as Krishna Bajaj's auntie. One slender, pretty Indian woman probably looks much as any other to her baby blue eyes.

But when Mini stands outside the glass wall of the tiny room where her new family is gathered, she is aghast to see how much Alka has aged in twenty-four hours. Always thin, now she's positively haggard, hair dry and brittle. Worry quickly etched its fingers deep and black below her eyes. She crouches to the side of Krishna's bed, clutching his hand. On the other side of the bed, Raj paces up and down, chewing on his lower lip, his contoured, round face framed by graying muttonchops. When Mini has seen him, he's been wheeling and dealing on his Blackberry, his paunch covered by a one-thousand-dollar pinstriped suit. Now, stiff with fatigue and grief, he looks as solemn and blank-faced as a death row inmate.

Sister or no sister, Mini doesn't feel she can walk into the room at this moment. She swallows hard and runs a tongue over lips gone dry.

The desk clerk directs her to a small waiting room where she finds Kakaji. Slumped in a distressed leather sofa, ivory beads clasped in his withered hands, chanting. Mini sits beside.

"Kakaji. Please tell me how Krishna is doing." Her voice is wobbly, disoriented.

Kakaji wordlessly shakes his head. Mini closes her eyes and begins to pray for Alka whose life had already been shaped by strident losses.

Waheguru. Waheguru. She tries again in a more supplicating tone. *You are Agam, Agochar and Apar. (My God is immaculate, inaccessible, and infinite. He alone knows what is in His mind.) Please help Alka.*

She's far away, deep in her prayer, when she feels pulled away. *Tom!* She opens her eyes to discover him standing right in front of her, staring down at her from the other side of a low magazine-strewn table.

"I didn't want to disturb your . . . " He seems unsure of what she'd been doing, sitting there with eyes closed next to Kakaji.

She turns. Kakaji has relaxed into sleep. She puts her finger to her lips and stands up to join Tom.

"I'm starving." Tom reaches for her arm and pulls her toward him.

Really? Her inner Sita raises an eyebrow impatiently and scowls at him. "Tom . . . " Mini gets no further, for Raj appears, framed by the window of the waiting room. He lifts his hand to acknowledge them, then turns back toward the unit. A moment later, Alka bursts into the room.

She throws herself at Mini and squeezes her desperately. She shakes and sobs in her friend's ear.

"Oh, Mini, Mini. My *beta*, my *beta*, my *beta*."

"Hush, my dear, hush." Mini holds Alka tightly to console her.

Alka clings to Mini, perhaps drawing strength from her. "Mini, I'm so tired—and the battle has just begun." Mini hugs her closer, feeling perilously close to tears.

After some time, Mini pulls back a few inches to look into her friend's eyes through her own. She lets out a soft cry, seeing up close Alka's pale, hollow face, where the giant thumbs of fate have pulled her cheeks downward.

"Alka, have you eaten? You must eat. Please, I'll get you something."

"Raj! He's going to the cafeteria to eat, I have to go to Krishna!" She gives Mini one last squeeze and runs from the waiting room.

Mini's tears will no longer be contained. She takes a shaky step or two toward the sofa. In an instant, Tom is there. In one lithe motion, he opens his arms wide and draws Mini close to him. He holds her in a strong, warm embrace. She leans gratefully against his sturdy frame for a moment, and then pulls away, remembering Kakaji and the nurse—who can see them through the window, touching intimately, despite the suffering of her dear friend.

In the cafeteria they see Raj sitting in a corner, huddled over a soup bowl. Tom doesn't want to sit with him. Mini can't say she blames him. But she must go over to say a few words. Talking with Raj was never easy in the best of times.

When they return to the ICU waiting room, Kakaji begins to reminisce about Krishna—as if he accepts that Krishna will die.

"What a sweet young man. My Krishna. My *beta*. I remember when he was a little boy he ran in the courtyard crying, 'Kakaji, Kakaji, catch me.' " Kakaji's voice is dreamy. "He would giggle and giggle when I caught him. And I spun him around." Mini listens politely, asking a question now and then. She can feel Tom at her elbow, restless, disapproving of the Hindi conversation that excludes him.

He touches her wrist and moves his hand softly on her skin to claim her attention. She turns and smiles.

"Can we take a walk? I'm feeling claustrophobic in here."

They go downstairs and walk through all the spaces the hospital has set up to distract and occupy people like them. Tom kisses her long and hard in one of the gardens, and invites her to linger on a stone bench. But the April night is chilly and they soon return to the dull quiet of the main lobby. For nearly an hour, they sit on a plastic loveseat, their arms rubbing against each other in a friendly way as they leaf through limp copies of *Time* and *Sports Illustrated*.

"Mini?" Someone interrupts an article about David Beckham's alleged sexual exploits. Reva and Seth Lal, whom the Bajajs know from the Hindu temple on Oakland Boulevard—her shocking pink tunic festooned with silver sequins is a bit exotic in the drab hospital lobby. Reva usually is.

Mini fills her in on what she knows about Krishna, which isn't much. While they are talking, Suman Bhatia and Sweety, her teenage daughter, from two blocks down on Carlmont Avenue show up. Sweety is carrying a bunch of daisies tied with a handsome yellow ribbon.

An auntie from the neighborhood Indian Association whose name Mini can't remember bustles in a moment later clutching a box of *prasad* that she's brought back from her recent trip to Banaras, India's most sacred Hindu city.

They are the advance guard of a steady stream of visitors that passes by. Mini becomes the greeter and explainer for the Bajaj family, as if she actually is Alka's sister.

Mini is constantly aware of Tom sitting right behind her, sure that he's impatient with her—and she's not going to introduce Tom to all these people. Some of them she barely knows herself. But she knows if he were Indian, he'd know how to meet and mingle. She sees him looking at his phone and feels a flash of irritation. Her inner Sita folds her arms across her modest chest and glares at him, seething with anger. *You're not going to say anything to him?* she screams. Mini shuts her down.

She insists they return to the ICU waiting room. Kakaji is still on the sofa with his beads, praying. Mini wants only to join him—but she knows instinctively that Tom won't understand that they are sharing in Alka's grief simply by being there. Inder would have understood this process of healing.

"You should go," she hisses to him when she sees him check his phone a second time. Then, regretting the harshness of her tone—it's not his fault that he doesn't understand their ways—she touches him lightly on the arm and gives him a wan smile.

"I mean it. You should go. You have to go to work early tomorrow. Kakaji will drop me home when I'm ready to leave."

Mini guesses that Tom is putting up a show of reluctance, while inside he's grateful. He hugs Mini tightly and strides to the exit. He hesitates in the doorway.

"Mini."

She's deep in conversation with the manservant again. She looks over and meets his gaze with a noncommittal smile. Then she sits down next to Kakaji.

Waheguru, she murmurs. Everything else dwindles.

She hears the clack of the door closing.

Please save Krishna. She closes her eyes.

CHAPTER *28*

Divya

Sham and I are constantly fighting. And lately I find myself snapping at my daughters for no apparent reason. Nearly two weeks after Alka's nasty taunt, the words keep reverberating in my mind with a staccato beat. "Why don't you buy a house then? What's stopping you? Why don't you buy a house then? What's stopping you?" When Maya carelessly drops a plate, which smashes to smithereens on the kitchen floor, my hand flies out unwittingly. The slap resounds on her cheek.

"Mom!" My daughter dissolves into a flood of tears.

"Divya!" my husband roars from across the room, shaken by my outburst.

I'm aghast at my own violence. I run from the room with a loud sob, snatching up my car keys from the kitchen counter. Tears streak my face as I drive around Washington Boulevard in aimless circles.

When I creep back into the house, all the lights are off. The shards have been cleared from the floor and the dinner dishes cleaned and put away. I hang the keys on the hook in the hallway and make my way softly into the girls' shared bedroom.

They are both beautiful, petite and slim like me. Serena, now thirteen, has bright brown eyes and likes to wear embellished headbands in her thick, black hair. In the last year, she's developed a sarcastic sense of humor to mask her discomfort with early puberty, and the unwanted attention it brings. She's taking hip-hop dance classes and enjoys participating in local competitions. She told me that dance is her one great passion, and she wants to pursue it as a career. I fake a smile and nod as if I'm in agreement. *We'll see, Missy! Mini Auntie thought so, too!*

Maya, two years younger, has always been small for her age. She has curly hair like Sham and a generally sunny disposition. She refuses to wear clothes that don't match and follows Serena around the house like a puppy. She puts smiley stickers on all her folders, and her work in school usually comes home crowned with A's.

I stroke Maya's forehead, gently pressing a series of feathery kisses on my daughter's temple. I prattle nonsense Punjabi terms of endearment and whisper, "*Gudiya, Gudiya,* I'm sorry," in her ear, but she's lost in her dreams, uncaring of my ministrations. With one backward glance, I glide noiselessly to the master bedroom. For once I'm relieved to find Sham contained on his side of the bed, snoring like a barrel organ. I slip soundlessly under the covers and lie awake for a long time, considering how I'd change the kitchen of the Danville house.

The sound of an incoming text on my phone arouses me from reverie. I look up from the fill-in-the-word second grade test papers I'm supposedly grading. Outside the teachers' lounge, children run up and down the corridor, the girls chattering and giggling in their cliques, while the boys race toward the gates like wild horses freed from their pens. The school bell peals loudly, signaling the end of the day.

My phone vibrates again. I fumble among the junk in my handbag to find the Blackberry. From Mini. Short and succinct.

"Accident involving Krishna. Come ASAP to Highland General Hospital. ICU."

My belly feels crushed in the mouth of a vice. Despite the chilling bite of Alka's scorn, my love for my friends' kids is unquestionable. Krishna is like my own child. I can see him now as I first knew him: a loving, playful boy of five, always neatly turned out in a periwinkle blue shirt and crisp navy shorts, the school uniform that Kakaji had creased into submission. He's now an introverted young man, slightly awkward, timid at times, but unfailingly polite to his mom's friends.

What's happened? Is Krishna Okay?

I scoot my chair back and get up, anxious and fearful. Sweeping the test papers carelessly into my briefcase, I stride from the room and out to the teachers' parking lot as fast as I can maneuver through the throng of children and parents reuniting.

CHAPTER 29

Priya

As the airplane makes its final descent into Indira Gandhi International Airport in New Delhi, Priya presses her nose against the tiny window, always wanting to see every detail of the landscape. They are two hundred feet above the tarmac. Then suddenly they are crossing the runway. And suddenly the pilot jerks them back up into the clouds.

A tinny voice resonates over the speakers. "Too many flights coming in at the same time. We have to wait for clearance to land." Disgruntled murmurs fill the cabin. After a twenty-one hour flight, nobody wants to spend even a minute more in the air.

After fifteen minutes in a holding pattern, they descend, until they break free of clouds. The runway looms below them at the same cross-eyed angle. Again the plane makes a stomach-dropping swoop back up into the sky. Now everybody's staring out the windows. On the third attempt, they are able to land successfully amid a swirl of distinctive jets. Lufthansa. Emirates. British Airways. Virgin Atlantic. Kingfisher. Japan Airlines.

The names blur by. Priya's feet are asleep, and pins and needles attack her left arm. The cramped chair has held her captive for too many hours. Since the layover in Munich, she's been counting each hour, waiting for her feet to touch ground again. As the passengers clear out from the main cabin, she crawls slowly from the window seat. She staggers out of the aircraft, stomping with each step to restore circulation. She stretches her lumpy arms and back, smooths her hair as best as she can without a mirror, and follows the throng of yawning passengers into the huge interior of Delhi's finest airport. She's exhausted, can't wait to lay her head on a pillow, but her heart is singing with joy.

It's been almost four years since her last trip home. Vik was always too busy with business. And besides, his tastes ran more to Hawaii or London than the teeming, jostling masses of India. As she walks out of the terminal, the pungent smells of decaying garbage, human sweat, and animal waste assail her senses. She squints, adjusting to the glare.

"Priya *Didi*. Priya *Didi*."

She looks for a familiar face amidst the endless sea staring at the gate. Her clothes, her luggage, her demeanor report she's an NRI—easy pickings for beggars, unscrupulous cab drivers, and the plucking fingers of pickpockets and street urchins. A wave of nostalgia envelops her at the sight of a pale-faced, thin man with scruffy hair and a sweeping black moustache. Raju, the family driver for thirty-odd years, is hurrying toward her with a smile that stretches from ear to ear.

"Priya *Didi*." He beams widely, standing in front of her diffidently with his head slightly bowed. Priya's eyes mist over, fond memories starting a prickle at the back of her eyelids: Raju carrying her Anya on his narrow shoulders like a princess. Raju playing endless games of marbles with her five-year-old son one long winter vacation in Delhi. She wants to hug him tightly, but she may only touch his arm gently.

More would disturb the ancient boundaries between master and servant, nonfamily and family member, no matter how long the relationship between them.

"How are you, Raju?"

Raju nods his head shyly, "*Acha Hoon, Didi.*"

He grabs the handles of the baggage cart from her, nimbly weaving his way through the milling horde. Her father's old Impala is parked right in front. Priya arrives a dozen steps behind Raju to an annoyed cop whacking the hood with a baton. "Move it. Move it." Raju heaves Priya's luggage into the trunk, then fusses over Priya for a few moments, to make sure she's comfortable in the rear seat. Satisfied, with a loud blast of the horn, he eases the creaking car into the midday airport traffic.

The highway is jammed. The car idles next to a slum colony. The shantytown quivers in the heat. Skeletal dogs skulk in and out of doorways that provide pathetic privacy to residents of the multicolored mud shacks. Children, malnourished and lethargic, make their way through wastelands littered with debris. The dust, the squalor, the smells reflect off hot corrugated tin roofs.

Priya feels a new sense of horror at the poverty, unapologetic and so abject. She's not one to walk away from responsibilities. She wants to do more. She yearns to do more. She realizes that even if she gave up everything she owned to help these raggedy children, it would only be a drop in the ocean of need. Helplessness overcomes her. *But this time I'm going to do more than just pray to the God of lesser beings to look after them. When I'm back home, I'm going to organize a neighborhood drive or a fundraiser at the temple. Something, anything, to help these children. They should be in school, not playing with marbles in the dust.*

Priya sees Raju glance at her from the rearview mirror. She takes a deep breath, bends her head so that Raju won't see the tears spilling from her eyes, and exhales. She resolves that this time around she will not allow herself to forget these scrawny children, barely clothed, who look at her with hollow eyes. Like the end of a storm, the traffic clears and Raju speeds them away from the slum toward South Delhi.

Two days later, Priya is sipping fresh-squeezed *nimbu-pani* in the airy green courtyard of her mother's home in Defence Colony. At her feet are littered sheaves of newspapers, dailies, and magazines. Having caught up with the latest in Indian politics and been satiated by her mother's cooking, she feels the forgotten joy of being loved and pampered. Her mom bustles out of the kitchen carrying a tray the maidservant has just cooked up: cheese toasts, samosas, spicy cashews, and Priya's favorite—fruit *chaat.*

"Mummyji," Priya groans, laughing. "I didn't come back home to become fatter than I already am."

"You're not fat, my sweetheart," reprimands her mom gently. "You're wholesome. Like a fresh bun just out of the oven. That no-good Vikram was too full of himself to realize that."

"Oh, Mummyji." Priya affectionately wraps her arms around her mother's shoulders, as happy as if her heart were flooded with sunshine. Her mom feels thinner, older—but she smells the same. Of clove shampoo and Johnsons' baby powder. Of warm cooking spices and sandalwood incense. Of home.

"Mummyji, sit with me for a minute. I want to talk to you."

Her mom pads silently over the marble floor, pulls up a comfortable rattan armchair close, and eases her body into it. She's dressed in a plain cotton *sari*, her gray hair tied in a bun at the nape of her neck, rubber slippers on her feet. Her skin, despite the expected wrinkles, shows no age spots. She wears a heavy gold chain on her neck, a gift from Priya's father on their fiftieth wedding anniversary, her only concession to adornment. She has worn the chain every day of the four years since he died in an accident on the Delhi-Jaipur highway, as though the feel of it around her neck represents his continuing presence.

Priya's father had worked as a CPA for Ranbaxy Pharmaceuticals.

Her mom had run their old, comfortable house with its wide-spreading trees and bright airy rooms in a posh colony in South Delhi, a bequest from the Government of India to Priya's grandfather for his exemplary service to the Armed Forces on the dangerous border with Kashmir. Having no mortgage to worry about allowed her parents to lead a comfortable—even luxurious life—on her dad's modest salary. They took family vacations every summer in the hill stations—though they usually stayed in low-end hotels and chugged along the twisting mountain roads in the antique Impala.

Priya's earliest memories were of waking in the pre-dawn hours—the city of Delhi still a foggy lunar landscape outside her window—and listening to her father padding down the hallway. A creaking floorboard, the refrigerator opening and shutting, the hiss of tea being poured in delicate English bone china cups, the chatter of the maidservants as one cleaned the dinner dishes and the other chopped okra and onions for the midday meal. The hinges of the aluminum closet as he removed his wool vest from the hanger and dragged his briefcase across the hallway table. Her mother's lighter step. Clink clank on the counter, a plate set on the dining table, then the rustle of the maidservant bringing in the silver tray neatly laid with the teapot and a plate of *Parle* glucose biscuits, and hastily retreating.

The voices of her father and mother talking quietly, a murmur punctuated by a laugh. The front door open, then shut. A minute later water running, the refrigerator again, her mother settling back into bed.

Sheela, the older maidservant, would come in, *sari* tucked untidily around her waist, at 7:00 a.m. and rouse Priya and her sister from half-sleep. Sheela gave the girls breakfast, inspected their uniforms, and ensured they'd brushed their teeth, then escorted them to the bus stop for school.

It was a welcoming, homey household. Her mom walked to the

produce market every day, choosing from ripe, just-picked okra and cabbage. Raju brought freshly slaughtered goat or chicken from the local butcher. Every meal was freshly cooked. In the kitchen, her mom and her grandma gave directions to the maidservant for grinding fresh *amchoor* powder for the chickpea curry, smoldering cumin in the skillet for rice pilaf, cutting up knobs of ginger for lamb curry, or squeezing lemons from the garden for succulent fish stew.

After so many years, her taste buds are tingling and her senses are assuaged by the foods she grew up with. Priya has been turning over an idea in her head. A tiny seed of an idea has sprouted just enough to talk to Miguel and her comrades at the farmers' market. Though she hasn't shared with the girls yet. Launching her own stall at the farmers' market in downtown Danville. *I will sell my specialties—Indian chutneys and curries. Maybe there's a market for it. Maybe not. I have to give it a try. Start small.*

"Mummyji, the reason I came here was to visit with you. But also I want to gather all the traditional Indian recipes from you and Grandma and take them back to California with me."

Her mother looks surprised as Priya pours out the details of her idea and her new circle of friends. Her mother smiles. "Come, my daughter, let's get started."

In the kitchen the air is scented with the flavor of roasting cumin. Priya opens up the new notebook she's brought from the States and grins at her mother.

"I don't know what you will write in that book, Daughter. It's all by instinct, not measure."

"I'll just watch you and Sheela." Priya settles herself into an overstuffed easy chair near the kitchen door. The room is large and uncarpeted, filled with the history of spices. Her definition of heaven.

Her mother hesitates as though Priya's presence unnerves her, then she grabs a bunch of freshly washed cilantro and cuts it with brisk confidence. She stirs the herb into a heavy pot filled to the brim with black beans. The sounds of sizzling and bubbling food, the intense scents—the rituals ancient yet familiar—soothe Priya's soul.

She asks an occasional question and records the nuggets of information connecting the generation of women. Many of their heirloom recipes have been told like adventure stories by three generations. When she was young, Priya had been too busy studying for exams or watching Bollywood movies with her girlfriends to bother. But now, free from Vik's petulant demands, she is unleashing her passion for cooking.

All her friends, including Divya and Mini, come to India and go berserk shopping. The gold and diamond jewelry and the hand-embroidered *saris* beguile them. They speed from one monster mall to another, or plunge into alleys in Old Delhi for well-crafted silver or wood—bargains if you know how to haggle relentlessly.

Vik had been a slavish consumer, buying, buying, like a rat drawn to a piece of cheese, and he had drawn her along. Priya's smile is small and ironic. *I should just have let my parents arrange my marriage. They and the astrologer would have done a better job than I in choosing a compatible mate.* Outside the *pipal* trees rustle, even though there is no wind, reminding her of the story of how Buddha gained enlightenment under a *pipal*.

I too have become a different person. With her eyebrows ungroomed, her long hair tangled in an unkempt bun, free of any makeup, she no longer looks like the upscale Indian-American woman visiting her homeland. In long, colorful tunics and flowing linen pants that conceal her ample hips, she ignores how she appears to others. The two weeks she has taken off from the demands of daily life are filling with recipes of her Punjabi heritage.

Steeping herself in her family's history does not mean she wants to cut herself off from the present. Her mom keeps up subscriptions to all the major dailies and a couple of magazines. Other news is supplied by visiting the produce market where she trades local, national, and international gossip with her friends. But at six one evening, Priya walks to the neighborhood Internet café. It's always bustling, so she has to wait a few minutes for a computer toward the back of the room, noisy with kids in their twenties.

She quickly scans through the two-hundred-and-fifty odd e-mails determining that the majority are spam, and then clicks one from Mini titled "Urgent." Even that word doesn't prepare her for the brief message.

> FROM: Mini Singh minisingh@aol.com
> TO: Priya Sharma
> SENT: April 20, 2011
> SUBJECT: Urgent

"I don't even know how to write this. Krishna is in a coma, he tried to jump off the golden gate but they savd him. he is aliev but jst barely. THeres nothing u can do but i had totell u.
LV
Mini

Priya reads the e-mail twice. The typos, the sloppy writing are so unlike her meticulous friend Mini that for a moment she thinks it's a hoax, some version of a Nigerian prince asking for money. But then she sees another message from Mini, subject KRISHNA!!!, then two from Divya and one from Reva Lal who's a member of the Hindu temple board with Alka, and one from Suman Bhatia who lives two blocks behind Alka on some-avenue-or-the-other, which name she just can't recall. KRISHNA! POOR KRISHNA! one message after another.

Her heart is pounding against the thin cloth of her tunic. The crowded room feels stifling. Her face and arms are covered in sweat. She holds onto her chair with shaky fingers. Papers and periodicals on the side table, which she inadvertently knocks over, scatter on the floor.

Suicide. The stark word blurs on the gray screen as she tries to make sense of it. *How could things have gone so quickly awry?* Priya's heart lurches again as she thinks of Alka, her oldest friend. Her head hangs with guilt. "Alka," she whispers. A moth-wing of a name. *In only two days, your world has turned upside down, and I was not there to hold your hand.*

CHAPTER 30

Alka

It's been one week since Krishna's attempt, yet even now she has to swallow a lump in her throat to get the "s" word across. Alka only left the hospital because Raj and Kakaji are both there with Krishna, and Raj insisted she go home and sleep. In just seven days, Alka's world has stretched, and then ripped apart. Her face is shadowed by hollows of fatigue, her black eyes burn in her thin, paper-white countenance. Her scant black hair is drawn severely over both ears, and her cheeks stretch like crepe paper over the fine cheekbones. She has lost more than five pounds that she can't afford to lose. Raj and Kakaji nearly force-feed her.

Raj and she have not lived together under the same roof for more than two consecutive days in almost two decades. Now that they are forced to for the sake of their son, an uneasy truce has fallen between them. She has a sense of gratitude in spite of the agitation which his presence has thrown her into, gratitude that he's there beside her. This past week when she lies in her bed—eyelids twitching frantically, sheets staining with sweat as she dreams of Krishna's death, screams shattering the night like a dropped bowl—Raj has been by her bedside with a cool glass of water to soothe her back to wakefulness.

This morning as she was straightening up from readjusting Krishna's bedside covers, her head was spinning. She grabbed onto something, a chair, to steady herself. Raj immediately was beside her, holding her carefully—though at arm's length. He looked full into her face, saw how pale she had gone with that small effort, and ordered her to go home. "You have to rest, Alka. You'll make yourself ill. That will not help Krishna."

At the house, she feels unbalanced, skittish, full of a nervous energy. She needs something to do. She walks with slow, intentional steps to Krishna's room. If ever there is going to be a clue to what possessed Krishna to attempt suicide, it would be here. Alka needs some answers, or she will go crazy.

A heavy plastic duty bag that the police brought in contains Krishna's belongings from that fateful night. Kakaji had dragged it upstairs and set it behind the heavy oak door to Krishna's room. Alka roots through the bag first. A bottle of Absolut Vodka, broken at the neck and side. Also the cork, the wrapper, the box. A plastic cup, cracked. Alka examines the bottle queasily. *Krishna drinks?* She plows on through the bag. Two halves of a soggy poetry pamphlet—*Into the Ocean* by Blue October—more pulp than pages, but it is Krishna's and Alka has to ask herself: *Will he want it when he wakes up from the coma?*

What if he doesn't . . . wake up? The insidious thought creeps unbidden like a stealthy cobra. When she comes back to herself, the hallway clock reiterates what she can see beyond the terrace. A darkening, with a scattering of clouds. She can only move forward if she believes Krishna will wake up—without a shadow of doubt. She concentrates on the sodden book in her hands. She will keep it. She can lay it out to dry in the sunshine that floods the terrace outside Krishna's room every afternoon.

From the bag Alka removes two Ziploc boxes still containing food. A half-eaten tandoori chicken wrap that she remembers Kakaji lovingly preparing for Krishna that morning. Had he eaten it before he jumped? Had his lips touched the *roti* that the chicken filling was stuffed in? Her eyes are dry, but her insides are dissolving.

The hospital staff had removed Krishna's soaked clothes and shoes and put them in a plastic baggie. She remembers the nurse handing the bag to her that night. *Kakaji must have put it in here.* Alka fishes. Krishna's battered sneakers. He's famous for buying a new pair of shoes every month. The size 10½ Converse All-Star leather sneakers are white and monochrome with a crinkled, vintage leather upper. His hulking feet had been in these shoes that morning. It's been a standing joke between Raj and Krishna that, like a puppy, his height had yet to match his rapidly growing feet. She and Kakaji will dry out the shoes and give them to Krishna, even if only for him to throw away.

Krishna's Blackberry is cold. Dead. But when Alka plugs it into the charger on his bedside table, the screen flickers to life with a melodious beep. She flinches. A bright picture of the globe flashes, making Alka's eyes sting with tears. Other teens have heartwarming pictures of their families, smiling parents, harmonious siblings, but not poor Krishna. He has only a generic image on his phone. Alka is coming apart again.

Put the phone away! But it's his cell phone. It's important. It could yield some clue about what caused him to jump. She checks the recent calls—calls from her at 7:02 p.m. and 8:07 p.m. to find out where he was. Calls from Kakaji at 6:10, 6:25, 7:01, 7:24, 8:03, 8:26, and 8:46—all seven phone calls unanswered. According to the police report, Krishna jumped around 9:00 p.m.

Alka checks outgoing calls. Had he tried to call someone before he jumped? Lord Ganesh, if he might have changed his mind. But the last outgoing calls had been placed the day before. Mom; Kakaji;

his Indian friend Mohan, who lives around the corner from them; Logan, who carpooled with him to school; and Dad. It felt suddenly like she was not looking for clues, but rather invading Krishna's privacy. Alka lets the sick feeling subside and then squelches it ruthlessly. This is her son. She needs to know. Alka's bewildered gaze settles on the large oak desk in the corner with a lamp in the shape of an elephant's head—a souvenir picked up from their last trip to India that had included a visit to Jaipur, the Pink City—shaded in parchment. Alka marches toward it, determined to find answers. She rummages through a messy pile of papers. Nothing but old news clippings and notebooks.

She pulls on the top right hand drawer, but it's locked tight. Alka sits down wearily in Krishna's chair and leans back. The desk is so big the movers had to bring it into the room in sections—and it has a lot of drawers. She gives the top drawer a savage yank. Its wheels jerk and screech before a loud snap lets her in. She rummages slowly, methodically. The desk is solely Krishna's domain. Neither Alka nor Kakaji have ever set a hand to it. She finds the drawer filled with five years of rickrack. Old letters from his *Nani* and his cousins in India—which Krishna had put aside to answer and never had. What once seemed so important now looks antique, even arcane. Postcards he'd bought in Hawaii on their visit two years ago. Stacks of college essays in varying stages of completion. Half a bag of stale Doritos. Envelopes, paper clips, credit card invoices. Stuffed at the back of the bottom drawer, Alka finds her answers. She furiously scans the rejection letters from Harvard, Yale, Cornell, and UPenn. Everything is draining away. Blood. Hope. Life.

She falls to the floor sobbing uncontrollably, the letters bunched in her fist. Everything is crystal clear, as if she were looking at life for the first time.

Under the full moon, she can see the rocks and shrubs in the garden bathed in silver. Just a few feet away, beyond the French doors, the Matsu tree they had lovingly planted together three years ago as a symbol of life and love—a project that his sophomore class had required—sways in the breeze.

"Oh, Krishna. Oh, my baby," she howls, her arms wrapped around her knees, rocking herself in a sudden rush of agitation.

"Forgive me, forgive me." Her eyes squeeze shut, and she falls to the floor in a fetal position. She rocks on the thick carpet, but it's no use. She needs to get out, get out, get away from the hideous pressure in her chest, the vicious roaring in her ears. Her stumbling, leaden footsteps lead her to the statue of Lord Ganesh, worker of miracles.

"Dear Ganesh, if you exist, please help me! Please bring Krishna out of his coma. Please, Ganesh, put me out of my misery. Dear Ganesh, I see that I have sinned. My unreasonable expectations. Please God, please God, forgive me. Dear Ganesh, please help me. If my son wakes up, Ganesh, I promise I will donate a million dollars and build a temple right here in Oakland in your name."

She prays urgently, sobbing quietly as she sinks to her knees at the feet of the bronze statue—praying for oblivion, praying for a cure for Krishna, praying for the pain to stop that has been wracking every part of her flailing, shuddering body for days now. The statue of Lord Ganesh was garlanded yesterday morning with fresh marigolds by Kakaji. His headgear looks like burnished gold, though it is only brass kept shiny by Kakaji's daily ministrations. Kakaji takes comfort and serenity in performing the rituals of the *puja*, especially in these trying days. Washing and drying the figurines of the gods. Sprinkling rice and fresh flowers around them. Burning incense. Offering *prasad*—sweets, nuts, fruit, sweet milk—in a silver bowl to be blessed. Lord Ganesh appears to look benignly upon Alka's entreaty. And Alka begins to feel a calm strength entering her.

CHAPTER 31

Mini

Mini and Divya, Alka and Priya, face each other across four steaming cups—how many times have they sat that way over the years? This time, though, they are perched on molded plastic chairs at a Formica table drinking bitter coffee from a vending machine. For the first time ever, they have run out of things to say. For ten minutes, they talk about nothing, each trying to make conversation. But there are no more soothing words to comfort Alka.

Seeing this fills Mini with heaviness. It's been two weeks to the day that Krishna went into a coma. That's how they refer to it— no one can name his act. Alka stays at his bedside almost every minute of the day, massaging his feet, stroking his unresponsive hands, caressing his forehead, singing lullabies and chattering foolish stories. In an outburst of grief, she even clasps his head to her bosom, admonishing him. "Wake up. Wake up, Krishna." She chants the words like a mantra, not caring that anyone might hear her undignified howls or see the tears rolling down her cheeks as she coaxes, then yells, at him to open his eyes.

Worse than pain is the helplessness she must feel as her son lies in that strange absence. With all of us watching—our proud Alka who's always kept to herself her problems, her desperations, the many days of private pain that must have preceded this public one.

But Krishna remains heedless of her pleas, and after she has rendered herself hoarse from crying his name over and over again, the wildness in her eyes raises the hair on the back of Mini's neck.

Raj intervenes. "Please take her to the cafeteria," he says to them. "Help her. She won't eat." Mini hears an unexpected depth of concern in his voice.

Mini wraps her arm around Alka's shoulders while Priya takes her right arm. They lift her almost weightless form from the chair beside Krishna's bed. Divya holds the door open as they shepherd the still-sobbing Alka into the practical, emotionless hallway. Mini catches a glimpse of Raj taking her place in the chair as the three friends shuffle through the doorway. His face is serene as he holds his son's slack hand, praying for a miracle.

As they lead Alka to the cafeteria, Mini broods on the image. Raj. That hard-headed, self-reliant individualist turning to the spiritual when he has no hope. *Is that combination an Indian thing?* And her next thought is of Tom. She's been coming to the hospital almost every day, but Tom doesn't understand her need to be there so often.

He still calls every day, but their conversation has lost its sparkle. For her, Krishna's condition hangs like a shadow over everything. He keeps pushing her to go dancing, have a night on the town "to cheer you up." When Alka's son lies so close to death's door!? She has explained and explained how the four of them are like family, how they all know each other's parents, each other's siblings, how they have known each other since they were sixteen—carefree, giggling teenagers. *He just doesn't get it, does he?* her inner Sita scowls at her, scrunching up her skeptical nose.

Surely there are Anglos who have such friendships. Mini feels distant from him.

She even told him Alka's story, how Alka had been a victim of the fates in her unhappy marriage, and Krishna had become her only focus. He seemed sympathetic, and yet he told her twice that he thought she was overdoing it. To Mini, being with Alka in her hour of need is as natural as breathing. And if Tom can't accept that, then maybe they are not meant to be together. Her inner Sita sits up and applauds.

Other differences have already challenged them—differences in families, in cultures. Six weeks ago, Tom's daughter had been a huge disappointment. Karen, a buxom blonde, had swept into Mini's house for dinner with her stay-at-home husband, Richard, and their son, three days shy of two.

She wore a black cashmere sweater dress, black tights, and high heels. She'd gelled her Meg Ryan pixie cut to spike the bangs, and many layers of makeup were expertly applied. Mini, in a loose, flowing turquoise top, dark skinny jeans, and silver ballet flats, felt frumpy and underdressed in front of the glamorous Karen.

A day trader by profession, she's vice president at a firm competing with Tom's. She dominated the conversation, limiting it to insider gossip and unintelligible arguments full of numbers and names Mini didn't recognize.

Richard and Mini skirted around various safe topics: how difficult it was to find reliable childcare, the rising costs of private schools, the declining standard of public education—but their easy conversation couldn't diminish the fact that they were being excluded from the father-daughter tête-à-tête.

Suddenly, Karen tossed her crisp blonde hair back from her face. *That brassy color has to be out of a bottle,* Mini's inner Sita assessed critically. Mini smiled even as she tried to shush her.

Though Tom, Mini, and Richard were in the middle of the tiramisu Mini had bought from Tom's favorite bakery Karen scooted back her chair, getting up unsteadily. *She's had one too many to drink.* Mini eyed Karen's empty wineglass—her fourth.

"Rich, be a dear and get William, will you? It's way past his bedtime," signaling the end of the evening.

In the entry as they bundled up the baby against the chilly night, Karen half-turned to Mini. "Thanks so much," she said breezily, addressing the top of Mini's head.

Then she turned toward Tom. "Bye, Daddy." She snuggled up to her father's chest and whispered something in his ear.

After Tom left and she was clearing the table, Mini noted wryly that neither father nor daughter had even touched the chicken curry, the one Indian dish she had dared to include. *And you have to like everything he likes?* her inner Sita shouted.

I don't know if I can compete with Daddy's girl. Or even if I want to. At any other time, Mini would have hashed all this out with her friends. Was it worth seeing this guy who didn't seem to get who she really is? How important is Karen in this equation?

She looks around. The overhead fluorescent lights are too bright. The clatter and chatter in the cafeteria continue unabated. Indistinct sounds—chairs sliding and dishes clinking—fill her ears with useless noise.

Alka is talking in low tones to her aunt who has called from New Delhi to ask about Krishna's condition.

Divya has a sandwich in front of her that looks about as appetizing as a cardboard box scraped across the floor of a UPS truck. Mini watches her take a tentative bite and put it down with a grimace. "I missed lunch," she whispers across the table. She missed lunch at the elementary school to get to the hospital early. Mini squeezes her hand. Divya has been skipping lunch all week so she can get her papers graded before the school day ends. As soon as the bell rings, she races back to the hospital.

Priya's chin lolls against her chest, and just as Mini looks over in her direction, she blares forth a snore worthy of a mean giant. *Still jet lagged, poor thing.* Priya hadn't thought twice—hopped on the first available flight out of Delhi when she heard about Krishna. The notion of the earth being round—people living on the other side—our day, their night; our night, their day. What was a concept to most Americans is a reality to NRIs. What can someone like Tom possibly understand about the bone-heaving jet lag that accompanies a trip back home?

The sound of an incoming text sends Mini and Divya into their purses and causes Priya's head to jerk upright. It's Mini's phone—a text from Tom.

She shakes her head ruefully, feeling like she'd put out some kind of vibe by thinking about him so much.

"Brain Trauma guy @ NY Presb Hosp. Pamiloxiprine new drug just ok'd by FDA reverses coma. Spoke with Dr. Nicholas Brown. Tell Krishna's doc call 212-998-0990. Use my name."

Her inner Sita, stretched out on a rattan cot, raises her head—watchful and wary. Mini looks up slowly, holding back the urge to shout or jump up. Alka has said good-bye to her aunt and sits hunched in the orange plastic chair, her gaunt face cheerless and defeated. Wordlessly, Mini reaches over and thrusts the phone into Alka's hand.

Alka pulls her hand away.

"Take it. Read it."

Alka reads the text. Once. Twice. Then again. Mini watches Alka's eyes light up with a hope so naked in its desperation that it's embarrassing to see. Alka grasps Mini's hand, painfully.

"Please, Mini. Call him right now. It might be the only way."

Mini takes the phone and hits Tom's number. *Tom!* Whatever else she can say about him, he has some amazing connections. She waits impatiently for the call to go through. *Maybe he understands me more than I give him credit for.* She can feel the strong pounding of her own heart as the phone starts to ring.

CHAPTER 32

Divya

"Mrs. Kapoor! Mrs. Kapoor!"

A shrill, insistent voice invades my fogged brain from a far distance. The tug of his hand on my sleeve tells me I'm not having a dream in broad daylight. It's Tommy Roth, but I knew that even before I rearranged my features into a smile and looked down. Every class has a kid like Tommy—a seven-year-old whose attention wanders endlessly, whose pencil breaks at least twice every period, who needs to go to the bathroom every fifteen minutes. Tommy's obsessively curious about what his neighbor is up to, his wandering eye can count every dead bug trapped in the fluorescent light overhead, but it's impossible for him to concentrate on the math problems in front of him. Poor little guy, he already has a label—ADHD or some other name.

"Yes, Tommy?" I manage to keep exasperation out of my voice.

"Brooke's stomach's hurting. She's crying, Mrs. Kapoor."

A barely audible, wispy sigh reverberates in my ears. I'm tired. Over two rows, Brooke is doubling over in pain, tears streaking her red, round cheeks, and she's clutching her belly with both arms.

I lean down, resting my palms on her desk to be eye level with her. She's looking green in the face.

"What's wrong, Brooke?"

"My tummy hurts, Mrs. Kapoor." Halting words that I have to strain to hear them.

"Let's get you down to the nurse's . . . " my words are cut off as Brooke suddenly lurches forward and spews her breakfast on my new, black suede pumps. *Shit.*

"Eeeew," comes the collective cry from the classroom. The girls surrounding Brooke cover their noses and squeal, "Ooh, that's gross."

"Sorry." Brooke is sitting back now, looking relieved to have stopped the pain so simply.

I motion Brooke to go to the bathroom. "No, not with Tommy," who has eagerly volunteered himself for the task. "Riley, would you help Brooke?" I scramble to the class phone and call the janitor for a clean-up, trying desperately to ignore, the revolting mess congealing on the $106.75 shoes I bought at Macy's last week.

When the long, terrible day finally ends, when I'm again lying sleepless in the middle of the night, I wish that I had stopped right then, marched my vomit-covered shoes down to the principal's office, and invented some pretext to go home. I'd have gotten into bed, pulled the covers up, and called it a day. Instead, I did what I always do: I kept on plodding, muddling through the rest of the day weighed down by exhaustion.

As soon as the kids are gone at the final bell, I rush out to my car and onto the freeway toward the hospital. The stink from my hastily cleaned shoes fills the car, but the traffic's so slow that opening the windows would only add fumes to the mix.

My head throbs. I'm burned out at work. I love the kids, but I have little to give them. And I'm afraid I'm short-changing my own kids as well. Racing home to cook dinner, especially now with Sham's parents in residence. So it's slow-fry Indian food every night. Preferably vegetarian. "Your dad has a hard time digesting meat at his age," Mom insists.

My daughters, on the other hand, look at the rice and beans or rice and lentils and wrinkle up their noses in disgust. "Indian again?" their long, ungroomed eyebrows raised in incredulity. When Sham throws them a glowering look, they slink away to their room for cereal with milk.

All the extra demands on me are grinding me down—stop by Walgreens to pick up medicine for Mom's wracking cough. Fresh, home-cooked meals for their breakfast, lunch, and dinner. Sit in the doctor's waiting room for two hours when Dad's arthritis flares up in the unusually cool May evenings.

I should have skipped the hospital this time. Later, I saw it so clearly. But the night before, Sham and I had tangled in a terrible row. I wasn't ready to face either him or his mother.

It had been another variation of the familiar issue: the enforced intimacy when his parents push us to the limits of our too-small town house. This time I'd been almost out the door to ferry Serena from middle school to basketball practice, when I heard the distinct sound of rushing water in the bathroom. With one glance, I saw the waters flowing from a clogged commode. My father-in-law is famously and incorrigibly overzealous when it comes to toilet paper. I jerked the plunger furiously. All the chores fall to me.

Over the splashing gurgles, my mother-in-law informed me that the fridge had rivulets running down its sides. I stomped into the kitchen and thrust the plug back into its socket. It has a tendency to fall out when the door is slammed. I swiped a mop across the floor and ran to the car. *Good! They'll have to climb to the upstairs bathroom till I'm good and ready to deal with the clog. They can use the exercise!*

Over the din of the toilet and my mother-in-law's unsolicited advice and complaints, I hadn't heard the phone. Who would have guessed Serena would choose that day to become conscientious? A thousand times I've insisted she call if there's a change in plans, and 999 times she's forgotten. But yesterday she left a message that practice was cancelled and she's heading home on the bus to save Mom the trip. Except that Mom is waiting in the school parking lot wondering what's taking Serena so long.

I finally call and find my daughter at home. I can hear the shrieking smoke alarm before I enter the town house. My mother-in-law is directly under it, hands covering her ears. Serena had heated a frozen pizza, but managed to burn it. Purse still dangling from my shoulder, I freeze in the kitchen doorway, overcome by the smells, the sounds, the sights.

Hai Bhagwan! I raise my eyes heavenward.

When Sham strolls in five minutes later, I explode. "I can't take it anymore. This house is too small for the six of us."

I gain momentum with every word. "We need to move. Like, yesterday. The next house I like we're going to buy, or they leave. and never return."

I translate from Sham's narrowed eyes and thinned lips that I've been unnecessarily belligerent. I can see him thinking as much. At this perfect opportunity to retreat, I flounce out of the room still seething.

My mother-in-law refuses to come out of her room—no doubt pouting, wounded by what she heard me shout. Sham goes to persuade her to join us for dinner.

Mama's boy.

But, she continues to sulk in her room. Dinner is consumed in brittle silence. Sham pours himself a second drink. Serena and Maya, having wolfed down the dal and rice set in front of them, hurriedly excuse themselves as soon as their dirty dishes are in the sink.

The cold silence between Sham and me continues. He pours a third drink right before we get into bed. The ice clinking in his glass may have cooled him, but I boil. Our townhouse is so still I can hear laughter from the neighbors next door to us. At some point, I fall asleep.

In the morning Sham is gone before I awake. Not a good beginning to my day. By afternoon, even the sluggish freeway and the depressing hospital seem preferable to rushing home again.

The hospital cafeteria smells of disinfectant and sour milk. Or maybe that's still my shoes. I take a bite of the vegetarian sandwich, but it tastes as bad as it looks. My head is throbbing in unending waves of pain.

Suddenly everything shifts. It's crazy. Mini gets a text from Tom that says somehow he's found a drug that might cure Krishna. Mini's beaming—happy and proud of her Tom. She passes her phone to Alka who starts crying hysterically again.

"Call him!" Alka says to Mini. Priya, fly-away hair electric around her face, is reading the text over Alka's shoulder.

"Let me see," I say, but Mini takes the phone back and speed dials.

"I have to tell Raj!" Alka runs from the cafeteria, trailed by the three friends who all but carried her there half an hour earlier.

The three of us end up in the too-familiar waiting room. Mini is murmuring into her phone over near the window. Priya and I collapse onto the sofa, with me claiming the deepest recesses of the cushions.

I awake with a start. Alone. When I stand up, I wobble. The weight of my head is hard to balance. I make my way down the hallway to the women's bathroom.

I'm stifling a wide yawn as I walk in. Priya and Mini are huddled in a corner, talking in low voices. They are so engrossed in their conversation they don't notice me.

"So, what's happening?" I ask.

They spring apart. They look guilty and embarrassed.

"What is it? What are you talking about?" My eyes bore into them, willing them to answer me.

Mini looks at Priya, then blurts out, "Alka broke into Krishna's desk. She found rejection letters from Harvard, Yale, Cornell and UPenn.

"Oh, my God. Is that why he . . . ?" I pause to let the idea soak in.

We're all thinking the same thing—that Krishna jumped because he couldn't disappoint his mom.

Mini nods in response.

Neither of them will meet my eyes. *They've known about it and they didn't tell me.* A cold, electric charge runs down my spine. *They weren't planning to tell me. I'm still the outsider.*

I can imagine the two of them dissecting the scene where Alka found the letters, speculating on her emotions. I can picture them in the cafeteria cradling cups of lousy coffee, their heads bobbing together. Just like when we were all at Jesus and Mary High School. Always the three of them—Priya, Mini, and Alka—eating lunches in the mess, laughing about some silly boy. The three of them excitedly hugging each other on the first day of school—Priya in a crumpled, shapeless dress worn over bell bottoms, Mini and Alka preppy in boot-cut denim and fitted-collar shirts. Waving to me cheerily from across the gymnasium with their sickly sweet fake smiles, their shiny, bouncy hair and sun-kissed skin.

I'm tired of being excluded from this clique, of being shut out of their secrets. We're no longer seventeen. It is past time for them.

"Well, that's what happens." I'm reminded of the old story of Ravana, who sought to burn Hanuman's tail and kindle a fire upon it, but later paid the price of watching his own city burned to the ground.

Mini's look implores me not to speak the truth.

"I'm not saying anything you haven't thought. When you push a child the way Alka pushed that boy . . . "

Priya's hands flutter. Mini flushes red as *sindur*. Priya lowers her eyelids. A sixth sense makes me spin around.

The bathroom door is ajar, Alka standing in the doorway. Her face is deadly pale, a knot working convulsively in her throat. I can't breathe. I take a step forward. "I'm sorry, I'm sorry," I babble, but Alka raises a long, thin finger and points at me.

"I want her out of here, Priya. Out. She's not my friend. She can go."

She spins on her heel and sweeps out. Mini rushes after her.

I am wounded. My throat is swollen, my eyes sting. A metallic fog has woven itself around me. I open my mouth to call out, to stop Alka—and the fog fills it like cotton candy. Loneliness candy which dissolves into nothing, leaving a taste both sweet and sour.

"I didn't say anything that's not true, and you know that, Priya."

In shock at the soap-opera scenario, Priya gives a noncommittal shrug and stares at the tile floor with God knows what encrusted in the grout. I know the conversation is at an end. I shake my head furiously. This is typical. *It's always my fault.*

I square my shoulders and look straight and unflinchingly at Priya, silently communicating defiance. Priya doesn't meet my eyes, but swallows hard and says, "Let's go."

She herds me to the parking lot and walks me to my car.

"It'll be okay," I mumble to Priya, who's reaching out as if to hug me. But I shake her arm off angrily, get into my car, and speed away.

CHAPTER *33*

Priya

After her divorce from Vik, Priya had imagined herself content to live out the rest of life simply—a spartan apartment with a large dining room table, a queen-size bed to spread out in, heat and air conditioning to keep her warm when cold winds blow or heat waves smother the town in a shimmering blanket, and a gas stove upon which to prepare lavish meals to feed her friends and family.

That was before Miguel. It's Miguel who has taken the time and trouble to convince her that her talent should not be hidden under a bushel basket. He pushed her and argued with her until she finally allowed him to escort her to the City of Danville's administrative office to apply for a permit for her own stand at the next farmers' market.

Standing in the afternoon sunshine, Priya is dazed by the swiftness of becoming a business owner. Miguel's dusty white cowboy hat shields the upper half of his face, but his lopsided grin is visible as he looks down at her. His face is sharp and chiseled, not quite handsome, with a blade-like nose that makes him look vaguely mean and a little wild. But then he takes his hat off and immediately pushes back the long, dark hair that hangs to his shoulders.

"Priya! You did it!" She basks in his accent. It isn't that strong,

213

but she can feel the sun and smell the rich, red soil in the gently clipped consonants. His brown eyes are warm, twinkling as he gazes into hers. Priya feels recharged by his wide, infectious smile. She smiles back, the momentary sexual tension melting away in the warmth of his high five.

Priya ogles his biceps as they flex and bulge when he moves his arms. He is wearing the Oscar De La Hoya T-shirt—which she takes as a compliment. He'd been wearing it the first time they ever talked, however many months ago. It still makes her smile to remember how shocked he'd been that some dumpy Indian housewife recognized that Mexican sports hero. Later, when she confessed she only knew Oscar because her son was a huge boxing fan, Miguel pretended to be disappointed that they wouldn't be watching the fights together.

I would never have thought I had it in me to start a business at this stage of my life. "Who knows what else you're ready to start!" Miguel is always encouraging.

The next night she has him over to dinner. A "sampling" she calls it, to get ready for the opening of her stand on Saturday. Coconut shrimp curry rests on a bed of basmati rice, cucumber *raita* on the side. Pistachio crème brulé for dessert.

He can't stop raving with each bite. He even eats with his right hand "to get the full depth of the pleasure." She couldn't have sought out a more appreciative audience if she'd tried. They sit, side by side, chatting companionably about their day. She tells him about her mother and father, and their steady love for each other before his tragic demise four years back. She tells him a bit about her girl-friends and how they ended up in California, carefully skirting the current conflict between Alka and Divya. She would never betray confidences. She mentions Vik only in passing—which surprises her until she realizes that though he had been a major part of her life for almost twenty years, he is so gone from it now—and her sellers' license certifies this absence.

Miguel tells her he's planted wheat and sweet potato crops on his forty-acre farm in Fresno. To wean his land away from corn.

"I may even try planting grapes next year. Then I'll be known as a sophisticated wine maker instead of a struggling farmer." He winks at her. A delicious shiver runs through Priya. She watches him help himself to the food, admiring the obvious strength of his large hands, the male ruggedness of his skin—so unlike Vik's urbane businessman glamor. She wishes the night to go on forever.

When it's finally over, he leans in and tries to kiss her good-bye, but she gently pushes him away. She is grateful to him, she explains haltingly, but she isn't ready yet for anything more.

"It's okay, chiquita. Thank you for the preview. It promises great success." Miguel wraps his arms around her for a moment, then turns on his heel with a tip of his hat in her direction.

Priya watches the darkness swallow him, her heartbeats quickened. He starts the engine of his old farm truck with its broken radio. As it rumbles away, she releases the breath she's been holding. She's bereft without his presence. She longs to feel his touch on her body.

It's a new feeling. Since meeting Vik in New Delhi in her early twenties, she'd had eyes only for him. Though he could be as difficult and demanding as a petulant child who sulked when he felt unappreciated, she had always been dazzled by him. He had the power to send her spirits soaring—and, as with mercurial men, the same power to pull her down.

Miguel makes her feel attractive in a way Vik hadn't in years. There is nothing like the first spark of desire. She'd forgotten the magnetic pull of another human being, the invisible force that holds her attention wherever he is in the room, and the sense of loss when he's out of sight. She closes her eyes, filled with the sense of his earthiness. Tangy and clean, that's what he smells like. Her nostrils flare as heat sweeps over her body. She wants to let his hands wander and explore, stroke her skin, quicken her breath. But she's afraid to let him see her body.

When she had fought Vik for a divorce and a fair division of their assets, she was his verbal punching bag. He mocked her and goaded her, said her legs were bulbous and she was ugly. No one would ever want such a fat, ugly woman. *Empty vitriol*, she repeatedly assured herself. *His way of dealing with her defiance.* But his words did more damage than a physical blow. By the time their marriage was officially over, her weight had become an obsessive, overriding concern. Any possibility that she could ever be with a man again was obliterated.

Priya wanders to her bedroom and stands in front of the bureau. She's always been plump, and for most of her life she was fine with her weight. Now, for the first time in ages, she finds herself staring into the mirror and wondering what someone besides Vik thinks when he looks at her. She doesn't look as bad as she's feared. The luxurious fall of her dark hair, still mostly black, flatters her strong features, and the shiny bronze lipstick makes her face look bright. The embroidered turquoise tunic has loose lines, and a few undone buttons reveal her still round breasts. *But do you dare to bare your fleshy skin to a man who's so attractive?*

With Miguel, she felt beautiful—like her weight doesn't matter. *But what if he's repulsed when you're naked?* She really isn't ready yet. She begins the task of preparing for bed. Alone.

The dreary winter had seemed to last forever: one rainy day after another, color faded from the landscape. Pines that lined the streets of downtown Danville, visible from Priya's regular perch on her kitchen stool, had lost their rich hue, turning black against the gray, clouded skies.

But on this May morning bright pink and purple azaleas have bloomed overnight, and she can see lime green new growth in the hanging baskets she has strung from hooks in the ceiling of the tiny terrace of her apartment. *Who would have thought that a banal task like chopping onions could give one so much joy?*

Priya's Curries and Condiments. She can visualize the letters emblazoned on the wooden board—bright red against a dull, gold background to represent the fire of the spices in her curries. She has carefully selected Corsiva font because of the slanting, cursive characters. It's silly to be so invested in just a name, but her life is beginning anew, and she wants everything to be just perfect.

The kitchen is fragrant with spices. Chopping the onions methodically, Priya wishes for the umpteenth time that she could talk to one of her friends about all of it. Miguel. How he makes her feel. Her fears. Vik's voice still ringing in her ears. And her business! None of them even know she has a business. They wouldn't believe it. Of course, she can't bring any of this up with Alka, who is barely hanging on under the weight of Krishna's condition. She doesn't feel she can confide in Divya, after the scene at the hospital. Anyway, she and Mini have both tried calling Divya and their voice mails have gone unanswered, as if Divya is shutting them out to lick her wounds in private. Priya knows she can talk to Mini, of course, but it seems almost petty to bring up her angst about her weight when one friend's son lies at death's door and another has created an emotional chasm between them.

Priya stretches the stiffness out of her neck and her upper arms and goes back to dicing onions.

CHAPTER *34*

Alka

The second week of May. The jacaranda trees on Skyline Boulevard are flowering in purple extravagance, and throughout her garden, Alka sees signs of new life: foxglove spikes above velvety moss green leaves of lilacs, translucent burnt orange of the Japanese maple, and clumps of perky peonies in a full rainbow of hues. It's a daily reminder that the seasons are changing, that the steely gray winter has given way to a bright, nurturing spring. Usually Alka loves this season when pink blossoms float through her yard like bits of cotton candy. But this year, time is not her friend. This year time is measured by Krishna's days in the hospital. Twenty-one have dragged across her spirit, till it is chafed raw.

As she walks purposefully down the corridor to Krishna's room, she recites the *Gayatri Mantra* to herself. In the last twenty-one days, she has memorized it, knows it by heart. She no longer needs to look at her prayer book, but she can still not bring herself to think the word *suicide*. She's aware of times a nurse or visitor glances at her—maybe curious, as her lips move silently, constantly. But she barely gives them any thought. *Save Krishna*—the words of supplication to Lord Ganesh lend her much-needed strength.

Her legs are shaky, and she can feel the beginning of a dull throb at the back of her head. If she allowed herself to close her eyes, she feels sure she would sleep for hours. She has to force herself to take at least a few bites of the complicated dishes Kakaji makes fresh for her every day. Her clothes are hanging on her, and in the mirror, she can see that her cheeks have hollowed out. Her recitation of the *Gayatri Mantra* comes to an end just as she reaches Krishna's door. She commands her lips to smile as she sees him.

"Hi, Kris baby."

She stands still and waits for him to stir, for any response to let her know that things are somehow returning to normal. But nothing happens, and in the long, empty silence that lingers, Alka feels a physical stab pass through her heart. Despair hits her like a hunter swinging a machete. Always. She shakes it off, summons her faith, steps into the room, and shuts the door behind her.

She opens the blinds, inviting sunlight to spill across the floor. There isn't much of a view—the room looks out on an overpass crossing the 580 freeway. Slow-moving cars drift past fast-food restaurants, and she imagines the drivers listening to music on the radio or chatting to friends on cell phones, or heading to work, or making deliveries, or running errands, or going to movies or church. People going about their daily lives. People lost in their own concerns. All of them oblivious to what is going on in Highland General Hospital. She had recently been one of them.

Alka straightens the covers on Krishna's bed, then sits by the bed and reaches for his hand. His skin is pale, almost waxy. His body seems smaller. Thin, spidery veins are showing in his motionless arm hooked up to the IV bag above his bed. His hand is soft as always. Most days she will hold it for hours, imagining what she would do if he squeezed hers in return. She watches him. She wonders what he's thinking—or if he was thinking at all. The world inside him is a mystery.

"Dad is doing well. He's home now. We're taking turns, as you must have noticed." Tears fill Alka's eyes as her voice falters, aware Krishna hasn't been up to noticing the changes in their household arrangement. But she determinedly plods on.

"Kakaji is with him. Before I left home, Kakaji told me that he was going to make fish curry for Dad for lunch. You know it's one of his favorites. Or maybe you don't, because he's been so busy traveling all of your childhood. That's one of my regrets, Krishna. Maybe things would have been different if your dad and mom had tried harder to make a better go of their marriage. I admit your dad did try, but I was too wrapped up in superficialities like how short and dark he is . . . " She stops suddenly, realizing that this is creeping into the realm of Too Much Information.

The medical community seems divided on whether Krishna has heard her. Some swear that coma patients can hear, and may remember, conversations. Others deny the possibility. Alka chooses to believe in the optimists, acknowledging it's mere belief.

She clears her throat and pitches her voice to sound conversational. "Anyway, I was saying that it's actually been really good to have your dad around these days. He fixed the overhead light in your walk-in closet—the one that kept flickering on and off, that Kakaji tried God knows how many times to fix. You remember how Kakaji went to Home Depot two or three times to find a replacement bulb that would work for that vintage fixture that came with the house?

"Well, the other day when I was in your closet looking for Blankie . . . " She holds up the washed-out baby blanket that Krishna had loved for his first four years, not allowing herself to picture his blissful little boy face. She takes a breath.

"Anyway, your daddy found me in there, and what do you think? He poked and pulled some wires at the back of the light and presto! It came on in full force and hasn't flickered once since then. I guess that's an engineer for you. Even though he hasn't used his engineering skills in so many years—too busy being the business head he is these days. I guess you never forget what you learned in college, do you?" She corrects herself, "or in high school."

Alka slides her eyes sideways and stares back at the bed. Krishna's eyes are vacant as ever. His body is as still as it has been for the past three weeks. She swallows past the lump in her throat and continues again. "His family was so proud! Oh *beta*, the way your grandma looked at your daddy! You never knew her, but for a simple woman like her to produce a son who made it into IIT Delhi! I wish I could tell you what it meant, so you could know." The lump in her throat is almost choking her now.

"For one whole year, the stories go, he barricaded himself in his room and refused to go to any family functions. His meals were delivered to his room, and all he did was study, study, study for the entrance exams, which are among the toughest in the world. He even missed his cousin's sixteenth birthday bash because he was so focused on getting into the Indian Institute of Technology! Harder to get into than MIT! Do you understand the odds he overcame? Your daddy competed against three hundred thousand applicants for the mere five thousand seats. Do you understand the odds?"

Alka's voice breaks, and she hangs her head. Tears slip down her eyes and streak her face. "I'm so sorry, Krishna. I'm so sorry. Please forgive me. I've made many mistakes and God has punished me for them. Please give me a second chance to make it up to you."

Her memory captures a Bengali poem Kakaji used to recite when he put Krishna to sleep.

Supposing I became a champa flower, just for fun,
And grew on a branch high upon that tree
And shook in the wind with laughter
And danced in the newly budded leaves,
Would you know me, Mother?
You would call, "Baby, where are you?"
And I should laugh to myself
And keep quite quiet.

I should shyly open my petals
And watch you at your work.
When after your bath
With wet hair spread on your shoulders,
You walked through the shadow of the champa tree
To the little court
Where you would say your prayers,
You would notice the scent of the flower,
But not know that it came from me . . .

Alka finally bows her head over Krishna's motionless hand. She weeps into the faded old blanket. There is a knock on the door. Alka struggles to contain her raging emotions.

"Come in." Her voice is muffled as she wipes her tears and grabs a tissue to blow her nose loudly.

It's Rita, the day nurse. She looks sympathetically at Alka and busies herself changing Krishna's IV bag, giving her time to recover.

"He's in fine form today," she chatters over her shoulder in a matter-of-fact tone that Alka finds comforting. "Did really well with his exercise."

Alka nods, grateful for Rita's steady stream of conversation as she tries to get her feelings under control. Every morning and again in the evening, one of the nurses comes in to flex and stretch Krishna's limbs. Bend the knee, straighten it out; flex the foot up, then push it down—doing this for every joint and muscle in Krishna's body. But Rita is Alka's favorite nurse. Unlike the others, Rita maintains an undying faith that the new drug will work and he will emerge from all this just fine.

"Don't give up yet," Rita had said to her yesterday morning. Alka couldn't imagine a moment when that would be possible. Believing in hope hurt, but not believing would hurt even more.

After she finishes hanging the bag, Rita checks the flow and adjusts the sheets, then turns to Alka.

"Are you doing okay today?"

"As okay as can be." Alka's smile is wan.

Rita purses her lips and nods sagely. A moment later, she's gone.

CHAPTER 35

Mini

SATURDAY, 9:30 A.M.

Tom arrives a little too early for her to be primping up on the weekend, but she prepared the night before and managed to pull it off. She set her hair in rollers before going to bed, and although sleeping on them was uncomfortable, she's pragmatic enough to know she can always catch up on sleep Monday night.

"You look great! Hot date, huh?" Tom asks with a leer. He stares unabashedly at the low neckline of her blouse and gives her a conspiratorial wink. A delicious shiver of anticipation runs down her spine. She blushes prettily and whacks him on the arm. "Oh, stop it!" But she's flattered and amused—she knows she's looking good.

She's wearing her favorite all-the-rage Lucky denim leggings, under a low-cut blouson top in turquoise and black. Pedicured and polished red toenails peep out from embellished, nude-colored sling backs with kitten heels. She fully looks the part of the leading lady heading off toward the horizon with a handsome man in his dashing red convertible. Top down. Mundane matters like sleep or fatigue are not permitted to intrude.

She sneaks a sideways look at him. *God, he must have a hundred pairs of them hanging in his closet,* she thinks uncharitably of his beige Dockers. A light blue Polo shirt—*again, no surprise there*—and a gray cashmere/silk jacket—*very stately looking.* Of course, Tom turns and catches her sizing him up. The boyish charm in his twinkling blue eyes captivates her. Her insides quiver. *Oh, my. Nice.* Mini laughs back at him, feeling giddy about the trip they are making down the coast to Half Moon Bay.

It's one of those impossibly beautiful mornings. The summer fog hasn't settled in yet. Perfect temperature, light breeze, not a cloud in the piercing blue sky. The waters of the Pacific embrace broad bands of white sand. A heron breaks from marsh grass and glides low above the sun-drenched water. A flock of pelicans burst from the ocean and soar into the sky. The exhilarating thrill of freedom courses through Mini's veins.

Tom is drumming on the steering wheel with his right hand, singing along in his slightly flat voice to the CD that's playing.

There's a backseat lover
that's always undercover
And I talked till my daddy say,
Said ya ain't seen nothin
Till your down on a muffin.

Since he's driving, he gets to pick the music—but his musical taste is one of the things Mini has to make herself accept. She could have asked him to find something else on the radio, but she doesn't want to sound demanding. She blocks out the grating sounds with the words of her favorite Bollywood movie, concentrating, willing herself not to be bothered by Aerosmith.

Tom's hand on her wrist interrupts her reverie.

"Beautiful day, isn't it?"

"Yes, perfect."

"You were far away there."

Not far enough away from your so-called music. It's all she can do not to bite back at him. She turns back to the passing landscape—the sky spread over water speckled with golden prisms of sunlight. There's hardly any traffic on Highway 1, and in no time they're breezing into the driveway of the Ritz-Carlton.

"Have you been here before?" Tom asks as they wait in the valet parking line for the rush of incoming guests ahead of them to clear.

"No. This is my first time."

"Then you're in for a treat," Tom responds with enthusiasm as the bellman comes to heave their luggage from the trunk onto his trolley.

Just a week before, Tom suggested they go away for the Memorial Day weekend. At first Mini hesitated, not sure where her relationship with Tom was heading. After all the stress with Alka and Krishna, and then the furor between Divya and Alka, it would be nice to get away. But she didn't want Alka to feel abandoned. On one of her every-other-day visits to the hospital, Mini had sounded out Alka about Tom's invitation, and the proposed absence from the routine they'd established. Alka sanctioned the trip with her blessing. Tom is the wonder boy in Alka's eyes after he used his connections to get Krishna started on the miracle drug. And although Krishna has still to twitch or stir, his brain has registered some activity that the doctors are buzzing about.

So Mini consented gracefully, and she has to admit that Tom has taken care of every detail.

Although it would have been nice to have been consulted, her inner Sita pipes in, infuriatingly.

He did consult me, Mini returns sternly, *but he's a take-charge kind of guy, and he likes to plan every detail just so.*

Tom has made reservations for a romantic, candlelit French dinner in the hotel. Mini smiles with excitement as the concierge points the way to the four-star restaurant. She's really excited. She's also as nervous as a six-year-old at a ballet recital, and just as clumsy. She's wearing froufrou clothes—a clingy black dress, major jewelry, and sky-high stilettos. Which is a mistake. She trips walking up the broad stairs up to the restaurant, then almost falls over a chair on her way to the plush, intimate red dining room. As she slides onto the banquette, she catches her heel in the knotted rug and drags the edge of the tablecloth to steady herself, disturbing the rectilinearity of the place settings. A swift-headed waiter prevents glasses and dishes from crashing into each other.

She frowns at Tom's glance of disapproval.

"I'd like you to move us to another table." That imperious note in his voice Mini has heard before, and dreads.

"I don't know if that's possible, sir. All the tables are reserved . . ." The waiter trails off helplessly.

"I want to talk to your manager," Tom demands.

Mini looks around embarrassed. She can feel other diners staring at them.

An unassuming man in a black jacket, black trousers, and a simple white shirt hurries over. "What seems to be the problem, sir?" he inquires politely.

"This table is too tight for us. I want you to move us."

"It'll be a twenty minute wait, sir. We're fully booked, as you can see." The manager spreads his hands out with a mournful look on his face.

Tom shakes his head, huffing disdainfully.

"But if you like, sir, I can send over a bottle of our finest champagne while you're waiting," he suggests, leaning closer to Tom.

"Okay, I guess that'll do."

The waiter uncorks a bottle and fills two flutes. Tom takes the glass from him with what Mini recognizes as barely controlled impatience.

"I don't like the taste." His face looks sour.

Mini folds her hands under the table and stretches each finger back as far as it will go, counting to ten.

Tom beckons to the waiter.

"It's okay, Tom."

Tom looks down his nose at her. She meets his glare, squarely, arms folded across her chest. Surprise replaces the anger on Tom's face, momentarily.

"It's not okay," he mutters, but continues to sip on his champagne. The waiter skulks away quietly.

They are served the first course, and, of course, Tom sends the consommé à poirot back to the kitchen—it isn't scalding hot. During the course of any meal, Tom invariably finds fault either with the seating arrangement or in food preparation. Tonight Mini notes they've hit the jackpot: they've changed seats AND he's sent back the first course. Mini has learned to not allow herself to become too comfortable in the first chair held out for her. It's the price of being with a man who demands nothing short of perfection, as Tom is fond of saying anytime she protests weakly that they are fine where they are.

"Nothing less than perfection." He has a way of looking down his regal nose that Mini finds pompous, no matter how hard she tries to suppress Sita's grumbling.

Nor does she need her inner Sita later that night to tell her their lovemaking is disappointing. She bought a new silk nightgown with a subtle floral design that goes from champagne to peach to deep orange. It looks particularly fabulous when her hair hangs loose. The Frette sheets and the marble bathroom create the lap of luxury, and she loves hearing the sound of the ocean right outside their room.

But she and Tom are out of synch. Out on the terrace, he leans down and reaches for her just as she starts to turn toward the railing for a better look at the whitecaps below them. Her shoulder hits his nose with a cracking sound that scares them both.

After icing his nose, they start again. Mini tries to generate some enthusiasm, but the event is tedious.

The plan for Saturday is for Tom to play golf while Mini enjoys the world-class spa and catches up on her reading. She loves romantic novels, particularly on a vacation like this.

"I see you brought one of your Masquerade stories." They are out on the terrace. A hesitant sun peeks through the bank of gray clouds. Mini nurses a cup of lukewarm coffee from the machine in the room.

"Call room service and get some real coffee." Tom bends down to kiss her cheek. She can't tell if it is an indulgence or an order. She's content with her book and her bland coffee and the gorgeous view.

The smattering of raindrops turns into a torrential downpour. Tom comes back from his ruined game, churlish and sulking. His pants are sodden, his shoes are saturated and muddy, and his jacket is dripping.

"Have a hot bath," suggests Mini, helping him peel off his wet clothes.

The shower helps, but not enough. He's made reservations at a highly reviewed Italian restaurant down the coast in Pescadero, but decides he doesn't want to drive in the rain. The same restaurant where they'd eaten the night before can seat them at six or nine. Tom chooses nine, but then he pulls a towering sulk all through dinner, whining over the vagaries of the weather, complaining about the inconveniences of life, petulance and disgruntlement in his every expression as he plays with his steak. "It isn't cooked well enough." "The bread isn't hot enough." "The table is too near the kitchen." "The restrooms are too far away."

It's tiresome, and Mini is glad to retire early. *My poor Mini. Did you really think this was a match made in heaven?* Her inner Sita sneers.

Flinging her hair over her shoulder, Mini climbs into bed, flops on her side, and pulls the sheet and blanket up to her chin, determined to avoid a repeat performance. Tom turns out the lamp beside him and settles into his own side of the bed with his back toward her.

Mini crosses her arms over her chest and stares at the ceiling while the puffing noise beside her indicates that Tom is already asleep. Her mind is whirling. *Do I really want this man?* Her inner Sita has nothing to add.

CHAPTER 36

Divya

The alarm clock goes off for the third time. I grope to silence it, wearily hauling myself upright. With an effort that requires every ounce of my strength, I throw back the covers and get out of bed. I pull my robe down from its hook on the bathroom door and put it on before I splash my face with cold water. I avoid looking in the mirror. Since that awful row with Alka, reflective surfaces are not my friend.

The world has tilted off its axis. Sorrow has become my silent sidekick—I feel its shadow beside me all the time. In the weeks following the spat with Alka, I held myself together by strength of will alone. That, and a schedule as tight and busy as a buyer during Fashion Week.

I keep myself moving—doing. Routine has turned into my salvation. Every morning I force myself up early, wake my girls and pack their lunches, make my husband and in-laws breakfast, and leave for work. By eight o'clock, I'm in my classroom going over the lesson plans for the day.

Lunch is a break in strict routine. Sometimes, if I'm really together, I bring leftovers in the orange and silver thermal tote. If the school cafeteria is serving my favorites—cheesy lasagna or chow mien—I buy lunch. Or I zoom out to the Subway and grab a pastrami on whole wheat.

Then it's back to the classroom until 2:45, dealing with recalcitrant children, slow learners, and disobedient brats—so it seems to my numbed state. I can't wait for the school bell to end the day. Groceries on my way home, take Serena and Maya to dance class or basketball practice or music lessons, by 7:30 sitting over whatever dinner I've thrown together. Without fail, I fall asleep by 9:00 but am wide awake before 3:30 with thoughts consuming me from the inside. My corrosive words buzz around in my brain like a swarm of vicious insects. If only I could swat them to a pulp!

Sham is worried about me. He throws me concerned glances every time I give him or the girls a cocktail party smile—more and more frequent each day. I can't even summon up the energy to go through the sheaf of new listings Jackie dropped off at his office when I failed to respond to a dozen voice mails. I have tried crying, but it doesn't help. Night after night, I wake with tears on my cheeks. I look out the window as the fog wraps its long silvery fingers around my *tulsi* plant. I cock my head to listen for something I can't hear. I'm closing down the compartments of my mind. Click, click, click. Ram was the pampered one in my mother's house, I one of the many daughters always fighting for Papaji's attention. Why should I expect anything different now? *Once an outcast, always an outcast.*

I want to not care so much, but I keep going on. Smiling brightly at work and moving from one chore to the next with a desperate zeal. It isn't until my in-laws leave for India, after three months, that I realize how exhausted I am by the pretense of ordinary life. *I'm failing in every area of my life.* Happiness seems as distant and unattainable as space travel. I haven't always felt this way. There have been long periods of time during which I remembered being very happy. But things change. People change. Change is one of the inevitable laws of nature, exacting its toll on our lives. Mistakes are made, regrets accrue, and all that's left are repercussions that make something as simple as rising from the bed seem almost laborious.

On Saturday morning, Sham wakes up about seven o'clock and turns on his side to look at me.

"Rough night, huh?"

I draw a deep, steadying breath and reply shakily, "Yes." The old emotions, the disappointment with myself, the resignation to Alka's anger have caused another restless night.

"Did I keep you awake?"

"No."

We used to sleep intertwined. Lately, we sleep far enough apart that one's restless night doesn't affect the other.

He squeezes my hand that clutches and unclutches the cover—a nervous habit I have developed. "How about I take you to see that Indian movie everyone's been raving about? The one with Priyanka Chopra and Shahid Kapoor." I know Sham's really trying—he has zero interest in these Bollywood actors whose on-again, off-again romance and living arrangements fill the Indian dailies.

"We can have lunch at Masala Grill and catch the matinee show."

"What about your golf buddies?" Sham meets up with a couple of friends just about every Saturday to hit a few balls.

"I can cancel it. You need a break."

It's a tattered version of my real smile. I'm touched, try to smile up at him.

"No, you go ahead. I have to make cookies for the bake sale at Serena's school. I promised her the pistachio creams that my mom makes for them every time we visit India."

I reach up, pat his shoulder, drag my lead-weighted carcass out of bed, and stumble to the bathroom. I turn on the shower and take a fresh towel from the folded stack in a wicker basket. I wait for the water to heat up. Suddenly, the big, black pustule I've been carrying swells to enormous proportions, threatening to swallow me. I long for bed where I can pull the covers over my head and escape this drowning feeling.

"No, no, no," I shake my head. "Snap out of it."

Quickly I undress avoiding the mirror, and step inside the steamy stall, melting into the warm blanket of water. I cross my arms tightly, hold myself together, willing my mind not to think. Pieces of my soul have been falling away, like religious leprosy.

My cheeks are wet. Wet with tears. Before my mind can amble down the tortuous path of regret, I shut off the shower and dry myself off. Toweling my hair dry as I walk into the bedroom, I'm surprised to see Sham still in bed looking directly at me.

"Shall I make you some tea?" I avoid his penetrating gaze.

He gets out of bed and comes up behind me. A silvered image of our faces in the tall mirror on the back of the bedroom door is reflected in the early morning light.

"You should call Alka. Maybe go meet her."

The words clatter to the faux wood floor of the bedroom. I have only given him a bare bones version of what happened, and thankfully, he hasn't pressed me for details. The awful exchange of words flits through my mind, seasoned with a pinch of grief. I'd tried to explain it to him before. *Sham, it isn't as simple as you make it out to be. Sometimes you tell the truth and everyone's hurt. Sometimes the truth forces you into places you never intended to go.* He thought we should "talk it out," whatever the hell that is supposed to mean.

In fact, I haven't tried talking to Alka since that fateful evening. Nor have I returned Mini's or Priya's phone calls. Maybe Sham is right.

"Okay, I will." My voice is small, but echoes with surprising resolve.

I won't try to call Alka, not even to leave a message, since my voice would break and I'd probably start to cry. So I sit down in front of my computer.

FROM: Divya Kapoor
TO: Alka Bajaj
SENT: May 29, 2010
SUBJECT: I'm sorry

Then I sit. What can I possibly say? Images flash in my memory: Alka as I first saw her—a beautiful princess to my naïve eyes. Alka laughing so hard we had to pound her back so she could catch her breath. Alka in her cold, perfect mansion. Alka weeping at her son's bedside.

I put my hands back on the keyboard.

Alka:

I should never have said those words. You should never have heard them. I am genuinely sorry. I hope you can forgive me. Please realize that I care as deeply for Krishna as for my own kids.

Love,

Divya

I hit the "Send" button. I instantly feel better. On its own volition, my mouth forms a real smile. For the first time in weeks, I feel galvanized. I open the desk drawer and retrieve the folder Sham has brought home filled with enticing photos and over-the-top descriptions of houses that are waiting for me.

CHAPTER 37

Priya

Priya is flying high. She's drifting on the solitary cloud she sees overhead, puffy and full as if molded from snow. She's the happiest she's ever been. Even if nothing comes out of this venture and she has no customers for her curries or her condiments, at least she has tried something different. A new experience. The next step in her evolution beyond a dutiful wife and loving mother—the mantle she dressed in for almost half her life.

It's a cool and blustery morning in Danville. Priya shivers slightly—not from the remnants of morning fog, but because she's revved up. The wooden stall which announces *Priya's Curries and Condiments* in red and gold letters is perched at the far end of the closed-off street.

"Not the best location for foot traffic." But even that practicality can't bring her down today.

Miguel strides up to her, smiling broadly. He's pushing a hand-cart loaded with blueberries, apricots, and tangerines. Torn jeans, dusty cowboy hat, and bulging biceps taut under a fraying T-shirt, he looks like any of the dozens of Latino farmers who transport their luscious produce from the Central Valley and the Delta to Danville. Except Miguel is taller than average, easy for Priya to spot even in a crowd. And when he grins down at her, displaying a row of perfect white teeth, her insides do a rapid somersault.

Huge, brown, and delicious. Cheeky indeed. Priya wonders at the direction of her thoughts. It isn't like her. Sex with Vik had always been a chore or a big production. She had never been remotely interested in any other man in all the years they'd been married.

Miguel bends down with a casual peck on her cheek.

"Ready to go?"

Old Spice cologne and a wave of desire course through her so strong that she has to put a hand to the wooden counter. She nods with a smile, not trusting herself to speak. Miguel whistles tunelessly and begins to prepare his own stall next door to hers.

At two o'clock, Priya mops the sweat off her brow with a harried hand. If she'd stopped to think about it, she would be reeling from the number of people who had come up to her stall and asked to sample her curries. She loves watching them while they let her ginger-infused chicken curry or her cardamom and orange-peel garbanzo curry melt in their mouths with a surprised, "Oooh." She loves the thrill she feels when they leave the stall with a jar (or two) tucked into an overflowing shopping basket or clasped tightly in a fist. She looks into the hazy afternoon, and Miguel catches her eye, winking at her with a quick, upturned thumb before turning back to answer a customer's query about the unusually early Fresno corn he's hawking today.

A warm glow suffuses her body. Just as Miguel had predicted, everything is flying off the shelves: *Andhra chicken curry, Goan fish curry, raw-mango-and-lentil curry.* And the chutneys—both the mint-cilantro and the tamarind. Even the yogurt-sour cream dip. She has almost sold out of several things and is calculating volume for the following week, as well as what other dishes she might try.

She has yet to tally the sales, but from the number of twenty-dollar bills stuffed into the steel cashbox, she has definitely made a tidy profit. She might even need to hire a helper if today is any indication of how busy she's going to get. It would be fun to have Mini help out for a little while. She smiles to think of her perfectly put together girlfriend mopping up chutney spills from her newest silk blouse. But it would be such a treat to have her girlfriends here to witness this triumph.

"Could I have a chicken curry with a slice of the potato parantha, please?" An older woman in a powder-blue UCLA T-shirt stands in front of Priya, a twenty-dollar bill clutched in her fist. Priya jumps up to fill the order and stays busy for the last hour and a half of the market.

But later, as Miguel helps her load leftovers into her mini-van, her thoughts return to her girlfriends. She wants desperately to call Alka, Mini, and Divya to regale them with the success of her little undertaking. But it doesn't take more than a moment's reflection for her to realize the truth. *Oh my Alka. You have so many of your own worries with Krishna still in a coma. How can I be so selfish as to burden you with my happiness?* Divya, still smarting from the row with Alka, has disappeared into silence, answering no calls, texts, or e-mails. She can call Mini, but as much as she longs to have one of their marathon chats over the phone or over dinner, somehow telling Mini and not the others smacks of betrayal in Priya's mind. She will tell them. But not today. She can only fix one life at a time—and she's starting with her own. So she invites Miguel to share the leftovers at her place.

Mostly they talk. Occasionally they touch. His knee accidentally bumps into hers as he leans in to fill her wineglass. He lets it remain there. She doesn't demur. It's too soon to make sense, but she feels an uncanny familiarity with him, a connection that grows. He doesn't feel like a new friend—it's as if they had met a long time ago, in another time, another place, and are picking up where they left off. Maybe some past life. The feeling gives credence to the possibility of reincarnation and karma. Miguel has no pretension, no need to impress. Unlike Vik.

Also unlike Vik, Miguel seems to have an intuitive feel for when to stay silent or when to respond. It's that feeling of engagement, Priya realizes, that draws her to Miguel in the first place. Of course, she's attracted to him. He's attracted, too—she can see it in the way his gaze holds hers, the way his hand brushes her face, lingers at her hair. She would swear electricity jumps between them from such simple touch. She can see he feels it from the way his eyes darken, the way his inhalation hisses.

At the end of the evening, she senses that he's about to kiss her and she quickly turns away. She becomes acutely aware of the sound of traffic, of crickets singing in the trees. He gently takes her hand in his, upturns it, and kisses her open palm—then closes her fist around it, tenderly.

She can't deny it. She's drawn to Miguel—it isn't just that he's ruggedly good-looking and that he makes her feel desirable. It has something to do with his natural exuberance for life and the way he invites her to partake in it. It's the fact that he's lived a life so different from hers, yet they still speak the same language.

Most people she's known, and certainly everyone from her high school, seem to live their lives as if checking off goals on a score sheet. Study hard, get married, buy a house, have kids—and until two months ago, she realizes, she'd been no different.

She opens the sliding glass door and steps onto her balcony to exchange a last good-bye wave with Miguel. *It's never too late to change things.* She feels as if somehow she's been given the chance to start over. The thought frightens her even as it excites her.

CHAPTER 38

Alka

Mummy, Daddy. You tell me why I should wake up. Give me a reason why I should reenter your world of silences. Of brooding glances and words unspoken. And it had better be a damn good one! For all my waking years, it seems like I've been a ping pong ball between the two of you. Swatted from one to the other while the silence between the two of you grew as wide and deep as the Pacific Ocean.

I have no idea what went wrong in your marriage, but whatever pulled you apart polarized you both, froze you both into positions with no visible way back to each other. In all my seventeen years, I wish I could remember one time when I saw you exchange a kind glance with each other, a lingering hand on the shoulder, a kiss on the cheek, or a hug. Try as I might, I can't for the life of me conjure up a memory like that.

All I recall is separate lives, with separate bedrooms. I can remember Daddy jetting off to Denver every week, every weekend, every month of my life. Mummy, skittish and nervous any time Daddy reentered the Bajaj household. Dinner a solemn, heavy affair anytime Daddy's in residence. A cathedral of silence held within your bodies. Each sitting apart, each uneasy, each holding the words back behind tight lips. The atmosphere so thick with tension it would take a scalpel to slice it. The mood so somber that I would quickly flee to my room, like a mouse caught in the kitchen when the lights come up.

Every day I feared I would arrive home from school to find that my dad had cleaned out his closets and left us forever. I can still feel the terror I experienced as a child when the two of you fought. I would try to soothe one of you, then the other, but nothing I did made either of you happy.

So, you tell me, Mummy, you tell me, Daddy, why should I wake up and join the world of the living? If I'm the only reason you and Daddy are together, maybe it's better for me to be dead. I know it will hurt at first. But at least you can end this charade of a marriage, this pretense of a united family, and go on to find actual happiness in your individual lives.

The black rush of abyss roars in Krishna's ears and a void of darkness reclaims him. He sees distinctly for an instant, and then he is yanked back. He sinks, vanishing into the black chasm.

Sometime later, Alka pushes the heavy door to Krishna's room. Warm bands of sunlight stretch across the room and drape themselves silkily over Krishna's placid face. She crosses the room to his bed, brushes a loose strand of hair away from his forehead. Her stomach rumbles, but hungry as she is, she can't bear the idea of eating. Her insides are perpetually knotted.

Every day Kakaji's curries end up in the trashcan or given to the gardener who comes on Wednesdays to mow the lawn and keep the flowerbeds pristine. Yesterday, Kakaji made Krishna's favorite dish to try to tempt her to eat—*Punjabi chole* with piping hot *pooris*. For Kakaji's sake, Alka took a few bites, but only a few. The tastes and smells reminded her too much of the past, of happier times with Krishna oohing and aahing over the *pooris* Kakaji placed in front of him. Her throat tightened as she remembered, and she covered her mouth with a napkin so Kakaji couldn't see she was gagging.

In the first weeks after Krishna's suicide attempt, she frantically attempted to take control of some part, any part, of this unbearable situation. She made sure that every nurse on staff had her and Raj's cell phone numbers so they could be informed as soon as Krishna woke up. She read every article and testimonial she could find online. She called every friend or acquaintance who had any tenuous connection to the medical world. After a month, when he was moved from the ICU to a private room, she was certain, Raj had been certain, that the change would surely wake Krishna.

But as the days pass with no change at all, her manic energy is replaced by a quiet, gnawing dread that's even worse. Google research has told her that six months is the cut-off. After that, the odds of waking from a coma drop dramatically. But it is still only six weeks. She still holds out hope. She reminds herself of the number of people who are praying for Krishna.

She's feeling cooped up, cut off from everything. Not ready to resume her vigil by her son's bed. She moves over to the large window opposite Krishna's bed and looks down at the hospital grounds. She imagines herself sitting on one of the benches under the squared-off leaves of a tulip tree. Maybe next time Mini or Priya visits she will sit with them there.

What am I thinking? While Mini and Priya still drop by once every two to three days to see Krishna, their conversations are stilted. Everything they say seems to be wrong. When they ask about Krishna's condition, she isn't in the mood to talk about him. When they try to talk about something else, Alka wonders why they are avoiding talking about Krishna. She knows she isn't being fair, but she's always struck by the differences between her life and theirs. Despite their kindness and sympathy, despite their professed empathy, she finds herself thinking that in a little while Mini will head home or to a date with Tom, secure in the knowledge that her daughters, Rani and Sophie, are happy, thriving girls despite their dad's death a year ago. And Priya's embarking on some new business adventure, and her Sameer and Anya seem to have sailed through their parents' divorce unscathed.

Despite herself, Alka is often angry in their presence. While she is forced to live constantly with the unthinkable, their concern can be switched on and off. And despite her best efforts and in spite of trying, she can't escape her rage at the unfairness of it all. She wants what they have, and knows they can never understand her loss no matter how hard they try. She hates herself for these thoughts and tries to hide her frustration. But they know her so well, Mini and Priya, her dear, lifelong friends. She senses that things have changed irrevocably, even if they are all uncertain of what that change is. Gradually, their visits have become shorter and less frequent. She hates herself for that, too, for the wedge she's creating, but she doesn't know how to mend it.

As for Divya, the fleeting memory of those cruel words in the restroom four weeks ago flares up briefly, but she determinedly pushes it aside. She has spared just a glance at Divya's e-mail of apology before squirreling it away in her My Folder. She doesn't have the mental acuity to deal with anything but Krishna at the moment. She forces her thoughts into the present. She needs to stay positive. Lord Ganesh has never failed her. She sits down and takes Krishna's lifeless hand in her own. She closes her eyes and focuses, then clears her throat.

"Oh, did I tell you that Dad got an offer for his company for two hundred and twenty million, Krishna? He's seriously considering it. He's said to me that he wants to slow down now. Retire. At first, I snorted in disbelief, as you can imagine. Your dad, not working?" A brief, unwitting smile lights up Alka's face.

"But now, I'm beginning to believe he's serious. You'd be amazed how much he's changed." She forces herself to continue. "He's so much more relaxed at home. The other day I even caught him puttering in my vegetable garden."

She hears herself chattering away, and with a jolt of pain, she has a vision of what might have been. The lines of Tagore's poem flash through her mind. Kakaji used to sing them when Krishna was a baby, while Alka rocked his swing and smiled down at him.

When after the midday meal
you sat at the window reading Ramayana,
and the tree's shadow fell
over your hair and your lap.
I should fling my wee little shadow
onto the page of your book, just where you were reading.
But would you guess that it was
the tiny shadow of your little child?

She leans her face close to Krishna's and whispers urgently, "I love you, Krishna, more than you'll ever realize. You're everything I ever wanted in my child. You're every hope and dream I've ever had. I know I've made many mistakes in my life. I know I've failed you as a mother. I know the home we made for you was dysfunctional. Daddy and I both love you, but even so, your upbringing was tough. So please, give me one more chance, my son. You won't regret it."

Her heart races. The words she cannot utter: *Don't die. Don't die.* She waits for a response, but there is nothing. There is always nothing, as if Lord Ganesh is telling her that her love is somehow not enough. She suddenly feels very tired. She adjusts the sheet, feeling alone and apart from her son, knowing she's a mother whose love has somehow failed.

"Please," she whispers. "You've got to wake up, *beta*. Please? Please, please. We're running out of time."

CHAPTER *39*

$\mathcal{D}ivya$

Who am I?

I feel restless and edgy as I inch my Prius into the gravel driveway of the Danville home we closed on the previous evening. I observe listlessly that the heavy rains we had last month have caused the rhododendrons in the front yard to burst into plate-sized blooms, and the azalea bushes planted all around the foundation are still bright with flowers. On this crystalline day, the twin peaks of Mt. Diablo in the background look close enough to touch. It seems impossible that they are more than ten miles away. I can see the apricots ripening among the leaves in orange and green in the late spring sun.

My feet drag as I unlatch the side gate leading to the backyard. A few dying leaves lie on the ground, tumbled from the branches of the giant trees framing the rear of the yard. Among the brilliant kaleidoscope of color from bounties of flowers—deep ruby red, rosy pink, and purple with flashes of orange and vermillion—the leaves look lonely and stark. I feel as desolate as those leaves, realizing suddenly, fearfully, that there is no group around me. This day should be the happiest of my life, but I feel I'm splintered into shards of anguish. Without my friends, I don't know who I am, nor even who I'm supposed to be.

Alka will neither speak nor listen to me. In two weeks, there's been no reply to my e-mail of apology. I dialed Alka's cell phone twice after that, but disconnected when it went into voice mail. I tried to summon up penitent words of remorse, or cheery words of hope, but at the last minute the corrosive words of our last encounter rise up like bile in my throat, suffocating me. In my last attempt, the ringtone gasped right into voice mail, as if making a mockery of my effort to makeup with her.

I keep my eyes tightly shut to keep the tears at bay. A cold ache tangles in the pit of my belly. I have done this thing, wrecked it all. My cruel, vengeful words, "Alka pushed Krishna too hard, too hard," keep clanging and banging in my noise-filled brain. And then Alka's accusatory voice, "She's no friend of mine. No friend of mine." All the time I play it in my head. All the time. Trying to change it, to soften it. But my own pettiness comes to mind in a strange, slowed-down way as if I were under water or behind a wall of wavy glass blocks.

Mini and Priya have kept in touch with me through occasional calls or texts, but their conversations sound stilted and guarded to my wary ear. There's an emptiness inside me, a gaping, ragged hole. Unless I reconcile with Alka, I know that my world is not going to right itself.

Sighing heavily, I scan the inside of the fixer-upper we finally decided on. It really is charming. The cleaning crew has worked its magic, and everything from the banister to the floorboards is burnished. The ugly old orange carpet has vanished—we had insisted on that in the negotiations. The painting crew is set to come in on Monday.

The house does not look like something out of a magazine spread yet, but I know that, in time, with a careful eye on my budget, I'll get it there. It has three bedrooms, smaller than what we wanted, but I'd taken one look at the beautiful roses climbing around the front porch, the walk curving to the front door, the live oaks in the backyard that shade the bay window in the downstairs guest bedroom, and fallen in love. I told Sham I liked it, tempering my enthusiasm in case I was disappointed yet again. It was the house I always wanted, and it was still on the market because escrow had fallen apart for an earlier offer. But the burning desire to buy a house has fallen beneath the wheels of this high-octane distress.

I've done a lot of looking over the last four weeks, and I haven't liked the woman I see in the mirror. I admitted, after a long bout of introspection, that I'd been jealous of my friends. I'd felt like the kid outside the candy store window while my friends were inside spending rupees. I'd believed that success and having their own homes was bringing my friends inordinate joy and serenity—even though it wasn't true—and that their days were easier. The resentment had been simmering in me so long that my throat had been filled with the silt of it. It hurts me that I hurt them.

I had been wrong to say those nasty words about Alka. I know that now. They may have held a nugget of truth, but it was not the time—nor my place—to cast aspersions on a grieving mom. I shake my head.

I walk through the house, inviting it to rise to the name. My Home. *Apna Ghar.*

I can see my daughters giggling to each other as they run into the yard jostling to get the first shot at the swing I'll hang from the apple tree. I can envision Sham on the laptop, perched on the granite countertop of the island in the kitchen, sitting on a wrought iron barstool with its rattan weave back. I saw the barstools yesterday in an IKEA catalog and intend to run out and buy them as soon as we move in. From the sunlit kitchen that looks out into the yard, I can see Sham's parents under the shade of the spreading oak tree, soaking up the ambient sun in a La-Z-Boy recliner that I'll place on the freshly clipped lawn. It's taking shape as a vision of my future. I trace the elaborate detail work on the heavy front door with a thoughtful finger. *Why does it make me sad?*

I miss my friends. I want them here with me in my watershed moment to share in my joy. I know what is the right thing to do, what I have to do. *I'll drive to the hospital right now and apologize to Alka. I'll even go down on my knees and plead with her if I have to.* A flicker of real, tangible hope courses through me. *Maybe Mini and Priya will be there, to see us reconcile.*

I trot to my car, dig impatiently for the keys in my oversized handbag, and then stop with a sharp pang as I catch sight of the time. The ghastly neon glare of the clock on the dashboard announces that it is almost 3:00 p.m. I have barely twenty minutes to make it across town for an appointment with my gynecologist.

For the past two weeks, I've been feeling achy and exhausted, a sharp, jabbing pain between my ribs as I walk. I'd put it down to the stress of my row with Alka, the chaos in my overwrought brain, and later, due to the closing on the house. But two days ago in the shower, while lathering myself, I'd felt a tiny lump in my left breast, almost pea-sized, but unmistakable in its shape.

I'm imagining things. I forced a laugh. Yet yesterday, when I'd almost convinced myself, I gingerly touched the spot and there it was—tiny, yes, but fierce in its presence.

This morning again I'd let warm water glide over my voluptuous boobs, filled both hands with enough soap to make my fingertips frothy, and then caressed my left breast. Smooth skin filled the palm of my hands. Feeling blissful as I massaged it tenderly. Until I felt the nugget again. I rolled the mass under my thumb and forefinger forcefully, willing it to dissolve into nothingness. But a minute later when I brought my nerveless fingers up again, as if mocking my efforts, it remained unmarred by my determination to crush it.

"Oh, fuck." The word startled me, but the situation warranted an expletive.

I wasn't sure why I told Sham, except maybe I needed someone to allay my fears, tell me I was overreacting. But, he was somber, agreeing it was a discernible shape. He insisted I call the doctor. I felt almost silly telling the receptionist what the matter was, but I'd promised him I'd go.

Now as I rev up the engine, I berate myself for making such a fuss about something that's no doubt nothing, but considering it's too late to cancel—they'll charge me sixty dollars if I don't show up—I might as well go.

I'll go to the hospital to meet Alka after the appointment.

The rest of the day passes in a blur. Dr. Severance, whom I've known for seven years or so, looks grim as he conducts the clinical breast exam. Over and over, he pokes and prods me with his large, soft hands, but there's no mistaking what I felt—a lump just over one centimeter long and very mobile.

"It may be a benign tumor without any worrying features, but we can never tell." Dr. Severance is solemn. Only the pain of a vise squeezing keeps my heart from sinking. My mouth feels like the Rajasthani desert. I've never been any good in a medical emergency. I remember the time Ma went to hospital for blood tests to diagnose "woman troubles."

I ran tearfully to our *puja* room as soon as the door closed behind Ma and Papaji, and sobbed my heart out in front of *Ganesh, Lakshmi, Krishna, Shiva,* stopping obsequiously in front of each of the figurines. "Please bring Ma back home to me and Ram," I blubbered in desperation. The gods had heard my prayers—Ma returned home after the biopsy revealed that the growth in her cervix was benign. I was relieved. *Without her, who will take care of that brat, Ram?* But the memory of those few worry-filled days is seared in my mind.

Turning now to my doctor, I ask in a low, trembling voice, "So, what do we do now?"

He is all business, laconic and brusque. "I'm sending you to Quest Diagnostics for a biopsy as soon as they can schedule it. I've marked it Urgent. If they get you in within a day or two, we'll know the results early next week and we'll go from there." His smile is faint.

Our eyes meet briefly and he says, "Chin up, dear," before turning to go. The door closes behind him with a small whiff and a sigh, tossing my emotions in a somersault like autumn leaves.

It's as if I'm watching the pageant of a life not my own. I plod to the lab and procure an appointment for the next day. I make my way home with groggy steps, my joy and optimism from just a few hours earlier dissipating as I dwell on what to do next.

Mini

Saturday night dinner with the family. Tom, wanting to make amends for his boorish behavior during their Half Moon Bay getaway—he's having a difficult time lately with some demanding clients in this sluggish economy, he explained—has organized a lavish dinner at Michael Minna's in San Francisco. His daughter, Karen, and son-in-law, Richard, along with Rani and Sophie, who's in town for summer break.

Dinner proceeds amicably, Karen doing a credible job of keeping up appearances. But when the men disappear for a cigar on the terrace, she peppers Rani and Sophie with questions. Mini is uneasy, but nothing she can put her finger on specifically. More the manner of interrogation makes Mini's skin crawl. Which high school did you go to? Who are your friends? What extracurricular activities do you pursue? Hip-hop? Choir? No? And then it comes out: What God do you pray to?

Mini gasps loudly. Her eyes flash. Her inner Sita bolts upright, shock sending her hair flying everywhere, mouth pressed into a hard line. *Are you crazy?* Her inner Sita glares at Karen as if she wished she could punch her.

Mini is a wounded tigress sheltering her cubs. Apprehension churns in her stomach. Sophie's body language—her expression frozen—shows that the question has shocked her speechless.

Before Sophie can fashion a response to the rudeness, Mini jumps in, choosing her words carefully. Jaw in a firm line, she responds with steely eyes. "Karen, every major religion—Hinduism, Sikhism, Islam, Judaism, Christianity—preaches that God is one. Which form one prays to is immaterial and," with a delicate pause before swiping claws across the woman's face, "wholly private."

Karen responds with a tight smile, but she holds her tongue. Mini's relieved but numb. She watches her daughters finish their dinner in silence. When the men come in shortly afterwards, appearances have been restored, but on the silent drive home Mini is seething as she remembers.

When Inder and she first settled in this country, they tried to adapt to the local values. American ideals were the goal, yet what to adopt and what to reject were a constant struggle. Born to a civilization five thousand years old, they had emigrated to one of the youngest. A virtue in one land was now a vice in another. In India, deference and modesty signified respect, but in America it was a sign of weakness. And the American notion that everyone is created equal? Not in India where people openly acknowledged regional differences and hierarchies of money, caste, and power. Life there was like a card game—one played whatever hand one was dealt.

She believed she'd done a bang-up job at assimilation—earning a decent wage, dressing in smart business suits, researching and typing legal briefs that the attorneys depended on, and living the American dream complete with white picket fence in her largely white neighborhood. To attest to her further Americanization, she even has a white boyfriend.

But Karen's question has brought bad memories long suppressed. That night she has the nightmare again. Her mouth is dry with terror as she relives the horror of the 1984 riots—the burning of Delhi in communal uprising against Sikhs. Her family huddled around the television as news of retaliatory murders leaked out, while Indian media showed only the pomp and show of former Prime Minister Indira Gandhi's family mourning her death by two Sikh security guards.

Mini's world had gone crazy. New Delhi—a modern, cultured, progressive, and tolerant city—descended into chaos. The assassination of India's beloved prime minister to avenge the Indian army's march into the Golden Temple, the Sikh's revered shrine, spurred hordes to align with the Prime Minister's Congress Party to attack. Hundreds of Sikhs were massacred and countless violated while the state administration was too immersed in grieving Indira Gandhi's death to pay attention to the slaughter of innocent citizens. Savagery escalated. Riots and looting in the poor neighborhoods were rampant. Homes were doused with gasoline and torched. Countless women were kidnapped, stripped, robbed of jewelry, raped. Sikh men had their hair chopped off and their turbans burned or were set aflame with tires around their neck. The bloodbath drove many Sikhs to shave their faces and cut their hair against religious custom,

Yes, there were many accounts of communal compassion and heroism—people who risked everything to save others, regardless of religion or caste. Mini's neighborhood organized a twenty-four-hour vigil against goons unleashed by the administration. Her parents' Hindu friends brought them food, stored their belongings, sheltered them from the mobs.

Mini was only seventeen when she lived through it. Americans never had.

She tries to explain all this when she meets Tom at Café Diva on Sunday morning. He turns to her with a frown. "You're sure you heard Karen right?"

Mini throws him a blistering look. "Does it look like I may have made a mistake?"

"She's the sweetest, kindest soul you could ever meet." He

expresses his helplessness. "You must have misinterpreted it." His tone is defensive.

He doesn't understand. There's too much of the past in my blood, like a sickness I still have to sweat out.

Mini turns away and buries her face in her hands, breathing deeply to keep the threatening tears at bay. Nineteen eighty-four taught her that there are lines that cannot be crossed. She's never experienced overt racism, to be honest, other than a patronizing comment by a senior partner about her accent. In the beginning, she'd been upset that she could not go unnoticed, and so she had practiced mimicking the American inflection. In time, her American co-workers began to listen to what she said, rather than how she said it. But 9/11 reestablished cultural divides all over again. Now the threat of racism is always present—like lava bubbling beneath the surface of a dormant volcano.

"Big Brother is watching you." America's Patriot act reminds Mini of Orwell's *1984*. Terrorists frighten her, whether Islamic fundamentalists or Hindu communalists, but so does the Act. No due process. No formal charges. No lawyer. No phone call. No innocent until proven guilty. Some margin of error is inevitable. Who would Tom choose to protect from terrorists or . . . a TSA agent? *Who do you think?* Her inner Sita rears her sardonic head.

Mini contemplates all this while Tom's silence fills the booth. Finally, she turns around, picks up her umbrella, and slings her handbag over her shoulder.

"I guess I better get out of here."

Tom makes no gesture to stop her. It's over.

Sunday afternoon drags heavily. Mini stares out the window despondently sipping a glass of *chai* and watching rain droplets slither down the window panes. Usually the warm sound of the rain on the rooftops wraps her in its soothing cocoon. Today she turns away from the wide-brimmed window sill in her spacious kitchen feeling melancholy and disconnected from everything around her.

How could Tom be so obtuse! How could he not understand how she felt?

She climbs the stairs and yanks open the drawer in her nightstand. She lovingly rubs the nose stud she'd tucked away, the one that "makes you look too Indian." Tom's criticism rings in her ears. It takes a few tries in front of the mirror until she's able to thrust it back in the hole. She twirls this way and that, admiring how the tiny diamond glints, as she often did since her *Nani* talked her mother into letting her have that small traditional pleasure. *Why did I change for somebody else? Give up a part of my identity? For a man?*

She strides out of her bedroom and sees the message light on the home phone flickering. She dials her password. Her nerveless fingers almost drop the phone.

CHAPTER 41

Alka

At eight in the morning, Alka is in the *puja* room. Her eyes are closed, her face a blissed-out radiance. She balances her *puja* tray with incense and candles in her left hand and sways to the music of the surround-sound hymn. "Lord Ganesha, remover of obstacles . . ." she chants. She feels the alive presence of God around her.

A hard, rapid knock on the door jars her from her reverie. Contrary to his usual behavior, Kakaji bursts into the room.

"I'm so sorry, *Didi*, but it's Dr. Lin . . . from the hospital. I told him you were busy, b-ut . . . he insists on talking to you."

Alka lays down the tray carefully and lifts the phone mounted by the door. Kakaji quietly backs out of the small sanctuary.

The ringer is turned off, but a flashing light indicates a call on hold. An ominous feeling sweeps over her as she raises the receiver gingerly to her ear. It's the first time Dr. Lin has called at home. Raj left the house twenty minutes earlier to meet with Krishna's specialist. Alka is to join him after she finishes her prayers. She steadies herself, then presses the button.

"Alka Bajaj speaking."

"Mrs. Bajaj, it's Dr. Lin," the head of the neurology department says. His voice is calm. Unreadable. "I think you and your husband should come to the hospital as quickly as you can."

A million thoughts race through Alka's mind: Krishna has

stopped breathing. He's taken a turn for the worse. All hope has been lost. Alka grips the phone to ward off whatever might come next. Her eyes are opaque as stormy water, and her face blank, like a room with the light switched off.

"Is Krishna okay?" The words claw their way through her throat.

There is a pause that lasts the blink of an eye, but whole pages of words and storms of emotions travel through her. The two words she hears make her drop the phone and scream Kakaji's name.

Her devoted manservant instantly rushes into the room, since he's been waiting just outside the door to hear what's happened. Alka looks paralyzed, her hands involuntarily quivering. Kakaji speaks anxiously into the shadowed silence of the room of prayers.

"What happened, *Didi*?"

Alka doesn't know what to say to him. She imagined this moment a thousand times, but now her eyes can't see, her mind is blank. She hears herself breathing. If she concentrates, she will even be able to feel her heart beating in her chest. But thought is beyond grasping.

Has she heard Dr. Lin correctly? Did she hear the words in the ecstasy of chanting? Has she misunderstood? She replays the conversation, to grasp the reality behind the words, but she can't even focus enough to identify her emotions. Kakaji's eyes are glued to her, which frightens her more. She seems to be falling through space.

Kakaji grabs her hands to stop their agitated wringing. Alka looks around the *puja* room, at the burnished statue of Lord Ganesha who is smiling at her, at Kakaji, at Lakshmi and Shiva. When her eyes stop moving, all she can do is repeat exactly what she heard on the phone.

"He's awake."

"Alka?" Raj's voice, hoarse and trembling, sounds hollower over the cell phone connection.

"Raj," she croaks back, "Krishna is awake." As the enormity of the words hits her, she breaks down, sobbing in heaving bursts. Raj is weeping, too.

She can tell he's trying hard to get his emotions under control. "I'm going to his room now. Do you want me to wait for you or should I . . . ?" His voice is barely above a whisper.

"No, no. You go to him now. Kakaji and I will be there in ten minutes."

After twenty lane changes and four traffic lights that were definitely yellow and perhaps even red, Kakaji brings the car to a halt at the entrance to the hospital. Alka hasn't spoken a word except for her brief phone conversation with Raj.

Alka hopes beyond hope, and is excited beyond measure. But she can't shake the thought that she's misunderstood. Maybe Krishna woke for an instant and is in a coma again. Maybe someone has gotten the information wrong. Raj will check for himself. For herself. For themselves—as Krishna's mom and dad.

Alka flings the car door open and runs toward the hospital entrance. She zooms through the revolving door. A quick right leads her to the elevator and she bounds in. Someone asks her, "What floor?" Later she can't even remember whether it had been a man or a woman. She answers automatically, and the button for the fourth floor lights up.

She becomes more wobbly the higher they get. As she exits, she sees both a female and a male nurse look up at her as she passes the nurses' station. Their expressions are excited. They want to talk to her, but she doesn't stop, though her legs are about to give away. She leans against the wall to steady herself for a moment, then takes the last steps toward Krishna's room.

His door stands open. The murmur of voices pours into the hallway. Stomach churning, she steps inside and Raj's face lights up. She can see traces of tears on his cheeks, his eyes shining with unsuppressed joy.

He's standing next to Krishna's bed, one arm embracing their son's shrunken shoulders. Propped up weakly on the raised bed, Krishna looks gaunt and much older than seventeen, but his smile when he sees his mother tells her everything she needs to know.

"Krishna?" Alka finally whispers.

"Mummy." Krishna wheezes. His voice sounds different, scratchy and croaky from disuse, but it's Krishna's voice just the same. Her boy's voice. Alka moves slowly toward the bed, her eyes never leaving Krishna's.

"Krishna?" she repeats.

She sits on the bed beside him, taking his pallid hand in both of hers.

"Krishna, my son. Krishna, my son, *my beta.*" Alka breaks down. Her hands curl around Krishna's, stroking it, caressing it, feeling the pulse drumming along his forearm.

Raj leans toward Alka, and when she feels his hand stroking her hair and then her back, she cries from a more secret sorrow. Raj engulfs her and Krishna in an embrace, the three of them a small, tight circle.

The closing lines of the *Champa flower* poem fill her mind, striking a chord in her heart.

When in the evening
You went to the cowshed
With the lighted lamp in your hand
I should suddenly drop onto the earth again
And be your own baby once more.
And beg you to tell me a story

Where have you been, you naughty child?
I won't tell you, Mother.
That's what you and I would say then.

She isn't dreaming. Krishna is awake. He's here with them, seeing how much he means to them. Seeing that what he heard her say when she was alone with him is true.

It's real, is all she can think. *It's real.*

CHAPTER *42*

Priya

Priya grins at her own reflection as she passes the hallway mirror. She's expecting Mini and Alka to arrive at her apartment any minute. Since Krishna's miraculous awakening two weeks ago, the three friends have created four occasions to meet, as though they needed to be together to share the joy and relief.

And last night, over a plate of hot *jalebis* that Kakaji placed before them, Priya revealed the news of her burgeoning relationship with Miguel.

"We're going to spend a night at his home, his farm, in Fresno." She couldn't quite look them in the eye as she spoke, but then Mini squealed with delight and announced, "Well, we're just going to have to come over and style you!"

Even Alka joined in, clapping her hands with obvious glee. "That's right. Try keeping us away, Priya!"

Priya studied Alka discreetly. Shoulders sharp and angular beyond a sleeveless blouse, but gone was the panic that had been lurking at the edges of her mouth, the desperation in her black eyes, the knotting hands that had characterized her six weeks in purgatory. Instead, she was swathed in joy, her eyes full of life and promise—in a way that Priya had never seen in all the years they'd been friends.

Priya, happy that her friends were happy, acquiesced to their makeover offer with a grin. The same grin stares back at her now from the hall mirror. She recognizes her old happy face from a long time ago.

She pads softly out to her kitchen and puts the kettle on to boil. She sets out the bone china mugs from India—the special ones that make *chai* taste more authentic.

As she reaches for the tin of tea, she notices, with a sharp intake of breath, that she's automatically brought out not three cups, but four.

Divya! A small sound like a moan escapes before her knuckles against her mouth can cut it off.

It has been almost three weeks since their last stilted conversation. After the normal niceties, the conversation slackened and the intervals of silence grew longer until Priya could stand it no longer. She bid Divya a hasty good-bye and aborted the call.

How had this come to pass? How had four friends who had been so close gotten themselves stuck, unable to say the things that needed to be said? Some things were beyond understanding. Divya's reticence made it seem as though she blamed Priya and Mini for deepening the wedge in their friendship. Sometimes Priya thought that maybe they had contributed to the rift.

Maybe they should all have been a better friend to Divya. Priya feels dizzy, off balance, like she's being thrust back in time. Ever since Jesus and Mary, Divya has sought their approval, and acceptance. To Mini and Alka, and yes, to Priya herself, she has always been the outsider, the new girl junior year, eager and anxious to belong. *Has Divya ever felt as if she belongs with them?* Priya wonders with an acute sense of guilt. Life is a bag of regret. A part of her yearns to turn back the clock so she can redo certain moments of her life.

She returns the extra cup to its place in the cupboard, but imagines Divya sitting across from her on her little terrace, laughing and excited about all the changes everyone has gone through.

Does she even know about Krishna? I have to call her tomorrow. I won't let this silence go on anymore.

The kettle whistles just as the doorbell peals. In marches Mini with two laden garment bags from Nordstrom across her arm, drawing Alka along in her wake, and an orange and gray animal print makeup bag as big as a tackle box.

"What's all that? I only told you guys about the date yesterday."

"We just happened to be shopping a couple of days ago, and when we spotted these . . . " Alka holds up the garment bags, "we knew they'd be perfect for you."

"It was an investment," Mini says. "We knew you'd eventually have to start dating and . . . "

Alka interrupts, "Remember when the Indian bank manager from Citibank asked you out? You were a wreck. You said you had nothing to wear, and that's when we decided . . . "

Priya collapses onto her sofa, giddiness and excitement replaced by a feeling she thought she'd left with Vik.

"*Bhagwan Jaane*, I'm hopeless." Her smile is gone, a heavy feeling weighing her down.

Mini sits down beside her. "That's where we come in." She squeezes Priya's hand.

Despite her descent into gloom, Priya lets herself be carried away by their enthusiasm and proficiency. Mini wields the curling iron like she's prepping tomorrow's top model, painstakingly straightening long, curly hair layer by layer until it falls in silken columns around Priya's face. Then she applies makeup—smoky topaz smudges beneath mascaraed lashes, a sweep of coral-hued blush, and rose-colored lipstick just bright enough to bring out the color of Priya's warm, brown eyes.

"Ta-da!" sings Mini, handing Priya a hand mirror.

"Wow." Priya smiles at her own reflection. Never has her face looked so good.

"Too bad my body still looks like a baby elephant. Maybe I should wear a burka to dinner." Her voice is falsely jovial.

Now it's Alka's turn. Like a magician turning a piece of string into a rainbow scarf, she whips the plain plastic bag off the hanger to reveal a flowing black chiffon sundress with a plunging V-neckline surrounded by tiny sparkles of black jet, and a crinkly skirt that swirls from an empire waist.

"My arms will show."

"So will your boobs," Mini clarifies. She urges Priya to shed the T-shirt that has obviously seen better days as well as her baggy sweatpants. Priya raises her arms and bends down to let Mini pull the fluid dress over her head. It falls easily into place. She turns to the full-length mirror and tries to see herself through Miguel's eyes. A dusky, big-boned woman with a pretty enough face, flabby arms, and ample cleavage. Absent a tummy tuck, this is as good as she's likely to look.

For a finishing touch, Mini plunges into Priya's dresser and finds an old favorite, a summer shawl embroidered all over with vines and flowers in a variety of blues and greens.

"Perfect!" Alka says when Priya drapes the shawl around her shoulders.

"Well, at least it hides my arms," says Priya, studying herself in the mirror. She turns to her friends and wraps them in a loving hug. "Thank you, thank you."

Mini backs away. "Don't mess up my handiwork!" she says. She squeezes Priya's hand in place of the hug and starts packing up all her paraphernalia so they can get out before Miguel shows up.

"Call us when you get back," Alka says as she and Mini walk out the front door.

Less than ten minutes later, she's opening the front door again. Miguel holds out an offering of her favorite flowers—wispy tendrils of night jasmine surrounding three yellow tulips, erect and jaunty.

She lowers her nose to breathe in the heady scent.

"Wow," she says. "Thanks, Miguel." She looks up and finds him gawking, as if he's been struck by lightning.

"You look beautiful." His voice—hoarse, strained—tells Priya that he's as nervous as she is. Somehow that calms her down.

"Shall we go?" she asks. He picks up the small red overnight bag she's placed near the door in one hand. Priya takes his other hand in hers, and he leads her out to his truck. They sit side by side with the ease of longtime friends, talking about their day. Miguel tells her about the tremendous grape harvest they're going to have. The vines have set fruit and the deep soil is holding the late rain. And with *Priya's Curries and Chutneys* selling off the shelves in two more nearby farmers' markets, she has the urge to spread her wings. She's dreaming of opening *Priya's Chaat and Chai* in a storefront that's sitting vacant.

The hour-and-a-half-drive seems to take no time. Miguel's house is old and lived-in, large for a single man, and well-cared for. His housekeeper has prepared traditional Mexican food. It's delicious, as is the sangria that Priya repeatedly lifts to her lips. Later, she has no memory of it. What stays with her is the kiss they share under the nearly full moon. The starry skies bear witness to her longing, as she looks up at him among rows and rows of spindly young vines, verdant and promising.

"Priya," Miguel says to her in a husky undertone she hasn't heard before. She turns. This is what she's been looking for. What she wants tonight. She hasn't admitted it to herself until now. She tilts her chin just a little, waiting.

The kiss is like nothing she's experienced before. It lifts her up and twirls her around and plunges her to the ground. She clings to him as she's never clung to another human being in her adulthood, as if he alone can save her.

Miguel lifts his head, slightly out of breath.

"I want you, Priya."

It's intoxicating to be wanted so passionately by this strong, substantial man. Her heart slams to a halt, then races pounding against her ribs. She feels the staccato pounding of his heart as he gathers her close.

He puts his hand around the back of her neck. His fingers are warm and unwavering against her skin. She leans back, feeling anchored by him. Held close.

"Do you want me?" he asks. The softness of his warm breath brushes against her lips.

"Yes," she claims her long dormant desire as it kicks alive with a vengeance.

Miguel lifts her off her feet, all one hundred eighty pounds of her, in one easy motion, and carries her into the rustic master bedroom, laying her down tenderly on the white coverlet. As he slips off the black chiffon dress, she opens herself shamelessly, crying out his name and clinging to him. Nothing matters except his body and hers, and how alive he makes her feel.

Later, they lie in the ticking night, Miguel embracing her and whispering sweet nothings until they fall asleep, curled up safe and sated in each other's arms.

CHAPTER 43

Divya

My new kitchen faces east toward Mt. Diablo. Some mornings after a wakeful night I get up to watch the sunrise from the wide window of my breakfast room, sitting with a cup of green tea. My backyard brims with sky-blue hydrangeas, and climbing roses drape the fence. The rising sun catches the symphonic colors of the flowers: purples, pinks, corals, and whites. How beautiful it is. My dream come true.

And yet I feel no sense of ownership of my dream house. *Ironic.* It's the perfect house. It has everything we wanted. Even within our price range. Sham finally said, yes, this was the one. And I agreed. We were already in escrow for the house when I did a long-neglected self-exam in the shower, part of my determination to turn over a new leaf, to live life the right way.

It was a tiny, tiny lump. The lumpectomy had gone well, but it turned out I needed chemo, because of the kind of tumor they'd found. My odds were very good; the doctors were upbeat. I did everything by the book, and Sham was there for me, more devoted than anyone might have predicted.

We'd barely moved in when I had the surgery. The kitchen and the bedrooms were fine, but my plans for the family room—the one room that needed work—were put on hold. The garage is still stacked high with unpacked boxes, and we are still eating our meals at the worn-out kitchen table I'd sworn to leave behind.

I haven't told Ma about my illness. I continue my long-distance communications in the normal chatty updates by phone, and new photos of the grandchildren e-mailed every couple of weeks. I hadn't intended to lie to Ma, but I couldn't say the words—I couldn't deal with my mother's fears on top of my own. I hate scenes as much as Ma loves them.

I overcompensate with my kids. Fake smile and false cheerfulness when I hum along to old Hindi songs playing on Zee TV, my favorite of the eleven channels we get by satellite from India.

I keep up a front with Sham, too, concealing my exhaustion, papering over my depression. I've spoken twice about it with the social worker attached to my doctors. The woman has been great, sympathetic but not pitying, and helpful.

Many days I fall back into bed as soon as Sham and the girls are gone. I feel weak and alone, stuck in a bad dream. The social worker is pushing me to join a support group, and I've admitted I need to try something.

The first chemo treatment this past Monday hit me like a truck. The nurse, who's efficient but humorless, tells me I have an extremely sensitive system. I feel I'm being accused of something.

The side effects kick in a few days after the treatment: nausea, fatigue, a fuzzy brain. It's impossible to pretend anymore that everything is all right. Sham works from home as much as he can, but he needs to be seeing clients, checking on his people in the field. He wants to call my second oldest sister, who lives in Seattle, to come and stay with us for a while, but I won't hear of it. Aditi is as dramatic as Ma.

Our new neighbors help out, driving double carpools, keeping the kids after summer school until Sham can pick them up. Mona Vora calls Sham at work on Tuesday to tell him not to worry about dinners, she has organized our friends and acquaintances into a schedule, and she's going to be the delivery person.

She shows up during the day on Thursday when I'm alone, curled up with a hot water bottle on the couch, watching *Sholay* with the sound off. Mona rings the doorbell, opens the door, and walks in. She wheels a cooler behind her filled with a dozen different casseroles—*matar-paneer, Punjabi cholay, asparagus kofta*. The beloved aromas make my stomach lurch.

"Mona, quick, get those into the kitchen!"

Mona clicks her stiletto-heeled Gucci ankle booties across my straight grain fir floor and into the kitchen. I press the hot water bottle against my stomach. The sounds of doors and drawers opening and closing reach me from the kitchen. Earlier that morning clumps of my hair had come out as I brushed it. I felt as bad as I can remember feeling in my whole life. I did not want to deal with Mona Vora.

I click off the television and rearrange myself so that I'm lying stretched out with my face turned to the back of the couch. I'm sick—I don't have to be polite. I cradle the hot water bottle and try to calm myself by reciting the *Gayatri Mantra: Om bhur bhuvaha*. I wear my amulet around my wrist now, and I touch it to center myself.

I'm only half-awake when I hear those heels clicking toward me.

"Divya," Mona whispers loudly behind her.

"Mmmmmmnnnnhh."

"I left the food in the fridge. I put instructions on stickies and left them on each different dish."

"Thank you." My throat feels dry, but I don't roll over to pick up my water bottle. I just want Mona to leave.

"Can I get you anything?"

I think about a cup of tea. "No," I say, "thank you."

"Okay," Mona says. "I'm going to go, but I'll come again in a few days with more food."

"Great," I say. "Thank you."

The heels click away, then turn back.

"I almost forgot," says Mona. Her voice seems very close. "Do you want to send any message to the Rummy Club?"

I stop breathing. *What did she just say?* When I don't answer, Mona continues on her own. "They told you I was taking your place, right? Oh," she says with that false laugh of hers, "not that I could take your place exactly, but I am the new fourth."

I can picture Mona's sly gray eyes. My own eyes remain closed. I don't utter a sound.

"Oh," says Mona, "you poor baby. I'd better let you sleep." She tiptoes loudly away. Finally, the door closes.

I don't believe it. They wouldn't replace me. Not with Mona Vora. Not with anyone. I don't believe it. And then I do.

All those unanswered voice mails, texts, e-mails. My silence. It was my fault. They reached out. Mini left a message just a few days ago about starting up the Rummy Club again. It was the first day of chemo. They didn't know. I couldn't tell them.

My mind feels as poisoned as my breast tissue. Guilt, anger, betrayal circulate with the chemo until I crumple into sleep. Sham comes home in the middle of the afternoon. He helps me change into clean pajamas, turning away from my surgery scar. Now I'm in my own bed, with mind still spinning, misery wrapped around me like a shroud and a vast amount of time to brood. I miss Alka, Mini, and Priya fiercely.

*Alka didn't accept my apology. I **am** sorry, I never meant for Alka to hear. Alka holds grudges. She has always held grudges. She never really cared for me anyway. I have always been an outsider, never belonged. Except really, Mini and I are close. Mini is my best friend. Why didn't Mini do something right after it happened? But Krishna is in a coma. I should have gone to the hospital. I should* *have apologized sooner. But I did apologize.*

Thursday and Friday are obsessive thoughts broken only by scratchy sleep. Fatigue is not an adequate description for this raw, ripped, wretched, restless statelessness. On Friday night, when I know the Rummy Club is getting underway, I give in and take one of the sleeping pills the doctor prescribed weeks ago. I don't want to spend this night tormenting myself. I take the pill, drink a third of a cup of chamomile tea, and escape for twenty hours.

Late Saturday afternoon, I feel my way gingerly out of bed and stagger to the bathroom. After I've peed and washed my hands, I stand still for a minute, trying to discern how I feel. No nausea. I take a deep breath. I turn on the water in the shower. It's been days since I took a shower. Sham knocks on the bathroom door.

"*Jaan*, are you okay? Do you need help?"

"I'm okay. I'll be out soon."

Cleaned up and wearing real clothes, I feel a bit more like myself. I twist my hair up and pin it to my head. I'll have to do something about this hair. That's a good question to introduce myself to the women in that support group.

When I go downstairs to the family room, my daughters jump up to greet me. "Mommy! Mommy!"

"You were sleeping so long, Mommy!" Serena throws her arms around me and bursts into tears. Maya follows.

"I'm okay, girls. I'm okay." At least in this moment, it's true. I really am okay. "Come on, *gudiya*, come sweetheart." I move over to the ratty loveseat that the Salvation Army refused to take, and my girls move with me, unwilling to let me go.

Sham is setting out a frozen dinner on the kitchen table, but I don't want to be near the food, and the girls don't want to leave me. After a few minutes of cuddling, though, they grudgingly join their father. They are soon back. Serena wants my attention for a new sequence she's just learned in dance class. Maya has a pile of A's to show me. I'm astonished at how much they seem to have grown in the few days I've been out of it.

Sham puts on a CD of *Daler Mehndi* songs. A couple of boxes marked "PHOTOS" sit near the brick fireplace in the family room. The girls drag the boxes over and proceed to pull out albums, books of slides, framed photos, and envelopes filled with random pictures—the whole history of our family. They love seeing the pictures of themselves as babies and toddlers. They love, in particular, the photos of our wedding.

"Look at Auntie Mini and Auntie Alka," Serena says, holding up a picture from my school days.

I study the photo. "They were just a few years older than you are now," I tell my daughter. It's hard to remember the feeling of being that young.

That night after Sham turns off his light, I say to him, "It's time. Monday evening I want you to drive me to Alka's house. I have to get through this. I don't want to lose my friends." Sham rolls over and kisses me, and tells me how proud he is of me. When he starts to stroke my hair, I push his hand away.

"My hair is coming out!" And then it's my turn to burst into tears.

"It's okay, *Jaan*, it will grow back." He wraps his arms carefully around me and holds me until I fall asleep.

CHAPTER *44*

Mini

Kim and Kourtney Kardashian are moving into their New York apartment, and Mini is trying not to cut her finger as she chops vegetables for dinner while peeking at the mini-television on her countertop.

She stirs the big pot of *Goan shrimp curry*, sticks her nose into the fragrant steam, tastes the coconut gravy. Something's missing, but she can't figure out what. It's Priya's recipe—she would know what's missing. Mini glances at the phone. No. Better not—Priya's probably busy cooking up a storm for the fourth farmers' market stall she's launching this weekend. Mini takes another whiff, another taste. No clue.

The memory of Tom's intense blue eyes as they parted ways blurs her vision. She can still conjure up his freshly shaved jaw, breathe in his clean scent. Her body still craves his touch, but the disastrous dinner brought reality home to her. Mini has never been ashamed of her ethnicity, her Indian heritage. *My native land will always be a part of me, those first colorful threads woven into the tapestry of my life.*

But breaking up with Tom Sanders and forgetting about him are two different things altogether. A part of her wishes that he'd tried harder to change her mind. He'd been totally understanding about their breakup, too darned noble about it. If only he'd yelled or cried or fought for their relationship. Maybe that was all she'd wanted—to hear that he refused to let her go, that he really wanted her. Then together they could have overcome Karen Sanders Blakely.

With "If this is what you really want," he let it die.

"Yes, yes, it is." So it was over, and she hasn't had a message from Tom since.

Must have already found a new gal. Somebody Karen approves of. Her eyes mist over again.

No, no, no. Snap out of it. Her inner Sita has finally shown up to help.

She inhales the aroma of the ginger she's added to the shrimp curry and takes another taste. The missing ingredient flits on the edge of her senses, an elusive lightning bug—now you see me, now you don't.

This is why I don't cook. She bangs the heavy serving spoon down. *And this is the last time I do it.* Her inner Sita frowns at her. *Arré. However will you find a nice Indian man if you don't try to cook, you silly girl?* Mini sticks her tongue out at her inner Sita.

She turns away from the recalcitrant curry and mixes a blender of mango *lassi* instead. *This much I can do well.* The mangoes in the US are not as fragrant or flavorful as India's Alfonso mangoes. But luckily there's always Alfonso canned pulp on the shelves of every self-respecting Indian market. She samples the *lassi.* Her face breaks into a wide grin. "Aaah, delicious."

She adds a few ice cubes, and she pours herself a tall glass. Sitting at the breakfast nook table, she blots her lips with a napkin and whisks her thoughts determinedly away from Tom, turning instead to the momentous meeting of the Rummy Club tonight. Which is why she's stressing over cooking, and why she's been feeling uncertain and anxious over and above the whole Tom thing.

It's their first get-together in months, the first since Krishna did the unthinkable. Six weeks after he's come out of his coma, thank the gods, the friends feel ready to sit together over a game of cards and confide and console, and gossip and compete—a declaration that normal times have returned.

Mini volunteers to contact Divya, convinced that she'll be able to reach her, coax her back into the game, and into their shared lives. She's left two emotional voice mails for Divya, letting her know how much she misses her, asking after her daughters, dropping a couple of tidbits Divya would want to know, updates about Priya and Krishna. She tries to imagine the Divya she knows and loves listening to those messages and then erasing them. She simply cannot picture it.

And yet, Divya does not call. Then Mini sent a couple of e-mails, short and sweet. Still no response. Mini can't figure it out. Yes, Divya and Alka had that spat between them—she's clear she's not going to put herself in the middle of that. With some hemming and hawing, she recently asked Alka if Divya had contacted her, but Mini recognized Alka's expression all too well after decades of intimate friendship. "Not really." Alka's tone was casual, almost indifferent, just the slightest tremble in it like a *sitar's* overtightened string. Only Mini, who knows her from childhood, can tell she's upset.

She and Alka have shared history since she was a gawky freshman at Jesus and Mary. That first day she had stood frozen, searching for a place to sit in the cafeteria amongst the jabbering crowd of "lifers"—those who started together in the nursery class of the Lower School. She could remember that day as acutely as if it had happened yesterday—holding the tray full of unfamiliar food in one nervous hand, tugging at her pleated gingham skirt with her other hand, feeling as though every eye in the noisy, cavernous mess was sizing her up. And then out of nowhere, Alka raised a beckoning arm from across the room. Spared the shame and humiliation of having nowhere to sit, Mini slid gratefully into the place Alka made for her amongst her friends.

Their families had known each other from Delhi, but until that day when Alka took her under her wing, the two of them had shared only the forced kinship of the second generation foisted on each other because of parental friendships. Friendly acquaintances, not really ever friends. Sharing the dorm, along with Priya, had changed all that.

Then junior year along came Divya. *And then there were four,* she thought. *And now three again.*

With a huge sigh, Mini realizes that she's feeling guilty. That's what all the stress and anxiety are about. They had all wanted to play rummy again and Divya would not respond, so Mini had gone ahead and invited Mona Vora to play tonight.

Mona is someone they know from the Indian parties and community events they all attend. Mini likes her. Mona's sense of style and humor jells with her own. Knowing about their Rummy Club, Mona has hinted several times that she plays rummy with her *Dadi* who visits from Mumbai and stays with her parents for months on end—and she'd like to join them sometime.

We'll see how it goes, muses Mini, downing the rest of her mango *lassi* in one smooth gulp and banishing all thoughts of Divya.

Mona Vora is at Mini's door promptly at seven, the first to arrive. *I should have known.* Mini grins wryly as she bustles around the house putting the finishing touches to the beautifully set table gleaming with her good silver.

Mona is an ABCD, "American Born Confused Desi." Mini and other immigrants often make a hard and fast distinction about Indians born in America and Indians from India. The good Indian girls versus their infamous counterparts corrupted by the West, Americanized. But Mini doesn't subscribe to most of that nonsense. Indian immigrants or American-born Indians—their shared heritage gives them a good start, a shortcut to finding common ground.

But even Mini has to acknowledge that Indian immigrants

loyally adhere to IST—Indian Standard Time—always showing up an hour later, while ABCDs are as punctual as their Western peers.

Giving Mini an air kiss on both cheeks Mona says, "Am I too early, dahlin'?" She sashays into the kitchen with Mini trailing behind her.

"No, no, not at all. Just in time," replies Mini, a tad too brightly. Her inner Sita rolls her eyes.

At five feet six with slate gray eyes, Mona Vora stands out in a crowd of petite, dark-eyed Indian women. A rising star among the premier associates at Morrison-Forrester, she gave up her career to raise her babies, but her commanding presence, sharp intellect, and engaging rhetoric still make others sit up straight and pay attention.

Some women are intimidated by Mona, but not Mini—she and Mona have talked about the law and its practice in general. Mini always comes away amused by Mona's droll observations of the celebrity lawyers and judges she worked with. Mini thinks Mona would be a charming addition to their group.

How wrong she can be. All the charm and intelligence and humor drain away after a few drinks, and Mona somehow manages to piss off the affable Priya. The conversation has been innocent enough until Priya refers, in passing, to her recent divorce.

"Divorce is so ugly." Mona pitches her voice low and dramatic, suddenly assuming a look of concern that strikes Mini as false. "The children always suffer." She reaches up to tuck a strand of her perfectly coiffed, beautifully highlighted, mahogany brown hair behind her ear. She pauses, hand in the air, to showcase the mammoth diamond on her ring finger. In a town full of big rocks, Mini has never seen one quite this impressive.

"How *are* your girls doing?" Mona won't give it up.

The rumor mill churns so efficiently in their small Indian community that everybody knows everything. A question along the lines of, "How can you be sure you haven't scarred your children permanently with your stupid mistakes?" is hardly a covert affront.

"Well ... I've put it behind me now." Priya strives to keep her tone light and dismissive, but her eyes are blazing behind her fanned-out cards. Mini is offended on her behalf. Priya, who's such a terrific mom, who's so much happier without that worm Vik. Why should she have to answer to Mona Vora?

This is how Indians think. Her inner Sita is righteous. *Priya could well be wearing a sign across her chest proclaiming "divorced and sullied."* Mini presses her lips together. *Then it's best if we protect her from these narrow-minded Indians,* Mini snaps.

Mona drops the subject of divorce, and the talk stumbles, mostly empty chitchat. Priya has withdrawn from the conversation. Alka, too, keeps her distance, her face stony, uninterested in the superficial subjects Mona brings up, and unwilling to discuss anything important in front of Mona.

The last half-hour is dominated by Mona regaling them with a detailed run-down of the relative merits of the new monogram Vernis leather Louis Vuitton bag versus the timeless appeal of Chanel bags.

That night Mini can't fall asleep, confounded by how wrong she'd been about Mona. *And about Tom. A year ago, I was Inder's wife; I was content in my life. I thought I knew all I needed to know.* Mini has somehow gotten in over her head, her judgment not quite as sterling as she'd always assumed.

She lies in the middle of her big marriage bed, drifting off and waking up again. She remembers a day during senior year at Jesus and Mary when the Rummy Club ventured out to a village not far from Dehradun to attend the *mela*, the annual fair. The day was scorching, the scene lively. The Hindu village women instinctively shrank back and covered their faces when looked at. In sharp contrast to the brazen high school girls in preppy skirts and low-cut tank tops, giggling as they wandered around. Stands sold everything from samosas to shish kababs to bottled mineral water. They stopped at a stall displaying row after row of shiny bangles and rattan baskets overflowing with colorful *bindis*. Loud voices bargained and yelled all around them, but what Mini hears in her mind is the laughter and delight of four friends. They loaded their arms with multicolored bangles and pressed the *bindis* on their foreheads—then collapsed in a heap at the ridiculous mash-up of traditional *bindis* with their oh-so-modern clothes. What had become of those laughing girls?

The next morning Mini is late getting going. She hurries to make Rani's breakfast before gymnastics practice. She's fishing a fragment of shell out of a frying egg when the images come back to her—the village fair, the bracelets and *bindis*. She rings Priya with one hand and manages the pan with the other.

"I regret inviting Mona last night." Just saying the name sends a spike of negativity through her as she remembers all that snobbish chatter at the rummy table.

"She didn't exactly fit in," Priya corroborates.

"I'm going to hunt Divya down today. We have to break this ugly gridlock and get back to how we were."

"You do that, girl!" Priya is enthusiastic. "Tell her I miss her."

"I will, but Alka—" Mini stops. Rani hasn't even touched the bacon and eggs, and she's almost out the door.

"I've got to go, Mom. Talk to you later."

After she showers and dresses, she drives to the Pleasanton Farmers' Market to pick up a dense bunch of the first red flame grapes of the season, a bouquet of mixed flowers, and a couple of jars of Priya's curries. The two young women in charge of Priya's booth know all about their product. Mini doesn't tell them that their boss is her good friend.

Saturday traffic on the 680 is heavy, but moving fast. It's a bright, cloudless afternoon, and Mini reaches the Fremont exit in no time. She finds a place in the visitors' parking lot and gathers up her gifts. She feels light, happy. She's doing the right thing.

Her heart is pounding as she walks up the curved concrete pathway to Divya's town house door. It has been over three months! How could time get away so fast? She rings the bell eagerly.

A man in a faded rugby shirt opens the door.

"Can I help you?" He speaks with a European accent, maybe Russian.

Mini stands on the front step, unable to speak. She has never seen this man before. "You are looking for someone? We just moved here three weeks ago."

Mini backs away. "Do you know where they went, the Kapoors?"

He shrugs his shoulders and shakes his head. After a moment he closes the door.

They moved. They must have bought a house. How could she not tell us after all these years? Mini feels foolish, standing there with her grapes and her jars of curry and her drooping flowers—all for a friend who didn't even call to say she'd moved.

Mini starts back down toward the parking lot when she sees Divya's neighbor, what was her name? Mrs. Parker? She's watering the geraniums in a row of pots on her front step and down onto the walkway.

"Excuse me," says Mini. "I don't know if you remember me—" The woman looks up from her watering can.

"Of course, I know you!" she says. "You play cards with Divya!"

"Yes, yes," Mini says, "but where is Divya?"

The woman seems taken aback. "Well, I assume she's at her new house. Unless this is one of her treatment days."

Frowning, Mini asks her, "What? What did you say?"

Mrs. Parker begins again, as if speaking to a small child, "I said, 'She's probably at her new house unless . . . ' "

Mini interrupts her, cutting her off mid-sentence, "No, no. What did you say about treatment days?"

"Didn't you know? She found a lump. She has breast cancer."

CHAPTER 45

Alka

"Shit," Alka says. "I can't believe it. I cannot believe it."

Mini is sobbing. The cell phone connection is tinny.

"Where are you now?" Alka asks. "Are you going to her house?"

"I'm still in the parking lot. I called Priya, and then you, and I don't even know Divya's new address. The neighbor is looking for it."

Alka's call-waiting beeps. She asks Mini to hold while she switches calls. It's Priya.

"Did Mini call you?" The background noise almost drowns out her voice, which sounds huskier than usual. She's probably been crying, too.

"Mini's on the other line."

"I got the address," Priya says. "Tell Mini I'll call her."

"Just give me the address, and I'll tell her." Alka is losing patience with the whole situation. She takes a deep breath to slow herself down. "Okay. Tell me the address." It's a street in Danville she's never heard of. "Who did you have to call to get this?"

Priya laughs. "I called Mona Vora. She knows everything."

Mini laughs, too, when Alka tells her.

"But I'm not going to be able to get over there until next week. Inder's sister and her daughter are flying in this evening from

Dallas for a college tour, and Rani and I will be with them for the next couple of days."

"Maybe I'll go with you next week," Alka says, relieved at the thought of Mini smoothing the way for her.

After she hangs up the phone, she feels the sudden need to sit down. She braces herself and waits for the initial shockwave to pass. *No wonder Divya closed herself off.* The image of Divya alone behind a high stone wall takes over Alka's mind. She tries to shake it off, but it stays with her when she checks in on Krishna, who's watching *Pulp Fiction* in the living room with his dad. *With the pure relish that only two men can summon for such mindless violence.* That thought and the wall image continue to nag her when she goes upstairs to change out of her summer uniform of denim capris and a white tee into comfy sweats. And it burns bright when she flicks off the kitchen light after Kakaji has served them a light summery dinner.

She climbs upstairs to the master bedroom at the front of the house. Kakaji has left the curtains pulled so the room is in complete darkness. She turns on the bedside lamp, creating a tiny pool of light in the shadowy, cavernous room.

Her mind is too active to turn in for the night. She slips off her shoes and picks up a book from her bedside table, goes down to the family room, and tilts back in the recliner. She's been reading an account of a trip to Peru, an amusing story of misunderstandings and dangers. She opens the book and stares at it—the image of Divya has not faded.

Alka can't remember a time when she hasn't struggled with anger. It's a constant battle—one she liked to believe she was winning. But the showdown with Divya clearly revealed that she wasn't. Maybe she had been so furious with Divya because what Divya said was true. Those words had hit a nerve; a live, pulsing wire. She *had* pressured her son. She was guilty. She had pressured him, and he folded under her pressure. And Divya had dared to speak the truth, which they could all observe.

Lost in her private reckoning, she doesn't sense Raj until she feels his hand on her shoulder.

"Coming to bed?" He leans in to whisper in Alka's ear, his eyes alert and inquiring as she twists around to face him. Alka closes her eyes and inhales the scent that is wholly Raj—a mixture of his custom aftershave and a touch of the cigars he enjoys after dinner. The rush of adrenaline disorients her. She still isn't accustomed to her body's new reaction to his presence.

As the lightheadedness passes, she recites a silent prayer. *Thank you, Ganesh.* She's awash in gratitude for the joy that has moved into their household. Alka has a faraway look on her face. Just like the love story of Jodha and Akbar, the Hindu princess who was forced to marry the Mughal emperor—their alliance a power pact. Their romance was the subject of a popular Hindi film and many soaps. It's like a dream come true, a miracle come to pass.

Krishna hasn't emerged from his coma unscathed, of course. He has lost a great deal of weight, his muscles have atrophied, and a numbness persists on most of his left side. It was days before he could stand without support. The therapy is maddeningly slow. He still spends a couple of hours each day with the physical thera-pist. In the beginning, he often grew frustrated that he could no longer do simple things like drive his car to the temple or to meet with his friends.

At those moments, Raj jumps right in, distracting him with a game of foosball or taking him for a ride around the Montclair hills in his Ferrari convertible. On a daily basis, Kakaji cooks up a storm of delicacies just for Krishna, to nourish his will and to strengthen him. Alka rescues him from bouts of darkness by walking with him in the woods behind their house. The bad moments are less frequent. And Alka is convinced that the changed atmosphere in their house has helped Krishna tremendously. It's like emerging out of the ragged countryside into a blooming Japanese garden with birds singing and crickets chirping.

A brush with death changes the way you look at things. It makes you more philosophical, less judgmental. There were things that seemed so important to me in my twenties, my thirties, even my early forties. Now I look back and see so many of those things don't matter at all in the long run. It was my ego, my judgments, that got in the way. Egos cloud our vision. We need to pierce the veil in order to see clearly. Krishna's coma did that for me. My prayers to help him helped me.

When Raj sat at Krishna's bedside and pleaded for him to wake up, promising to give him the happy family Krishna wanted them to be; when he flexed Krishna's legs to stop his muscles from atrophying; when he spent every waking moment calling, texting, e-mailing every friend and business connection to sniff out a new drug that could bring Krishna to life—then it no longer mattered that he did not fit her expectations of a worthy match for her—how tall he should be, the shade of his complexion. What mattered was that he stood by his family through thick and thin. Raj had supported her and Krishna in every way. What mattered was that they continue to take care of each other and their son. Grow old together. To her that is the ultimate expression of love. Everything else pales.

As she pads upstairs to join her husband in their bedroom, she thinks again of Divya behind that wall of silence. *How thin and fragile is the veil separating each of us from misfortune.*

Alka wakes up early on Sunday. She showers and goes down-stairs to breakfast. Kakaji has prepared *pooris* and *alu*, a Bajaj family favorite. By nine, Alka is ready. She hasn't told anyone her plan in case she chickens out. Krishna and Raj are working away at their laptops, facing each other across Raj's desk. Alka stops herself from peering over Krishna's shoulder. He's signed up to take a couple of general education classes at the local community college that begin next week. Alka takes a deep breath and reminds herself to say a prayer of thanks.

She backs her BMW out of the garage and zooms out of her driveway. On the passenger seat lies a bunch of white roses she cut from her garden earlier in the morning. A peace offering? Maybe. She cracks the windows and cranks the air conditioning. She inserts a CD of the *Gayatri Mantra* to calm her nerves and forces herself to keep going.

She cruises down Diablo Road through the heart of Danville, where new construction is superimposed over old. Widened roads. Bulldozed trees. New traffic lights at the intersections of new neighborhoods. A parade of five-thousand-square-foot-plus homes squashed together onto tiny, impeccably manicured plots. Many old homes, decrepit and squatting on prime acreage, have been demolished, replaced with McMansions.

Abruptly, her GPS directs her off the beaten track onto a winding, two-lane road that ends in front of a two-story Tudor. A gingerbread house. Can she eat the walls? The fence and gate are laced with overhanging roses, like a satin gown swishing over bare hips. Alka pulls into the driveway. Her fingers tighten around the steering wheel.

She can see the crest of Mt. Diablo in the background. *Must have a killer view from the back porch.* Divya has found a house as singular and unconventional as her personality, and Alka is delighted. At the same time, she's awash with a bittersweet feeling, for she's not been present to celebrate her old friend's joy.

Wiping her clammy hands on her jeans, she walks toward the arched entryway and walnut double doors. The morning sun throws striped shadows across the lawn, shadows of the pine trees along the property line. In the front yard, flower beds bloom. The smell of potted gardenias fills the entry porch. Alka rings the doorbell.

The door opens slowly to reveal a quizzical Divya. Alka's eyes scan over her. She's so thin. And her hair, her lush, shining hair looks wrong, disheveled and dry.

Oh God, help her. The chemo's already begun. She thrusts out the roses, hoping Divya will see them for what they are, an olive branch. Alka's hands keep steady, but inside she's shaking.

Her tongue tastes coppery. She mumbles, "I . . . I was just . . . I wanted to . . . ." All the noble words she's prepared disappear from her mind.

Divya's wide eyes mist. Blinking, she takes Alka's peace offering stiffly, balancing it in one hand. There's only a single beat of awkwardness, a clumsy pause, before Divya locks her thin arms around Alka in a tight embrace. And they are hugging, their chests heaving. They sob and laugh, and look at each other. And then Divya takes Alka's arm and leads her friend proudly into her new home.

Epilogue

The jaunty red and white awning above the sidewalk café flutters in the breeze. The Open For Business sign proclaims that *Priya's Chaat and Chai* is ready to take the chic residential neighborhood in Orinda by storm. The interior has a lived-in feel of an eccentric friend's house—with stacks of books and magazines and exotic decorations, many from India, contributed by her friends and delightedly tacked up by Priya herself.

The vibe's chill and arty. Mini admires it as she steps into the boisterous interior. The party's already in full swing. She spots a thinner Divya and a fuller Alka huddled at the corner table, and makes her way toward them. Alka stands as Mini approaches the table, throwing both arms around her tightly. Divya doesn't stand, but reaches up both arms invitingly, and Mini wraps her in a loving embrace, bending over her a little. Divya's long-sleeved sweater brushes Mini's bare arm as she draws back slightly to look Divya full in the face. Her cheekbones are angular and sharp, and her hair is short, cut into a bob.

"The style suits you." Mini flicks back a black strand of the wig.

"Oh, yeah? A lot of people have said that to me. I may get my own hair cut into a bob when it grows out." Divya turns her brown eyes up to Mini uncertainly. Emotion tightens Mini's throat. She nods back at Divya with vigor and squeezes her fingers for reassurance.

"You should try that for sure." Mini's voice is thick. Divya turns away, wiping at her own brimming eyes.

They watch as Priya weaves her way among the full tables, stopping to speak with every friend, family member, and acquaintance who has shown up to support her new venture.

Even Vik makes an appearance with his latest floozy draped on his arm. He quickly sizes up Miguel, who's manning the busy bar, and leaves, breezily blowing Priya a kiss.

"This is great!" he shouts at her across the room. "Let me know when you're ready to expand. I've got investors."

Priya's smile freezes. Her entire face feels encased in a plaster cast, but somehow she maintains her smile.

"Of course, you do, Vik." Her teeth are clenched, as she waves him out the door with a relieved sigh.

Priya finally makes it to their table. She smothers first Mini, then Alka, and then stoops down to give Divya a full body embrace.

"I was hoping you would all show up." She has an enormous grin on her glowing face.

"Hoping?" Mini arches one perfectly plucked eyebrow. "I know an order when I hear one. What about you?" she asks, Divya and Alka.

"Oh, she definitely ordered us here," Alka mocks a serious tone.

"Oh yeah," chimes in Divya, bobbing her head Indian-style but slowly. She has to avoid sudden movements, or the chemo pain in her head will fill the circumference of her brain.

"I don't know why you three are total bitches," Priya grins. "You know you're going to be helping with the dirty dishes, don't you? Thank God you're cheap labor!" Priya pulls out a chair and asks the waiter to bring her usual from the bar.

"Miguel knows what I like," she purrs confidently with a coy wave to Miguel, who winks and waves back.

Mini catches the intimate gesture between the two and can't stop the pang of envy. She's happy that her friend has found the happiness she deserves, but Mini feels lonely without a man. Clearly not Tom, but she doesn't know yet what she wants. Only that as she is being hurled into her mid-forties, she doesn't want to live out the next chapter alone.

Maybe the Facebook connection will work out. She's going to India in the fall for a whole month. Her parents, in superb health for their age, are both in their eighties—their bonus years—and Mini wants to spend as much time as she can with them.

On a whim, she contacted an old flame from college whom she'd spied on another classmate's Facebook page. Ravi and she had gone steady for almost a year in college, but their burgeoning relationship had died a natural death when his father, who worked for the Navy, was transferred to another state. Ravi had valiantly tried to keep the love going with letters and long-distance phone calls, but she was lukewarm—a total out-of-sight-out-of-mind-kind of gal.

He'd settled in Mumbai, married, and had a couple of kids. Now, he's divorced and back in Delhi. His reaction to her "friend" request was everything she could have hoped, and more. A strategically glamorized picture of her on her profile page had no doubt aided the enthusiastic response. Now, she couldn't wait to meet up with him again and see where this adventure might lead.

Rani is going to stay with a friend in the neighborhood. Being a senior in high school means she can manage for thirty days without Mom. In fact, her sullen teenager is looking forward to escaping Mom's watchful eye. The plan has been in the works for several months, and Mini is restless to embark on her sojourn, heady with its promise of romance and face-time with her old friends. A time for nostalgia and a time for homecoming. Her inner Sita looks hopeful, almost bashful. What might come of it? Maybe, a suitable Indian boy for this minx? Her inner Sita smoulders, unheeded.

Divya sips apple cider and listens to her friends chatting about the new Bollywood movie in town: *Zindagi Na Mile Dobara* (Life Doesn't Come Twice) featuring the heartthrob Hrithik Roshan. The conversation turns to the kids and what they're up to come the fall. A couple of tables away sit Krishna and Anya, with her roommate, shoveling volumes of Priya's voluptuous chicken *biryani* into their mouths while the girls jabber away.

"Krishna's put on weight. He looks good." Mini's minx eyes twinkle. Her nose pin glints as she tosses her hair.

Alka nods. "Thank the gods." Though she hasn't accepted her son's sex appeal.

"Anya will look after him at Cal," Divya assures her.

"And we'll look after him at home." Mini and Divya each grab one of Alka's hands and hold it tight.

Kakaji, watching from the kitchen door—he's here to help Priya *Didi*—wipes at his tears. *God is Great, who would have thought that after the tragedies they've been through the house of the Bajajs had so much happiness in store.*

Divya floats in a sense of peace. The last three months have been a journey through hell. A better journey because Alka and Sham have been there to see her through the darkness. Alka took over driving her to her chemotherapy appointments, holding Divya's hair out of her face as she vomited on the side of the freeway. Alka sat with her through the hours in the infusion room, bringing her whatever she needed, running for the nurse when Divya needed help, holding her hand or plumping her pillow. So much talk and tears, so much catching up—not without pain and gratitude. Sometimes, they talked about the old days, when they'd been too young to know that they were young—when the whole world seemed open to them and dreams were as easy to pick as pansies. Sometimes they just sat in companionable silence.

When Divya developed an infection from all the infusions and had to be hospitalized, Alka came to keep Sham company while he paced the crowded waiting room. And it's Alka who recognizes the fear in Sham's face and fatigue in his posture and puts her hand over his. Sham, who usually maintains his stance of masculinity, is stilled by grief. While Alka pats his back comfortingly, his emotions come under his control.

After every treatment, when Divya can barely move from the nausea and the pain, Alka comes over every day. Helps her to the bathroom. Helps her dress. Chants the *Gayatri Mantra* to her while holding her hand. When Divya gave in and had her head shaved, Mini brought dozens of bright headscarves. Priya has stocked the Kapoor's freezer with dozens of single-serving dishes so Divya never has to cook and never has to count on Mona Vora again. During the whole ordeal, Divya's mantra has been, *I'm amazed—I'm not alone.*

And Sham, when she comes home, is altogether incredible—so gentle with touch and with words. Divya doesn't want him to see her body, but he sits beside her and says, "We're going to grow old together, Divi. We may lose our hair, our teeth, our memories, a few body parts here and there, but we'll never lose each other." *After twenty-odd years together, you think you know everything about a person, and you come to find out there are still mysteries left.* Divya is astonished at the twists and turns of her life.

It's the same thing with her friends. The shared history that only they can remember forms the community that sustains her and makes her recovery possible. *With time and love, emotional scars can heal. Life goes on like a train that waits for no one. I can't alter its course, but I can alter the way I've chosen to travel.*

Priya takes a sip of the skinny Margarita that Miguel has sent with a lustful leer across the room. She smiles. *I could stay in this moment forever.*

Priya can't believe her good fortune, and this time she's determined to give back. Whenever the restaurant starts paying for itself, a portion of the proceeds have been earmarked for a charity she's established in her father's memory. The Balraj Dutt Foundation will clothe, feed, and educate underprivileged children in the slums of New Delhi. Priya knows Dad would be proud.

She looks at her closest friends sitting around her—her friends who listen without judgment, understand with compassion—supporting her by showing up, as always. *There is nothing in the world more healing than friendship.*

"A toast to us." She raises her glass, and they all clink in unison.

At that moment, the Eurythmics come blasting from the sound system, belting out: "Sweet Dreams Are Made of This." Mini grabs Priya and Alka's hands, pulls them up from their chairs and spins them in time to the music. Divya claps her hands in rhythm. It's a flick of a switch—a spinning back to the 'eighties' when dancing to that "cool" music had been a part of high school dances.

Divya shuffles up to them slowly, pushing her way between them and taking the lead. "No way you are dancing without me, *saheli*. You know I'm the one with all the rhythm."

"Comes from all that hip bumping you did with what's-his-face." Mini laughs at her. Divya doubles over, holding onto her sides, her shoulders shaking mischievously beneath the arms Mini has wrapped around her. It's uncanny how a song or a dance or a look passed between friends can give the whole of your life back to you.

The evening passes in a blur of familiar snapshots—laughing, chattering, sipping wine, sampling bites of spicy-hot appetizers. Miguel, personable and agreeable, moves comfortably into their group. They come together, then apart in smaller groups to chat and reminisce. Mini looks at the four of them. *I could stay in this moment forever.* Her inner Sita snaps her fingers to the music.

"Do you all want to eat dinner here or in the kitchen?" asks Priya as the remaining guests file out of the restaurant, leaving a wake of joy and relaxation.

Mini pretends to debate the question, though the decision is moot. Here or there, they will all be together. She's with her girl-friends whom she loves—and who could need or want anything more than that? Wherever the soulmate train takes her, she will always have her friends.

Acknowledgments

To Laura Wine Paster, my writing group mentor and editor: Thank you for giving shape to my jumbled words.

To David Colin Carr, dream editor: Thank you for managing to wrest every ounce of Indian-ness from me, for making the narrative richer and deeper, and for wringing the best performance out of me.

To Sumant Pendharkar, my friend and author of *Raising Yourself: Making the Right Choices*, who led me by the hand and cut a swath for me in the publishing jungle.

To Lita Mikrut, my amazing website developer.

To Rajesh Relan for his awesome first cover that was the inspiration and basis of the final cover.

To Cathy Cutler, my dear friend and comrade who was the sounding-board for my stories, for her boundless support and enthusiasm for this project.

To Cynthia Leslie Bole, Mary-Ann Diffenderfer, Paula Santi, and every member of my writing group whose nurturing presence gave this story life.

And to Gemini Wahhaj, an extraordinary writer whom I'm lucky to call a friend.

About the Author

Anoop Ahuja Judge is an attorney whose first book *Law: What It's All About and How to Get In* was published by Twenty-Twenty Media in New Delhi, India as part of a series of Dummies-style books about different careers open to college grads.

She serves as Legal Advisor to Home of Hope, Inc., a non-profit based in the USA that supports more than 2000 destitute, orphaned, and otherwise disadvantaged children in India. Anoop has been featured in many Indian publications (*India-West*, *India-Post*, etc.) and has made several appearances on satellite television (TV Asia, Womennow, Sitaara TV) for her work with the organization.

She has lived in the San Francisco-Bay Area for the past 23 years. She is married with two nearly grown and fully admirable children.

www.therummyclub-anovel.com

Gloucester Library
P.O. Box 2380
Gloucester, VA 23061

CPSIA information can be obtained at www.ICGtesting.com
Printed in the USA
LVOW12s1156200714

395169LV00002B/244/P

9 780991 081011